TO MY BEST FRIEND (ALL 5 OF Y

Green Lama

Mystic Warrior

AIRSHIP 27 PRODUCTIONS

The Green Lama-Mystic Warrior

An Airship 27 Production
www.airship27.com
www.airship27hangar.com

Editor: Ron Fortier
Associate Editor: Ray Riethmeier
Production and design by Rob Davis
Promotion and Marketing Manager: Michael Vance

ISBN-13: 978-0692223406 (Airship 27)
ISBN-10: 0692223401

Printed in the United States of America

10 9 8 7 6 5 4 3 2 1

the Green Lama Mystic Warrior

CONTENTS

the

in

Shiva Enangered

by Kevin Noel Olson

Chapter One

Yeti in the Mist

Crawling down the mountain, the mists pressed slowly and lightly against the wall of jagged, glacier-deposited boulders surrounding the village. Ravikiran pointed his thirteen-year-old eyes toward the white peaks to the north as he stepped from his hut. Ravikiran wondered how many pairs of eyes he had in his transmigration through lifetimes; how many found wonder at the scene.

The sun waited on his right hand, peeling the layers of dawn away to display the majesty of the Hindustan countryside. Smiling, he walked to a grazing cow and patted it lightly on its dusty, tan back. He nodded at üüthe blessed day Brahma provided and walked past the other huts. He considered the beautiful lessons of the Bhagvat Geeta he learned from the monks in the temple. He could not read the sacred scriptures himself yet hoped one day to join the monks in learning more wonders of the world.

He walked to the well and lowered the pail by rope. When it felt full, he pulled the rope to the top and untied the pail. His mother didn't feel well and she needed the water. Ravikiran did not mind performing the task as he had done it every day since he was too young to remember.

The low rumbling started down the road as a cloud of dust in the distance. It caught Ravikiran's attention. He saw a row of large trucks climbing down a hill. He increased his pace to return home. "Mother!" he shouted before reaching the door. "Mother, someone comes along the road!"

His mother, her illness only slightly diminishing her angular beauty, stood uneasily to her feet and wrapped a sari over her bed clothes. "Come, Ravi," she said to the boy as she walked out the door. She joined in staring at the Juggernautical row of trucks. Her eyes widened. She stifled a cough before saying, "Let us take a walk up the mountain."

"Who are they, Mother?" the boy asked. "Is there trouble?"

A tear touched his mother's eyelid. Her lips pursed as she smacked him with her hand. "You will obey, Ravi!" She softened at seeing Ravikiran's face fall. "We must hurry, my beloved child." She strode quickly after him as he headed for the mountain range.

His mother directed him to a thin crevice leading up the formidable mountain next to their village. "We will remain out of sight if possible."

Ravikiran felt the gravity of the situation, though he did not fully understand. Looking back through the trees he watched the trucks pull into the village. One of the trucks towed a flat trailer carrying something large hidden by a brown tarp. Men wearing black coats and pants, pale in complexion with closely-cropped hair, alighted from the vehicles. Flat, round hats with short brims in the front decorated their heads. Red armbands with the Jain symbol of the Fylfot or Swastika decorated their arms, yet they didn't look at all like the gentle, white-robed Jain monks that came through on their travels.

Ravikiran saw the weapons the men carried; vicious-looking guns more frightening than those of the British hunters that came through in search of tiger pelts. Ravikiran's father, his mother told him, was a Sherpa. He fell prey to an attacking tiger while hired as a guide by hunters. That was a few months before the birth of Ravikiran.

He turned to continue walking, but his mother grabbed his shirt and pulled him to the ground. Her finger crossed her lip like the Jain symbol. Ravikiran remained silent and watched.

Three of the men walked to the small-yet-majestic village temple with elaborate statues of Hindu deities embedded in its walls. Ravi spent hours imagining them moving about, performing the business of gods.

An aged and balding monk appeared at the door and seemed to deny the men entry. Sitting behind him, Ravi's mother put her left hand over his mouth and her right arm around his chest. He did not understand until the rifle began spitting repetitive noises. The monk twisted and fell beneath a volley of bullets.

Ravikiran wanted to scream. His mother's hand precluded it. Only a clear drop streamed from his eye. He realized after all this time of listening to the wise monk he never knew his name.

"Tushar Das!" his mother whispered harshly. Tempered mourning fluttered in her voice. Ravi remembered hearing the name, yet was not certain it belonged to the monk. He sighed beneath his mother's hand as he reminisced about the monk saying to him one day, "The entire sky is yours, my child, yet nothing is all you have. The world, our very life, is in our care; yet we cannot place it in a vault for protection. Life is held in the tree, not the box made from the tree. The vault of our hearts," the smiling monk pressed a finger gently into Ravi's chest, "holds the sky, the tree, and the very earth. Hold it gently."

Ravi's mother retained her hold on him. They watched as the three soldiers walked into the Temple. The others soldiers remained outside. They leaned against the trucks, laughing and smoking cigarettes. The death of the monk lacked sacredness to them. A tall, imposing man dressed in a crimson monk's robe stepped from the passenger's side of the truck with trailer in tow. The man scanned the area with beady, piercing eyes. His gaze locked on Ravi and his mother. His lips twisted as he pointed. "Kill them!" he bellowed. "No one must know we were here!" Six of the soldiers obeyed the orders and headed up the mountain.

His mother pulled Ravi after her as she headed further up the mountain and into the dense mist. He could barely see his feet in the haze. He allowed his mother to pull him along as he made certain of his own footing. The soldiers followed them, yet failed to move quietly. Shouting in a strange tongue, stumbling and occasionally falling to the ground, the men persisted in their pursuit. Ravi heard the clatter of their boots against the dirt and pebbles. Despite their audible clumsiness, their voices grew louder and louder.

Ravikiran and his mother moved silently through the trees, searching for a means of escape or shelter. A scream split the air, followed by excited shouts from the soldiers and sporadic, staccato gunfire.

His mother moved faster. She pulled back as the figure of a soldier flew in front of them and smashed into a tree.

Ravi put his hand over his mouth. "Yeti!" he said.

"Silence, beloved!" his mother whispered. Her eyes searched the misted trees. "Yeti do not travel so far from the mountain snow!"

Ravikiran fell silent. He did not find his mother's words comforting. They climbed a steep section of the mountain when another scream filled the air, followed again by gunfire and strange exclamations. "It is Yeti, mother! Sachi told me they have come before!"

"Silence for the sake of the trees," his mother said. "That was long ago. If it is Yeti, our travails only begin!"

A soldier appeared out of the mists and rushed toward them. His gun pointed steadily in their direction. Ravi's mother pulled her son close and fell to her knees. "Mercy!" she said in English. "Mercy!"

The soldier, his eyes widened in terror, rushed blindly between Ravi and his kneeling mother. A large figure coated in white appeared from the mist, a low growl preceding its form. Ravi could not help himself. "Yeti!!!" he screamed.

The white mist fell off the fast-moving figure as it rushed past. Beneath the vanishing mist moved a white man dressed in a green robe like those of the holy Lamas. With swift strides, he easily overtook the soldier and collared him with a red scarf. The soldier fell onto his back, eyes widened with terror. The green-robed man held his hand palm-out, still holding the ends of the scarf securely about the soldier's neck. "Peace and stillness," he said in a deep voice, young in years yet inflected with the wisdom of eons. "You will speak to your purpose and wish no violence."

As Ravi looked on the scarf glowed a barely-perceptible green hue, shimmering like ocean waves. The soldier dropped his gun to his side. It swayed gently from its straps. His eyes glazed over, turning the same color emanating from the scarf. He spoke in broken English, of which Ravi knew a slight bit from schooling with the monks. "My name is Gustav. I come in the name of the *Führer*. We come to seek the Jade Tablet and the secrets of Soma."

The green-robed man clenched his jaw. "Sleep." Gustav fell into a deep sleep. The man removed the scarf from the soldier's neck and returned it to his own. "Fools," the man murmured. Looking into the mist, he took a grenade from the unconscious soldier's belt.

Another soldier rushed from the fog, his gun rattling bullets around the man in green. The tiny bits of metal sent splinters and sawdust through the air as they chewed at the trees. Unperturbed, the man threw the grenade and struck the soldier on the head. The gun and the soldier fell silent and to the ground, the unarmed grenade landing harmlessly beside.

Ravikiran and his mother looked at their rescuer. "Who are you?" the boy asked in rough English.

"I am the Green Lama," the man replied.

"The Green Lama?" Ravi repeated.

The man nodded. "It is an honored title bestowed upon me by my teachers." He looked toward the top of the obscured mountain and pointed. "I trained here to learn the ways of the Lama. I returned when I discovered a Nazi plot to retrieve the Jade Tablet. I hired a plane and flew directly from America to protect the area. I came as fast as I could." He closed his eyes and breathed deeply. "Not soon enough to save my old friend Tushar Das."

"A Lama uses no violence," Ravikiran said, more by rote memory than deep conviction. "How can you strike another?"

Green Lama smiled wisely. "A Lama understands justice." He flourished his hands to indicate their surroundings. "If a man falls against a rock travelling through the fog, is it not violence against him by the rock? Is the mist misused by nature as a tool for karma?" The Lama shook his head. "No, my son. To protect the innocent is merely nature using me as the rock and the fog."

"I have heard no monk speak as you," Ravikiran said. "Is this a new teaching?"

The Green Lama laughed, his teeth bright. "I am not at a place where many monks are. It is to my shame I cannot see as they do."

"Yet you are powerful," Ravikiran's mother said, "though you do not follow the teachings."

The Lama nodded. "I have learned the hidden mysteries of the masters, yet my passions are a mist and a rock within. I must face them. I will not stand by to permit injustice." Voices in the village met their ears. "I must go and teach those in the village before I can learn my lessons."

"There are no more in the village but the men with guns," Ravi replied. "They are lost to anger and ambition and will not listen to wisdom."

The Green Lama smiled. "Who more needs instruction to leave the mist and avoid the rocks?" With this, the Green Lama moved swiftly. The mists coated and transformed his figure into the swift, clouded creature that first appeared to Ravi and his mother. "He becomes the mists!" Ravikiran exclaimed.

His mother shook her head as she embraced her son. "It coats and comforts him as a mother. We must remain quiet, Ravi." They walked down to the edge of the mist to observe.

Walking to the village, the Green Lama left the mist behind. It fell off his shoulders to wander the ground. He approached the soldiers and the large man clad in a crimson robe. In the crisp, silent air their words wafted to Ravi and his mother.

"Be calm," the Green Lama said in soothing tones. "Violence will fail to further your purpose."

The tall man stepped forward, his smile remained cautious. "I am the mystic Adaulfo Kellen. Our cause here is in accord with the purpose of all. Who are you, monk?"

"I am the Green Lama. What do you desire to take by force that may not be freely given?"

The tall man's face fell into a sneer. "We will have what is necessary to bring alive a greater world, and will have it by hook or crook! The Nazis do not answer to," his lips curled, "an upstart American, as I discern from your accent. You are unwise to act superior to the Master Race of Areounus from Atlantis!"

Green Lama smiled. "One of a Master Race need not feel insulted by an inferior's opinion. I am an American. There is no need to feel superior when the seeds of nature humble us all."

Adaulfo gritted his teeth. "It is merely humbling to those who do not understand," he returned. "For those open to the secrets of the leaves, the meaning is plain."

The Green Lama simply nodded and smiled.

The German mystic twisted his neck. His head lowered to the side. His eyes peered at the Green Lama from beneath his brow. "Kill him."

"*Om! Ma-ni pad-me Hum*," the Green Lama said quietly as he began to spin in a circle. The Nazis pulled their guns to bear. The bullets clattered through the air, tearing at the spinning Lama's robe.

Adaulfo Kellen's voice drowned beneath the din until the machine guns halted. He waved his arms angrily. "Stop! Stop, you fools!" The soldiers let their guns rest at their sides.

Adaulfo walked to the still-spinning robe and yanked a sleeve. The robe fell like a tent, a metal pole clanking to the ground. "Imbeciles! *Dummkopfs!*" Adaulfo fumed at the soldiers. "It is a fakir's trick! Mere prestidigitation! The Lama left before you pulled a trigger!"

The confused soldiers stood open-mouthed. "How?" one asked.

To illustrate, the mystic held the robe in the air. "Sleight of hand! You concentrate on the top of a spinning robe while its erstwhile occupant escapes through the bottom!" Kellen threw the robe to the ground in disgust. "Hitler chooses the SS men from the very best! If this is the elite among the Nazis, the plans to restore the ancient race is doomed!" He stared down the captain standing there. "You are a disgrace, Adelbrecht!"

The door opened on one of the trucks and a Nazi general alighted. Stepping through the soldiers, he stepped to the mystic, his jaw set. "You will not speak to my men with such deprecation, *Herr* Kellen!" He pulled out his luger and pressed it into the mystic's neck. "You are not so invaluable as to abuse my men!"

Adaulfo calmed, his eyes widening. "I…I…" Kellen stammered, his eyes moving to the pistol at his neck. "I lost my serenity, *Herr* General Kannenberg. It will not happen again."

"See it does not," the General replied as he placed his pistol in its holster. "We are here on direct orders from the *Führer*. Your free manner opposes our precision. You may serve at our leisure, *Herr* Kellen! It may go well for you should we find the artifact," General Kannenberg shrugged. "It may go ill for you if we feel dissatisfied."

"*Herr* General," Kellen ventured, "we must find this Green Lama and the boy. They may be the key we need!"

The general looked toward the mist. "Did no one see where he went?" The soldiers and Kellen all shrugged their agreement on the matter. "Go search the mountain," he ordered three of the soldiers and Kellen. "The rest of you," he indicated the four remaining, "come with me to the temple!"

Chapter Two
Between a Mystic and a Predator

Ravikiran stayed close to his mother as they climbed the mountain. The mist started to thin, making it more difficult to stay hidden.

"Come, Ravikiran," his mother said. "We must reach the summit."

Ravi nodded. "Yes, mother."

As they walked up the mountain, Ravi looked to his right. He gasped at seeing the Green Lama suddenly walking beside them. "I did not hear you following us, Green Lama," he said. "You move silent as the silence of night." Ravi's mother looked to see Green Lama, but said nothing. "How did you retrieve your robe?"

The Green Lama smiled as he put a finger to his lips and nodded. "I move, yet do not disrupt," he said softly. "Others follow you who imbalance nature about them." He tilted his head and listened. The sound of a branch cracking drifted through the air. "See?"

Ravikiran looked about, his eyes wide. "Is that them? Perhaps a branch broke off a tree."

The Green Lama shook his head. "Everything sounds exactly as it is. Did it not sound as a pursuer stepping on a branch?"

Looking at the ground, Ravi thought deeply. He returned his gaze to the Green Lama. "Yes!" he whispered harshly. "It did!"

Green Lama smiled. "You are wise beyond your time, young man, and learn quickly. Now, we must move swiftly."

"Green Lama, you can destroy them," Ravi said. "We have seen your power."

The Lama shook his head. "My purpose is to preserve rather than destroy. These men may be in error, and perhaps we can show them the right path. Letting them discover life's twofold path is much better than destroying theirs."

Ravikiran nodded. "I think you are right, Green Lama."

The Green Lama laughed. "You can call me Jagmohan."

"Is that your name?" Ravikiran's mother asked.

"It is not," the Lama replied. "It is an appellation I chose." He examined

Ravikiran's mother as they walked along. "I do not know your names," he smiled. "I can decide on some for you if you prefer."

Ravi's mother smiled. "This is my son, Ravikiran. I call him Ravi." Blushing, she looked at the ground. "I am Pari."

The Green Lama stopped. He placed his gloved hand beneath her chin and gently pulled it up. "There is no need for shame. Pari means pretty, does it not? The universe swells with pride at the beauty it contains." The Lama cleared his throat and continued walking, pointing up the slope. "We near the snowline. A small Lama's retreat is not far."

Within moments, white snow crunched beneath their feet. The icy peak they climbed toward offered a steeper slope. They approached the jagged rocks. "Can you climb?"

The mother and son nodded. "Good," The Lama said. "I will follow." Ravi went first, with Pari following. The Green Lama grasped a rock in his gloved hand and pulled himself after them.

The Green Lama stopped again and listened. Ravi listened, too. "I hear them, Jagmohan!"

The Green Lama nodded. "They are close now." He looked up the jagged peak. "The ascent has many places to hide. They dare not fire their guns. It would start an avalanche."

"Perhaps they will not follow," Pari said. "They can fire at us as we climb."

The Green Lama shook his head, his face grim. "They will follow. The mystic is driven by hubris. That may be his undoing and our salvation. Speak only when necessary now. The energy is for the climb alone in this thin air."

The Green Lama followed the family, impressed at their deft ability to discover foot and handholds. "You seem to have climbed before," he observed.

Pari nodded. "We have lived in the mountains' shadow all our lives, and we must to survive. Save your words of praise."

They climbed in silence until Green Lama said, "Our pursuers begin their ascent." Pari stole a glance as did Ravi. They could see Kellen lead the soldiers with gusto. The soldiers, their guns slung over their backs, were more cautious.

Green Lama pointed toward a more difficult area to climb, following a long cliff. "That way," he said. "Those soldiers will not be able to make it. They will have to turn back."

Ravi instantly started the way Green Lama pointed. "It is child's play, Jagmohan."

Grasping a rock, the Lama shook his head. "No, Ravi. It is serious. Take caution and no chances."

Below, a scream pealed through the air. The trio turned to look as a soldier lost his footing and fell over the precipice. The Green Lama shook his head. "Why did he not stay behind?"

Ravi continued upward, looking down the rock face to the river far below. "He did not control his passions, Jagmohan."

Green Lama nodded as he climbed. "A lesson for us all to learn, yet I suspect his driving passion was fear of Kellen. We must all master our passions." He stole a glance at Pari's face, hidden by her collar.

Chapter Three

What Immortal Eye

Another noise met the party from below. Looking down, they saw one of the soldiers had twisted his leg into a shape broken and unnatural. They rested as they watched Kellen bend over the soldier and remove the man's pistol from its holster. Callous to the condition, Kellen shot the man through the temple. Green Lama's teeth ground together as he drew in a breath of cold mountain air.

"Come, Jagmohan," Pari whispered. "There is nothing to be done now."

His face still twisted in anger, Green Lama nodded. "Yes. Nothing to be done now."

Ravi continued his climb, pulling himself over a ledge and out of sight of Pari and the Lama. He let out a sudden yelp of fear. Green Lama climbed past Pari. "Wait here!"

Green Lama pulled his body over the ledge to see a powerful leopard looking at Ravi, its fur spotted black and white.

Ravi stood very still as the snow leopard sniffed the air. It watched the Green Lama and the boy with anticipation, a low snarl escaping its clenched, knifelike teeth.

"Don't move, Ravi," Green Lama said softly as he stepped between the boy and the leopard. The creature's green eyes seemed to glow in the thin mountain air. The Green Lama's muscles tensed beneath his robe. His eyes locked with the leopard's, as they moved in a circle, sizing each other up.

The leopard snarled lowly before hurling itself at the Lama. The Green Lama was prepared as he rushed between the massive claws and embraced the leopard by the chest. The combatants fell to the ground as both rolled

Green Lama stepped between the boy and the leopard.

to gain dominance. The leopard's claws slashed the air, the pits of its arms pressing against the Green Lama's shoulders and thus the powerful thrust diminished into the Lama's muscles. Still, the claws managed to tear at the green robe and shred it. If the claws dug deeper, the Lama's veins would be exposed to tearing and bleeding.

The leopard found its jaws and thrust its head toward the Lama's neck. The Lama pulled away, the beast's hot breath warming his throat. The Green Lama brought his hands to the leopard's neck and grasped it, attempting to deprive the creature of air.

The leopard rolled over and over with the Lama on the narrow ledge. It twisted its head from side-to-side as if attempting to break the neck of prey caught between its teeth. Green Lama pressed hard to ensure his neck did not end up between the ferocious jaws.

Ravi stood in a cleft gouged through the rock face. He watched with eyes wide, helpless to aid the Green Lama. "What can I do?" he asked.

The Green Lama shook his head as he rolled with the leopard toward the ledge as the beast struggled violently. "Care for yourself and your mother, Ravi." The Green Lama and leopard rolled off the ledge and out of sight.

"Jagmohan!" Ravi exclaimed as he rushed to the edge and lay on the rock, looking down. His mother joined him.

Their eyes beheld the Green Lama grasping onto a rock jutting from the cliff face with his right hand. Far beneath him, the distant, misted ground lay obscured. The ends of his red scarf wrapped his left glove tautly. The scarf's material cradled the snow leopard about its belly as it dangled below the Lama. Suspended above a death-promising distance, the once-ferocious creature now slept like a kitten.

Ravi smiled nervously. "Jagmohan! You did not die!"

The Green Lama grimaced, sweat on his brow. He looked up to see the face of the young boy and his beautiful mother. He smiled and nodded lightly. "I am alive, Ravi. For the moment."

Full of a motherly concern, a frown crossed Pari's lips. "How can we help, Lama?"

The Green Lama looked at the beast cradled in his scarf. "I need to get the leopard to safety. She is calmed by the scarf, yet also a heavy weight on my shoulders."

Ravi almost laughed, the situation being too grave for mirth. "The leopard!? What about you, Jagmohan?"

"If I do not have the strength to save others," Green Lama said, "I am helpless as a child."

Ravi bit his lip. “Yet the leopard tried to kill you!”

The Lama nodded. “Yes. She meant only to feed herself and her family.” He chuckled. “I cannot blame her for a desire so natural.”

“Can you not levitate?” Ravi asked. “I know Lamas often can.”

Green Lama shook his head. “I can. It takes much energy. If it did not, the Lamas would fly everywhere. My strength would wane, and I might not be able to help you and Pari. I cannot allow harm to come to you.”

“If you die,” Pari said, “harm is likely for Ravi and me. Saving the leopard may well doom us three.”

“Then you do understand my predicament,” the Lama replied, “yet there must be a way to save all four.”

“I do not see how,” Ravi returned. The Green Lama left the words unanswered as he closed his eyes and fell into meditation.

“Are you meditating?” Ravi asked. Pari responded with a harsh, whispered, “Shush!”

The Green Lama shook his head. “Not quite,” he replied to Ravi’s question. “I am praying.”

“What difference is there?” Ravi asked.

“Meditating is when you go inside yourself to find God waiting for you. It is calming to your spirit, yet I am calm. Praying is when you go to find God waiting outside of you, in everything.” He opened his eyes and smiled. “Faith can move mountains if only the size of a seed in the wind. I only ask for the strength to move a leopard. If I handed the scarf to you two, would you be able to pull it up?”

Ravi and Pari nodded. “It is not so heavy,” Pari said. “We have carried goats from the mountains.”

Sweat fell from Green Lama’s brow. “It is not so heavy, yet in catching it I broke the bone in my wrist. Your ability to lift her is not so outlandish as my ability to lift her with one broken arm.”

“We can climb down,” Ravi offered.

Green Lama shook his head. “Only the leopard and I are in danger right now. We need not complicate the matter by adding lives unnecessarily.”

Pari nodded gravely. The sinews pulled as the Lama started to lift the leopard. The scarf dug into his fingers as he lifted it over his shoulder. Ravi and his mother watched with bated breath. As soon as it was near, they clasped the end of the scarf.

The Green Lama freed his hand from the scarf. The hand fell with force to his side, drained of its strength. The sudden shift in weight caused the rock in his other hand to give way and break off. Green Lama dropped quietly into the mists.

Ravikiran's eyes widened as he watched the Lama disappear into the mist. "NO!"

Pari placed her hands over her son's shoulders. "He is gone," she said, her voice breaking. "We must continue without him."

Ravi looked at the snow leopard, still sleeping with the Lama's scarf around its midsection. He shuddered and turned away to continue staring at the mist. Slowly yet inexorably, the Green Lama began to rise out of the mist. Like a balloon he wafted back and forth in the air, drifting on the breeze. Great strain showed on his face. His skin wrinkled as he concentrated.

"Jagmohan!" Ravi shouted. Green Lama shook his head. A sudden wind pushed him toward the mountain. With a heavy thud, he struck the cliff face. His black gloves found handholds some thirty feet below the ledge and held tightly.

The Green Lama breathed in deeply through his nose and exhaled. The lines in his face began to disappear as he stole a glance upward to see Pari and Ravi's faces staring down at him.

Ravi clapped his hands together. "We are pleased to see you, Jagmohan!" he laughed.

Pari nodded and wiped a tear from her eye. "How will you get to the ledge?"

"He will levitate again!" Ravi said.

Green Lama shook his head. "No," he replied. "It takes much energy, and only in an emergency or in quiet meditation does it make sense. We will need my energy to defeat the summit."

Carefully searching the sheer rock face, Lama found the tiniest handhold above him and reached up to grasp it. His gloved fingertips found slight purchase, yet it proved enough. He pulled heavily and lifted himself a few inches, his feet resting against identically-thin outcroppings less than half-an-inch deep. He continued this painfully slow process with urgency in his face. He traversed the rock face with the celerity of a fly, and soon pulled himself onto the ledge. Pari and Ravi helped him as he seemed entirely exhausted. He fell onto the flat surface of the ledge next to the oblivious snow leopard. He began to shiver.

Pari laid her body on top of him, though he tried to push her away. She smiled at him. "You need warmth, Lama."

Green Lama nodded and welcomed the proffered warmth. "What can I do, Jagmohan?" Ravi asked.

Green Lama smiled as he gently removed Pari. "You can thank your mother, as I do." He looked into the woman's eyes. "You have strengthened me. Now, we must go on."

Ravi looked at the leopard. "What of the great cat? Will it stay asleep?"

Shaking his head, Green Lama pulled the scarf from beneath the creature. The snow leopard stood to its feet and looked at the Lama. The Lama stared into its eyes and nodded. "We have no more to fear from her."

The great cat turned and leapt to the next ledge, righting itself as its back paws slipped on the snow. It turned to look at the three humans, inviting them to follow.

Ravi went ahead, followed by Pari and finally the Green Lama. The snow leopard blazed a trail for them to follow. Ravi followed cautiously, yet fearless of the great beast.

Green Lama looked behind to see Kellen ascending the steep slope far below them, a machine gun slung over his back. "It looks like he has lost his companions," the Lama said. "He can move quickly alone."

Kellen pulled out a luger pistol and fired. The Green Lama gritted his teeth. "He is insane! He will bring an avalanche on all our heads!"

Kellen laughed loudly. "Indeed!" he shouted; dangerously in the delicate area. "I can hear you on the wind Lama! I can read your thoughts as well! YOU have the Jade Tablet, and I will it and the secrets of Soma to be mine!"

Green Lama shook his head and urged the others on. "We must get out of his range of sight and stay there!"

Ravi moved forward as fast as possible and as carefully as urgency allowed. "Is it true, Lama?" he asked. "Do you have what he seeks?"

Lama shook his head as he helped Pari climb ahead of him by lifting her feet in his gloves. "He is lost and knows not what he seeks. I do know where the Jade Tablet is, and how Soma is made. His finding it will not fulfill his search, or save your life or that of your mother. He is mad, and madness is not satiated."

"What is Soma?" Ravi asked.

"It is an ancient potion that gives a man enhanced strength of body and mind," the Lama explained with a shrug. "It could possibly be used as a serum to create super-soldiers. That is why the Nazis must not have it."

Passing around a large boulder, the group moved around a corner and out of Kellen's sight. Kellen retrieved the machine gun and fired it at the boulder. A rumbling began as the white of the mountain slid downward, angry at the disruption. They clung to the rock as snow and debris fell over them and turned everything white. Kellen's mad, cacophonous laughter drowned in the deafening noise.

Chapter Four

Buddha's Awful Silence

Snow drifted away from the empty space where the Green Lama stood with Pari and her son moments ago. Avalanche sounds continued to echo faintly through the Himalayan peaks. Triumphant, Kellen wedged the butt of the machine gun he carried between a pair of rocks and pulled himself onto the ledge.

The dislodged snow and rock rested on the narrow ledge. Kellen stood on the surface, smiling at the destruction. He looked down to see the snow shift. He dug in the snow with his right hand. "I am pleased you have survived, Lama. It will give me the pleasure of...OW!"

Kellen retrieved his hand with the growling snow leopard still attached. Blood spurted where the fangs settled into the mystic's arm. "Let go, you bloody beast!" Kellen snarled. He retrieved the pistol by reaching over his midsection. Now free from the snow, the claws of the great cat began slashing at Kellen.

The Nazi mystic attempted to draw a bead on the leopard. The massive cat shook its head viciously and tore into the flesh of Kellen's arm. He managed to take aim. The bullet tore through the air. Kellen found the gun leaving his grasp as the burning metal missed the leopard. The mystic looked to see a red piece of cloth wrapped around his wrist that had caused him to drop his weapon.

Still attempting to extricate his left arm from the cat's teeth, Kellen turned to face the Green Lama. The Lama shrugged free of the frigid prison. "You!" Kellen hissed through gritted teeth. "I will kill you!"

"Stay your hand, mystic," the Green Lama ordered. The scarf glowed slightly as Kellen struggled against it. "You are under my control." The Lama stared at the leopard, the great cat relinquishing its grip and stepping away.

Kellen's arm bled from the wounds. He seemed unconcerned as he stared at the Green Lama, hateful defiance escaping his eyes. "You think I am like a kitten you can tease with yarn?" Kellen yanked his hand free of the scarf. "You have no idea of my power, Lama!"

"You could show me," the Green Lama said while retrieving his scarf. He looked at the mystic. "Your bluster indicates most of your power is in intimidation. You do not intimidate me."

In reply, Kellen leapt to retrieve the revolver from the rock's surface. He pointed it at the Lama. "I will show you bluster!" he fumed.

The Green Lama laughed. "Your power is not very subtle to rely on a weapon."

Kellen nodded. "Subtle, it is not. It is exceedingly effectual, Lama. Prepare to die."

The Lama crossed his arms. "I am always prepared for death. Most humans fear it, yet as a Lama, we welcome the experience."

Kellen pulled the trigger on the gun. Its only response was a metallic clicking sound. The Lama shook his head. "Your weapon fails you."

Kellen threw the pistol at the Lama. "It is not the way of a Lama to mock!" He rushed at the Lama. The Lama moved forward to meet him.

"I am like no Lama you know," the Green Lama said as he grappled with Kellen, his green robe in stark contrast with the Nazi mystic's crimson one.

"You fail to be humble, Lama," Kellen said.

"To say I am unlike other Lamas is not said from pride. It is said with humility and regret."

Kellen sweated from his brow as the pair grappled. "Say it with a postcard from hell!"

The leopard ignored the combat and began clawing at the snow. Gently, she pulled the ice and rocks away until Ravi pushed through the pile and climbed out. The leopard immediately began digging in another area of the pile. Shivering, Ravi took stock of the battle between the Lama and the mystic.

The young boy turned again to the leopard and saw a hand sticking out of the snow where the great cat pawed away the debris. "Mother!" Ravi exclaimed and rushed over to dig with the cat. He uncovered Pari's ice-covered face. He attempted to free her unconscious form from the debris. "Mother!" Ravi repeated. "Wake up!"

Pari opened her eyes and looked at Ravi. "What is it, my son?"

"We were in an avalanche," the boy informed his mother. "We survived," he looked at the heated contest between the Lama and Kellen, "yet the Lama continues to work to ensure we are free from danger."

Pari pulled herself free from her icy encasement. Seeing the Green Lama thrown to the ground by Kellen, she stood to her feet. "We must help him, Ravi," she said, her eyes stern. "We must help him as he helped us!"

Froth claimed the corners of Kellen's mouth as he straddled the prostate Lama's chest. His fingers compressed around the Lama's neck. "I will have the secret you hold!" he seethed through clenched teeth. "You will tell me where the Tablet is and how Soma is made!"

The Green Lama succumbed to the abuse and passed out.

"NO!" Pari screamed. She brought a rock down on Kellen's head. "You have killed him!"

Kellen fell next to the Lama, blood the color of the mystic's robe leaking from the wound. With incredible celerity Kellen rushed to his feet. He knocked the stone from Pari's hand. It tumbled into the deep, clouded abyss below.

"He is not dead, ridiculous woman! I have merely rendered him unconscious! I need him alive to tell me what he knows!" He grinned viciously. "You, however, I do not need. I will ensure you and your son are quite dead," he broke out in dark laughter. "Though only after I have done with amusing myself with your tortured screams"

Kellen moved toward Pari, hands prepared to grasp her. She withdrew and brought her hands up in defense. Kellen grinned.

A hardly perceptible whistling sound joined the rushing wind. Kellen's grin turned to a grimace with blood at its corners. The mystic stumbled forward, an arrow sticking out of his back.

Pari moved away as the Nazi sympathizer lost his footing and tumbled over the ledge. He repeated the misty fall that the Green Lama had taken earlier. Amazed, Pari and her son looked at the arrow's direction of origin.

Out of the dimming twilight the short, solid form of a Sherpa strode toward them. Accompanying him, the slender, muscular figure of a Native American held a bow in gloved hands, its string still vibrating. The Indian wore a leather flight jacket, black pants, and heavy leather boots. The two odd figures waved at the Green Lama and his company. "I see ill has befallen my Lama friend," the Sherpa said. His long mustache teased the wind like reeds in a river. "I hope you are well."

The Sherpa knelt next to the prostrate Lama. He took a vial from beneath his rugged wool coat. He blew the powder into the Lama's face. Breathing deeply, the Green Lama sat up with a start and coughed. The Sherpa steadied the Lama so as to keep him from tumbling off the ledge.

"Green Lama," the Sherpa said, "it is your companion, Tsarong. I followed your path when you did not return. I used the mystic powder to revive you." He nodded toward the indigenous American. "Twin Eagles has accompanied me. Despite my wishes, he has felled your apparent foe with an arrow."

The Indian nodded gravely to the Lama. "I do only what is necessary. I do not kill for pleasure."

"What of Pari and Ravi?" the Lama asked. "What of Kellen?"

Pari and Ravi rushed over at their names. "We are well, Jagmohan!" Ravi assured. "You need be concerned with only yourself. Twin Eagles shot Kellen with an arrow." He pointed to the clouded abyss. "He fell as you did, yet he has not returned."

"I did not mean to injure him," Twin Eagles assured. "It was meant as a warning shot."

The Green Lama stood to his feet, patting Tsarong on the shoulder as he did so. "Thank you, Tsarong. And thank you, Twin Eagles."

"Call me Mike," Twin Eagles said.

The Green Lama nodded. "As you wish. My debt to you both mounts higher than the Himalayas themselves. Yet, I suspect we have not quitted ourselves of the Nazi mystic." He examined the area. "We should continue traveling so long as there is light. Perhaps we can reach the Clouded Temple, or at least ground we fear not to leave precipitously."

The party strode onward and upward, this time aided by Tsarong's climbing equipment. A storm arose and whipped their faces as they challenged the arduously steep terrain, yet all five proved worthy climbers. Some hours after dark, light from windows tore through the blinding snow and darkness.

"There," the Green Lama said as he pointed at the light, "the Clouded Temple!"

Chapter Five

The Clouded Temple

Ravi could not tell if they had traveled many miles or a handful of steps, yet he was pleased to be welcomed into the warmth of the monastery by a bald, aged monk clad in a blue robe. "Welcome, blessed ones," the monk smiled. "I am Lama Puneet. You will not find my hospitality dulled by solitude. Your comfort is an eager pleasure for me. Anything asked I will attempt to provide."

The Green Lama clapped the monk on the back in a familiar manner less Asiatic and more American. "It is well to see you, old friend! Thank you for accommodating my companions. Is our pilot friend awake?"

Puneet shook his head. "Mister Masters sleeps."

Twin Eagles stretched his arms."I will go join Rick. That flight and today's adventure sapped my energy." Familiar with the temple already, he moved to find his sleeping quarters. "Good night, all."

"You honor the Clouded Temple with your visit."

The monk bowed his head toward Ravi and Pari. "You honor the Clouded Temple with your visit. I am certain you are hungry and wish for warm tea."

Ravi rubbed his arms."Do you have some?"

Puneet laughed. "The life of a monk is not so austere as to preclude sustenance. Please to follow me," he waggled his finger and began walking. "You can eat with the others."

The Green Lama stayed behind with Tsarong. "The Nazi mystic believes I hold the Jade Tablet. He is correct. I must keep its secrets from him."

Tsarong nodded. "There is little danger his retrieving the Jade Tablet, yet I agree. Caution is of great importance."

"The decoy remains in the basement, I presume." The Lama pulled off his hood to reveal dark brown hair beneath.

Tsarong nodded. "A mendicant would believe it real. The Nazis we anticipated may not be fooled for long."

The Green Lama pulled at his chin. "We will have trouble. Kellen survives, and he reads my thoughts. He will not listen to reason. Madness is his true love, yet he knows it not."

Tsarong nodded. "Trouble will find us." He looked toward the door where Puneet took Pari and Ravi. "Perhaps we should remove ourselves from the country. Mister Masters will help."

The Lama shook his head. "There is no time. If this weather holds, even the skills of our guests will be worthless. We need to prepare a defense for the Temple. The false tablet might buy us time. We can scarcely hope it is time enough."

"My friend," Tsarong said with all seriousness, "the Temple is prepared for peace. It is not a fort to be defended. The monks will not fight."

"We have no choice," the Lama replied, "and neither do they. It must be. We must be vigilant; else the Nazis will create an unstoppable force against the world. If that occurs, there will be no peace aside from the peace of the boot and the bullet." The Green Lama punched a fist into his palm. "Though the secrets are ineffable, we cannot risk they may be discovered. We must fight to maintain peace!"

Tsarong shook his head. "You have much to learn, my friend. How you are skilled in the mysteries beyond the monks is a wonder when you cannot control your passions."

The Lama nodded. "It is true, Tsarong. My journey is not complete. I have time to learn perfection. Now, I desire the protection of innocents and the destructive force in our charge." He looked to the window where falling snow drifted through. "If the storm breaks by dawn, there may be another way."

Tsarong nodded. "Perhaps the light will shine to us."

"Let us hope and pray it is so," Lama said. "For now, we must rest and meditate. Dawn will come with storm or clarity. We must prepare to welcome it."

The Lama walked to the hall where the monks ate together. Passed out from exhaustion, Pari held Ravi in a blanket near the burning fireplace. Tsarong followed him in. "They are resting," he stated.

"They will need it for tomorrow," Lama replied. "Whatever trails the rising sun or darkened clouds the day brings."

The Green Lama excused himself. In his sparse room with stone walls, he assumed a lotus position. He fell into a deep meditation to prepare himself for the following day.

As the night drifted toward dawn, a slight whirring drifted through the thin, cool air. A small tank carried aloft by overhead propellers landed in the soft snow outside the Clouded Temple. It took aim at a high, candlelit window and quietly ejected a shiny metal canister through the nozzle of its cannon.

In the dining room of the Temple, several monks rested comfortably in their lotus positions. Pari and Ravi stayed by the warm fire, wrapped in a blanket. The metal canister flew through the unglazed rock window and clanked to the floor. An identical projectile soon followed. A monk stirred, choking on the yellow gas escaping from the metal cylinders. He rushed to the prayer bell, yet fell to the ground. The effort only caused the gas to go into his lungs and bloodstream more quickly.

The other sleeping monks stirred before falling into a deeper rest than before as gas filled the room. Pari and Ravi did not stir. Canisters fell into other windows as the strange tank aimed from beneath the propellers.

Moments later, Kellen and a Nazi pilot strode into the dining room wearing gasmasks. Kellen saw Pari and Ravi sleeping soundly by the flickering fireplace. He nodded. "How perfect!" he said with muffled voice. The pilot remained at the door as Kellen strode past the sleeping monks to the mother and son. "This is exactly what I came to shop for." With powerful arms, he lifted first Pari over his left shoulder. He folded Ravi over his powerful right arm. "Let us leave, Captain Adelbrecht."

"So soon, *Herr* Kellen?" the pilot replied. "We could kill everyone. We have already retrieved the Jade Tablet!"

Kellen shook his head in mockery. "You lack imagination and subtlety,

Captain. It is well you can use your skills as a pilot for the Rotor Panzer. You are unskilled in contemplation. You are a fool to think we have the true Tablet." Kellen shook his head. "No. They are protecting it. This will require greater finesse to cause the Green Lama to reveal it to us. We must remove him from his place of power. This Temple offers him resources. We will cause him to follow us to retrieve the woman and the boy." The mystic began to walk out the door. The captain followed.

The Green Lama smelled an odd scent in the air, and knew something was amiss. The yellow glow washed in through a West-facing window, indicating it was late in the day. He expected to return to consciousness far earlier.

The Lama moved through the building, noting the monks sleeping in the dining room. A round metal canister the size of a soup can rolled lazily back and forth over the uneven floor, impelled by the cold air blowing through the chimney. Ashes drifted from the extinguished fire. Green Lama rubbed his chin as he lifted the canister. He spun it around in his hands, examining it. "*Om! Ma-ni pad-me Hum*," he muttered. He continued through the Clouded Temple.

"Twin Eagles," a gentle voice said as Mike tried to open his eyes. "Twin Eagles," the voice repeated as Mike rolled onto his back. He pushed himself into a seated position on the austere mat of straw and cloth barely disguising the rock floor. His eyes cleared to a green color and focused the irises to see the Green Lama shaking his shoulder. Mike leaned on his hands to sit and looked at the man. "What is it, Lama? Is it time for you to return to Ceylon?"

Green Lama smiled lightly at the strong-framed, sharp-featured man. "No," he said, "not yet, Twin Eagles. There are problems."

Mike swallowed a yawn and stood to his feet. He glanced at the dark-haired man sleeping on the mat across the room. "Why wake me up first, Lama? Is Rick okay?"

"Rest easy, Twin Eagles. Our friend sleeps comfortably."

Mike stood up to face the Lama. "Look here, Green Lama-Jethro Dumont! Drop the Twin Eagles crap, okay? Yes, it's my name. I don't care for how you go around acting like an Indian! It's not like there's some connection there because I'm pure Seminole and you've learned the fakir stuff! India is Hindi, you dope, not American Indian. You're not either one no matter how much you learn! Two things to remember: I prefer to be called Mike except by my friends; Two, I'm not saying you're not a friend, but remember you're a client."

Green Lama smiled lightly. "Please, Mike. I mean no offense and we have no time to quarrel. As I mentioned, there are complications."

Mike's keen eyes wandered to the sleeping form of Rick Masters. "What's up with Rick? He never sleeps so long in the afternoon. In fact, I don't either!"

Green Lama handed Mike the round cylinder in explanation. Mike turned it over in his hands, reading the words in large letters. "*Schlaf*-Gas!"

Green Lama nodded. "Yes."

Mike offered a frustrated shrug as he knelt next to his friend and business partner. "What does '*schlaf*' mean? Is it laughing gas?"

"No. It means 'sleeping.'"

"Sleeping gas?" Mike shook his head. "No such thing."

Green Lama nodded. "It appears to be exactly what it claims. My brothers all slept soundly when I found them. Now awoken, they appear fine. The gas bears no ill effects; it seems I feel in good health." Green Lama stretched. "Even a bit refreshed."

Awakened from Mike shaking his shoulder, Rick sat up and smoothed his straight, black mustache before running his hand through his hair. "What's going on?" He glanced at the window. "Looks like I overslept!"

"We have suffered a sleeping gas attack," Mike said. He helped Rick stand to his feet. Mike looked at the Green Lama again. "Jethro says there's trouble, but he hasn't said what."

The Green Lama nodded. "We rescued a woman and her child from Nazis. They sought the Jade Tablet, yet I suspect it has become more of a vendetta situation." He looked at Twin Eagles. "Mike accidentally shot their accompanying mystic, a madman named Kellen. The rescued boy and mother disappeared while all slept."

Rick Masters nodded and looked at Mike. "You shot him by accident, Twin Eagles? You must be slipping." Mike grinned slightly. Rick breathed in and stood. "Well, let's start attempting to find them. What clues do you have?"

The Green Lama smiled. "If you would be so kind as to follow me, I will show you."

The three walked to the entrance of the temple and outside. The fresh snow covered the ground, interrupted by occasional jagged rocks thrusting through. The light of the azure blue sky reached them without interruption. The thick air and other obstructions known at lower elevations did not exist here. Each step they trod followed the Lama along the path of the Nazi invaders' footprints. The Lama halted in front of a large impression in the snow. “Here,” he said, “is our clue.”

Mike furrowed his brow. “Is this some type of joke, Lama? I know what these are from the Great War. These are tank tracks, but there’s no trail coming or going! It’s impossible!”

Rick Masters shook his head. “No it’s not, Twin Eagle. I worked with the Brits on a top-secret project like this. They wanted to create a gyrotank based on Cierva’s gyroplane designs.”

“Did it work?” Mike asked.

Rick shrugged. “Not when I was on the project. Who knows that the Germans didn’t hear about the idea and make it happen?”

The Green Lama scratched his head. “The Nazis had something on a flatbed truck in the village. This must have been under the tarp.”

Mike nodded. “Doesn’t seem like helpful information, Lama. How are we going to find a flying tank?”

Rick cleared his throat. “In the air, I expect.”

Chapter Six
Predatory Avalanche

Rick Masters slipped into the pilot’s seat of the British-built Armstrong Whitworth Whitley bomber. On the outside, the plane resembled an elongated, military-green brick with wings. The inside seemed only slightly less utilitarian.

The Green Lama stood regally yet humbly behind the pilot’s chair. “I have been meaning to ask how you came to own this plane.”

Rick shrugged. “I didn’t get it in pristine condition. I swapped a B-17 I used for transport with the Brits when I was working for them. These Whitleys,” he tapped the instrument panel as one would pat a beloved dog on its head, “aren’t as fast as some bombers their size, yet they are reliable and perfect for transports. The Mercedes engines practically fix themselves. It’s not so pretty as a gal you’d like to marry, yet a man couldn’t be happier if he married a wife that took care of him as well as she does.”

Mike walked past the Lama and slipped into the co-pilot’s chair. “The anchor is released,” the Seminole co-pilot informed, holding up a small, three-pronged anchor on the end of a rope rolled into loops.

Rick drew a deep breath and released. His lip curled slightly. “Time for another harrowing and original aviation miracle, Twin Eagles.”

Mike nodded. "Yes, Rick. Landing on the side of a mountain was pretty tricky, but taking off again might be tougher." He turned to look at the Green Lama. "You should sit down, Lama. This will be a death-defying attempt."

The Lama shrugged. "Then I defy death with you. If you have need, it is better that I remain free to assist."

"Twin Eagles is right, Lama," Rick said. "If nothing else, it is most disconcerting to have a holy man standing behind us. We need one-hundred-percent of our attention on this take-off."

With a smile and nod, the Green Lama sat on the floor in a lotus position. "I can be ready from here if needed."

Mike huffed slightly before turning his eyes toward the downward slope in front of them. Rick flipped a toggle-switch and the engines rumbled to life. The propellers spun in rhythm, agitating the fresh snow into a mini-storm. The plane moved slowly forward. It began sliding down the slope on its skis.

A rumbling sound joined the sound of the engines. Rick looked into an ice-encrusted mirror outside the plane to see a building avalanche of boulders, ice, and snow pursue them in a furious pace. "It's an avalanche!"

"Can we outrun it?" Mike asked.

Rick gritted his teeth. "I certainly hope so! I'll give the plane everything! If we clear the cliff in time, we'll be okay."

Rick pushed the engines to the outer limits. The plane shook under the strain as it rushed over the uneven surface of snow and ice, shaped by jagged boulders beneath it. The rumbling sound increased as the avalanche neared. Sweat appeared on Rick's brow as the plane approached the edge of the cliff. The avalanche increased its pace toward them.

Spurting through the air, the first and fleetest pieces of ice and snow began battering the tail of the plane. The uneven, pelting rhythm indicated an urgency and hopelessness.

"Lift off now, Rick!" Mike said.

Rick Masters shook his head. "Not enough speed yet, Twin Eagles! We must outrun it, and the engines are pushed beyond capacity as it is!"

With a sneer, Mike stole a glance at the calmly meditating Lama. "If you've got a trick, holy man, we need a miracle now!"

The Lama continued meditating. Mike turned his attention back to the cliff's edge rushing toward them. "Damn!"

A cracking sound rocked the aircraft. Rick looked in the mirror. One of the plane's skis tumbled behind and disappeared into the avalanche that relentlessly hunted after them. The plane seemed a great black swan; the avalanche a tiger preparing to sink frozen teeth into the flesh of its wings. The plane at least reached the speed that it did not need the skid. Rick skillfully kept the wing floating above the ground.

Rick felt the tip of the rolling mass of snow, rock, and ice lift the tail of the plane as it continued down the slope. The avalanche had overtaken the plane, and so near the cliff's edge!

Chapter Seven

The Shape of Air

The plane disappeared into the avalanche's drifting mass. The avalanche hurtled over the edge of the cliff, accepted into the yawning depths below. Bursting through the roiling snow, the airplane appeared, twin engines roaring, and took flight!

Inside, Rick struggled to right the plane with a laugh of joy. "I won't even say that was close, Twin Eagles!"

The co-pilot gave Rick an angry expression before bursting into laughter. He turned and struck the Lama on the back. "Hey, Lama! We did it! It's a miracle!"

The Green Lama breathed in and opened his eyes. He nodded knowingly. "The miracle you requested and I meditated upon."

Still smiling, Mike nodded. "Yeah, sure, holy man. I won't question it!"

Rick looked back at the still tumultuous cliff face as the avalanche continued to create a waterfall of glacial rocks and snow. "We can use more miracles if you've got them, Lama. We have to find a flying tank, and land this plane again with a missing ski!"

"We're missing a ski?" Mike queried.

"Yes," Rick nodded. "It broke off just before the avalanche caught up to us. It will be tough to land without it." He shrugged. "We can figure out how to cross that bridge when we come to the canyon."

"Maybe we oughta land a.s.a.p.," Mike suggested. "We could get another plane."

Mike shook his head. "We're losing time as it is. The tank tracks were fresh, but we don't know where they were headed. Our only chance is to catch them in the air. Let's hope they are still in it. If not, they'll disappear on the ground."

Mike nodded. "I guess you're right, Rick. Which way do you think they went?"

Rick shrugged. "You can land a gyroplane anywhere. It's a small tank, judging by the track print. Even a small tank means a heavy load. They wouldn't have much range. They could land anywhere there was fuel available."

Mike rubbed his chin. "A hidden base?"

Rick nodded. "Possible, yet a base would need a road or airstrip nearby to build, I suspect."

The Green Lama stepped forward. "I know these mountains, and I have an idea of a spot that fits all requirements to build a significant support base. Let us follow the mountains." Rick turned the bomber to run parallel to the range.

The Green Lama stood in the aisle, his eyes seeking the pointed mountain peaks and abrupt valleys describing the treacherously beautiful Himalayas. He breathed deeply, causing Rick to look over at the holy man. "You're a cool character, Lama. I'm pretty good at seeing when a person's not happy."

Lama shook his head. "I am not unhappy, yet I am concerned for the young boy and his mother."

"Seems to me," the pilot returned, "there's something else in your eye. Are you in love, Lama?"

Mike looked at the Lama's face and chuckled. "He is, Rick! I'm green with envy!"

The Green Lama smiled. "I will admit an infatuation with the woman. A Lama is sworn to not allow his passions to rule. The pair remains under my protection, whatever my sentiments. It is my duty to ensure their safety."

All the while he spoke his eyes scanned the area. "Over there." He pointed his finger toward a dark spot staining a snow-white peak. "It is in the air yet."

Rick pointed the Whitley's nose to chase after the moving dot in the distance. "I'm not sure what to do if we catch it," he said. "Do you have any ideas, Twin Eagles?"

The co-pilot shrugged. "We still have the machine gun hooked up, don't we? The Brits said we could keep it to protect us on midnight runs through Naziland."

Rick nodded. "We do have it. For all the good it will do against a flying tank's armor."

"Please," Green Lama interjected, "use no violence."

"What!?" Mike exclaimed. "They're gonna use violence on us! You expect us to take it!?"

"No," the Lama said. "You forget that there is a child and a woman on board. If you manage to destroy the craft, you will destroy our purpose here."

"He's right," Rick interjected. "We can't bring them down without injuring their prisoners. Perhaps we can land and perform a clandestine rescue operation."

Mike shook his head and pointed. "I think if we wanted to keep it a secret, we should have shut up some time ago. I think they heard us."

They watched the spot turn and head directly toward them. As the two craft drew closer together, the Nazi vessel came into clearer view. The props battered the air over the black Nazi tank. Decorated with German crosses, the tank was not large, and its profile deceivingly low. A cannon turret rested a few feet below the propeller, apparently swiveling on the same axle. The tracks jutted out freely from the tank's armored body. A rear fin and tail steadied the craft as it flew along.

"What kind of tank is that?" Mike asked. "The Nazis like to make 'em big, but this one's not bigger than a lorry!"

Rick shrugged. "To carry worthwhile armor and weaponry through the air, they couldn't make it too large. Looks like a stripped and modified Panzer One. It's got enough bulk to hurt and run. That little cub could be a tiger."

Mike nodded. "Probably can't fire its cannon from the air. The recoil would rip it apart."

The barrel of the tank's gun swung quickly to find its target and fired. A large blast rocked the Whitley, proving Mike's words wrong as a shell exploded outside.

"Whoa!" Mike said. "That's close enough for a Burma Shave! Guess I was wrong about them not being able to use their gun, but how?"

Rick shrugged. "Looks like the Nazis have developed a cannon with diminished recoil." Mike looked at Rick. "We've gotta fire up the machine gun! The next blast could be our last!"

"We're not out of tricks yet, Twin Eagles," Rick replied. He pulled the Whitley into an extreme climb as another blast rocked the erstwhile night bomber. The tank followed, gaining altitude by moving in a vertical fashion and keeping its nose level.

"They can't aim at us through their props," Rick explained. "I figured that would be too risky a design."

Mike nodded. "Now, we know they can't point the gun up or down except in a limited range. The tank needs to be on the level with its target.

"A large blast rocked the Whitley."

I hope so anyway."

"That's right, Twin Eagles," Rick replied. "I don't know all their capabilities yet. I can guarantee they'll run out of gas before we do. Unless they've landed somewhere and refueled, they've got to do it soon."

Green Lama nodded. "It is true. Of course, it will be worse if they land. We will face them on the ground, where the tank will perform on more familiar turf."

Mike's face turned grim. "That's if we can land this thing in the middle of nowhere with a missing skid."

Rick nodded confidently. "After that avalanche debacle, I can land it on top of a wedding cake between the bride and groom. It's a cinch!"

The Green Lama smiled. "Landing it safely will be enough, my friend. Your prowess as a pilot is not in question."

Rick brought the plane level and let out a sigh. "I'd wager you're right. This is not going to be easy, no matter how you slice the cake." He watched the rotatank level at the Whitley's altitude to pursue the bomber. "We're stuck playing cat and mouse, but we're the cat and a bit unwieldy. That mouse carries quite a poison bite. Maybe we can use the cloud cover to buy some time."

Rick and the Lama looked out the side window. The rotatank's gun spun in their direction. Rick pushed hard on the stick, sending the Whitley into a sharp dive. "I should have stayed in bed," he grumbled.

A tank shell exploded outside the plane. The windows and walls rattled at the vibration. The Lama gritted his teeth and stared out the window, leaning back to maintain balance. Though the angle seemed incongruous to standing, the Lama remained so. "I feel you, Kellen," he said into the vast space separating the Whitley and the rotatank.

Mike snorted. "If you can talk to him from here, tell him to knock it off! That, and tell him I'll slug him in the nose first chance I get!"

Standing in the rotatank, Kellen smiled as he looked out the small, forward window view. "They are diving," he noted to the rotatank pilot, Captain Adelbrecht. "Follow them down."

He turned to the rear of the small compartment, staring at Ravi and Pari tied with rope into two separate bundles. "Let my mother go," Ravi pleaded, tears in his eyes. "She will not harm you!"

Pari stifled her tears. "Hush, child. He is without mercy. His heart knows only ambition."

"Ah!" Kellen held his chest to feign injury. "You cut me to the quick, woman! I am a very kind person." He chuckled lowly. "Of what kind, it would take long to explain. I took you because the Green Lama seemed to have an attachment. I can use that to retrieve the Jade Tablet. While all slept in the Temple, I found the pathetic ruse they left to dissuade the imbeciles." He shrugged. "I also found Masters' pilot license, though he is well known as a transport flyer."

Kellen rubbed his chin. "I did not see the plane, but felt certain the Lama could follow. Knowing he could follow, I likewise knew he would. I could have kidnapped the Lama and tortured him, yet this is more poetic, do you not agree? To a man like the Lama, it is also exceedingly more torturous."

Pari moved closer to Ravi. "Just be still, my son," she whispered. "All is as Brahma directs."

Captain Adelbrecht turned to Kellen. "They are leveling out, sir."

The mystic nodded. "Good. They cannot continue to run. We must force them to land or crash. Try to strike a wing. It will give them time to bail out with parachutes and we will pick them up."

The pilot reached over and pushed a shell into the cannon, clicking the hatch shut. Using a periscope to aim, he turned the gun and pushed a red button next to the handle.

The shell whistled through the air and exploded near the right wing of the Whitley. The aircraft rattled under the force. "That was close!" Mike announced.

Rick shook his head as he struggled with the stick. "It was more than that, Twin Eagles. It was a hit somewhere!"

Looking out his window, Mike nodded. "The wing's on fire!"

"It is possible we will crash," the Lama said calmly.

Rick nodded. "It's possible. I can control it for now. Fire damage to the engine is the biggest concern. The plane will crash if that happens." He shook his head. "If we could put out the fire, we'd have a fighting chance."

Turning to the back of the plane, the Lama nodded. "Leave it to me. Just keep it as steady as possible."

"Where are you going?" Mike shouted at him. No reply came. Wind reached the pilot's compartment as a door clanged open in the cargo hold. Mike stared at the wing. "He's on the wing!"

Rick's eyes opened wide. "What the heck!? Is he nuts!?"

Mike shrugged, a slight smile on his face. "Maybe. He's just walking toward the fire!"

The wind tore at the green robe. The Lama seemed to not notice. Near the large Mercedes engine, the fire burned. The Lama held his arms above him, his sleeves threatening to tear under the violent wind. He stared upward and closed his eyes. The fire seemed to prefer the Green Lama, and it crawled toward him and away from the engine.

"You gotta see this!" Mike exclaimed with his eyes riveted on the Lama.

Rick gritted his teeth. "I am flying a damaged plane here!"

Mike watched as the flames abandoned the wing and engulfed the Green Lama. The flickering fire seemed calm in the ripping wind forces. "I thought you said 'damn plane' for a moment, Rick. This here is a damn sight, let me tell you!"

Rick moved over and grasped the co-pilot's stick so he could see, too. "He's on fire!"

As Rick said this, the fire went out abruptly. Rick and Mike stared as the Lama walked back toward the fuselage. Rick shook his head clear and returned to the pilot's chair. The Lama walked into the compartment.

"That was some crazy stuff!" Mike laughed to the Lama. "How the heck did you do that?"

The Green Lama smiled. "Just some fakir stuff, Mike."

"Call me Twin Eagles," Mike replied with a smile. "I've seen Houdini get out of straightjackets when I was a kid. That was a trick. What you did was real!"

The Lama shrugged. "Twin Eagles…friend. Houdini and I are much alike. He uses sleight of hand, yet he understands more deeply than most."

Rick saw the rotatank to the left of the plane, lining up the gun. "One thing I do understand is we've got to get away from that flying iron lung or one of us is gonna be out of air! Putting out the fire on the wing only puts us right where we started."

The Lama looked out the window at the rotatank and nodded. "Yes. We have to solve the issue at hand."

"How will we do that?" Mike asked. "Without using the machine gun, we're a sitting duck!"

Rick shook his head. "Not necessarily." He turned the enormous bomber to face the rotatank and gunned the engines.

"What're you doing!?" Mike demanded.

Rick shrugged. "Sorry, Mike. I'll need you for this. You've got your bow?"

Mike nodded. He mechanically reached behind the co-pilot's chair and pulling out the thin case carrying his bow and arrows. "What do you want me to hit? It's gonna be a tough shot with everything considered!"

"The electrical box on the outside," Rick said. "I saw it earlier."

Mike studied the approaching rotatank and nodded. "Crazy they'd put that on the outside."

"It's probably in its experimental stages still," Rick said. "This might be a field test where they didn't expect combat, but they needed the shells to test the cannon. Nazis don't want their secret weapons shown off, and the wilds of Asia aren't exactly Times Square."

Mike sighed. "We can talk about it over tea and strudels if we can knock 'em down," Mike said. "Just get me close enough, Rick. I can hit it. But they'll probably blast us way before we get there!"

"Are you always an optimist, Twin Eagles?" Rick continued on his heading. "If they do, they can't guarantee we'll miss them. They need to decide on a defensive or offensive move now, and I'm betting it'll be defensive."

"Hitting the box won't do much anyway," Mike shrugged.

"That might be enough to kill the engine," Rick replied.

"They'll crash!" the Green Lama protested. "Pari and Ravi will be killed!"

Rick shook his head. "A gyroplane can land safely even without power." He nodded with admiration. "That was the reason Cierva designed them in the first place."

Mike walked toward the hatch leading outside. "Just get me in a good range. I'll take it from there."

Removing his red scarf, the Lama fell into step beside the Seminole Indian. "Let me help keep you steady, Twin Eagles."

Mike looked at the Lama. "I'd appreciate that, pal."

Mike opened the hatch. The wind slammed it against the side of the Whitley. The Lama wrapped his scarf about Twin Eagle's waist. The Seminole warrior notched an arrow and waited until they got in range.

He saw the rotatank coming toward the plane in a head-on course. It quickly ascended just as it became clear the bomber would not turn. Straight as an arrow, the Whitley flew undeterred through the air beneath the tank. Twin Eagles pulled the string of his bow as taut as possible. He aimed far in front of the tank to account for its motion and the strong wind force. The bow twanged as he let the string go. The arrow flew at the rotatank and struck the box squarely in the bottom, causing sparks to fly. Twin Eagles smiled slightly as the rotatank moved quickly over them. The rotatank dipped slightly, narrowly missing the Whitley's tail fin.

"Did you get it?" Rick shouted.

"I got it," Mike returned the shout. "Let's see if it got the job done!"

The Green Lama continued to watch the rotatank as its barrel spun around. It aimed directly at the plane as the flying tank drifted slowly lower. "Rick!" he shouted. "They've got us clear in their sights!"

Rick twisted the stick just as the ship rocked with another explosion.

This time the dancing flames engulfed the left wing.

The Lama stood still as Mike dove out of the way. The flames washed through the open hatch, coating the Lama for a second time. He remained unharmed as the flames dispersed. Smoke rose from his robe.

Mike shook his head before turning it toward the pilot's compartment. "I think the engine's damaged, Rick!"

"Think what you want, Twin Eagles!" Rick shouted back as he wrestled with the controls. "I know the wing's damaged! So is the engine! We'll be lucky to land!"

Mike rose to his feet, walking briskly to the cockpit. He slipped into the co-pilot's chair. "What should I do, Rick?"

Rick nodded professionally. "Watch the dials. Try getting an engine back. Keep your eyes peeled for a soft landing. I'll keep us gliding and land us as soon as I find a place—sooner if I don't! This hawk just became an albatross around our neck, but we can't cut the strings just yet!"

The Green Lama walked into the cockpit. "Can I assist in any way?"

Mike gritted his teeth. "You can pray, holy man! Your fire-eating act won't help here!"

The Lama assumed a lotus position and began muttering.

Mike scanned the mountains and valleys. He pointed to a narrow canyon with a dry and ancient river bed. "Can you land it there, Rick? It's straight with a flat bottom!"

"Are you nuts or soup?" Rick asked. "There's only a foot or two for the wings!" He laughed. "Of course I can make it!"

Rick Masters steered the plane carefully to aim toward the river canyon. The plane dropped toward the canyon, as the tip of wing broke off with a loud *crack*. Unbuckling his seatbelt, Rick stood to his feet and pulled at the stick. "This is gonna get rough!" The stick rattled in his hand, the plane following suit. The plane leveled out as it glided between the canyon walls, tilting toward the left. Rick's arm muscles strained as he pulled against the Armstrong's unwieldy weight.

The right wing struck the side of the cliff, breaking off to the dead engine. Sweat poured off Rick as he desperately tried to correct, to no avail. The plane tilted sideways. The dry river bottom came toward them.

The plane struck with violence and thrust Rick toward the window. He struck it with force, violently shattering the glass. The shards flew through the air and coated Mike and the still-meditating Lama. The Lama did not flinch from his lotus position.

The fuselage continued to slide down the riverbed as it slogged through the silty, damp sand underneath the surface that had appeared from the air to be solid. The left wing broke of entirely now as it struck the side of the canyon. The Whitley came to a restful halt at the end of its toilsome journey.

The only sounds heard at first were the tired creaks of the crumpled fuselage. Mike breathed in deeply and audibly. He unbuckled and rushed over to Rick's prostrate form. Cradling his friend, he wiped the blood carelessly from his face, the glass digging into Mike's hands and Rick's brow. "Are you okay, brother?" Rick's breathing offered the only reply.

The Green Lama arose to his feet and observed Mike and Rick.

Tears in his eyes, Mike snarled. "Come on, holy man! What tricks do you have to save him?"

The Lama knelt to observe Rick closer. After a moment he stood again. "He will be healed. He is only unconscious. Help me carry him out of the plane."

Rick coughed blood and blinked the crimson liquid from his eyes. He grimaced as he stood to his feet. "Like hell. I'm just resting my eyes." He spit out blood with bits of broken glass that clattered on the floor. He pushed his back against the wall to rest. "If any of you two jokers knew about medicine, you might have known to pull the big chunks of glass out of my mouth." He chuckled, but it quickly turned to coughing again. When he stopped, he said, "I think I just invented a new type of sore throat nobody needs." The Lama grasped Rick's arm to steady him as Mike did the same.

A whirring sound filled the air as they opened the hatch. Mike looked down the canyon. "We've got bigger headaches."

The rotatank floated toward the ground, its gun aimed at the damaged remains of the Armstrong Whitworth Whitley. The Lama shook his head. "They remain without power."

Mike gritted his teeth. "Yeah, sure. That's how they shot us down!"

Rick coughed blood. "They'll have manual controls for the gun. They can still fire a shell."

The rotatank drifted to a landing. The nose of the tank sunk in the wet sand, burying the barrel. The Green Lama looked over at Mike, releasing Rick's arm. "Can you get Rick behind those rocks, Twin Eagles?"

Mike nodded. "I'll take care of him. Where are you going?"

His robe billowing behind him as he walked away, he said, "I am going to finish this. Now."

Twin Eagles waved after the Lama. "Take care, my friend!"

Chapter Eight
Jewel in the Lotus

Breathing deeply, the Lama approached the sinking rotatank. The hatch on the top sprung open. The Lama smiled at the figure presenting itself before recalling the weight of the matter. Pari's form pushed through the round opening, a Hindu goddess with sad eyes.

A German-manufactured pistol pressed into Pari's back as the Lama focused on Kellen following behind the young woman. The Nazi mystic smiled fiendishly. "I cannot tell you how glad I am you followed, Green Lama. I wanted you to, of course."

The Lama nodded. "Of course. Otherwise, you would have taken me from the Clouded Temple and tortured the secret you desire from my lips."

Ducking to avoid the slightly rotating props, Pari crawled onto the rotatank. Tears fell copiously from her eyes. Kellen kept the pistol trained on her as he shook his head. "No, Lama. That would not do. You are too headstrong to have fallen that way. Besides, think not that I am unsporting. You are the hunter, I am the leopard."

The Lama shook his head. "A leopard is a majestic creature. You have no honor, no sense of justice."

Kellen laughed. "Honor? You sound like a Japanese Samurai! You are like no Lama I have heard." Kellen shook his head mockingly. "You speak as an American, with none of the subtle beauty of a humble Buddhist! As for justice; Germany has waited too long to receive justice! Now it is our turn to take that which is rightfully ours!"

"Let the woman and child go, Kellen. I will give you what is rightfully yours."

Kellen smirked. "Certainly Lama. Take the woman," he shook his head, "it is too late to give you the boy. He is dead." Using his boot, he kicked Pari off the tank. She rolled to the sand, weeping.

The Green Lama's eyes widened. "What!?"

"Have you taken a monk's vow of dumbness instead of silence? The boy is dead." Kellen laughed at his own joke. "You could have just given me what I wanted, Lama!"

With the roar of a leopard, the Green Lama traversed the distance separating him and the tank with uncanny speed and celerity. "*Om! Ma-ni pad-me Hum!*" he shouted as he ran.

Kellen fired twice at the Lama, yet the bullets failed to find purchase. The Lama leapt onto the tank and knocked the gun from the Nazi mystic's hand.

"You wanted the power of the Jade Tablet, mystic?" The Green Lama's eyes glowered. "Very well then," he seethed. "I will show you!"

The Lama pushed Kellen through the tank hatch and slid in behind him. Surveying the scene, the Lama's eyes halted for a moment on Ravi's lifeless body, slung into the cramped corner of the small tank by the violence of Kellen's bullet. Captain Adalbrecht pulled his gun, too slow to fire. Kellen tried to stand as the Lama smacked the pistol out of the pilot's hand. The Lama grabbed the pilot's jacket and threw it and the pilot through the open hatch with a great, barely-human force.

Kellen grasped the pilot's Luger and fired at the Green Lama. The Lama pushed Kellen against the wall and yanked the gun from his hand. "I am going to show you what you wanted to know." He threw Kellen into the corner and removed the glove from his right hand and displayed a rainbow-colored finger-ring made of woven hair. "The six Sacred Colors," the Lama explained, pointing them out as he spoke. "White, green, yellow, red, blue, and black."

Kellen tried to charge the Lama, yet met the resistance of a Sherpa boot. "Calm down," the Lama said. "This will be over soon."

"Get on with it Lama," Kellen sneered. "Show me the Jade Tablet!"

"If you will stay still, I will." The Green Lama gently slipped the ring from his finger and set it on the floor. He kneeled and began to unravel the hair of the ring, making a square mat about two-feet-wide. "You see, my excitable friend, the Jade Tablet has power. Indeed, removed pieces are fashioned into green jewels of power used to defend the innocent. The information written on the Tablet is the true power, and like the Gutenberg Bible, it can be copied."

The Green Lama continued to order the threads of colored string to reproduce a pattern framed by the green hair. When done, he put his hands on his knees. "It is true, the copies are not as powerful. You see, I would have gladly given to you my Jade Tablet. You could not read it except if on a few points of knowledge. There are billions of ways to place the strands of hair, and only one way they read correctly." He shrugged. "It takes a Lama an entire lifetime to learn to do this. I am blessed to have memory of my transmigrations and have perfected the rite through many centuries. This will be the last time I see you on this road for quite a while."

The Green Lama stared into Kellen's eyes. The Nazi mystic shriveled beneath the gaze. "What are you going to do, Lama?" Kellen's quivering voice asked. "You cannot kill me! You cannot stop me!" The mystic was thwarted in his attempt to stand by the Lama's left palm against his chest.

"Peace, Kellen," the Green Lama said, his eyes closed in meditation. The mat of hair on the floor fluttered as the Lama held his right palm toward Ravi's unconscious body. The tank shifted as it sunk further into the soft, damp sand. The hatch cover slammed shut at the motion and Ravi's body slid forward to answer the call of gravity. The Lama's hand reached out to grab the arm of the corpse. He gently pulled toward him, still pressing his other palm against Kellen.

The Nazi mystic licked his lips. "What are you doing, Lama?"

"I am not doing Kellen," the Green Lama kept his eyes closed serenely. "I am undoing an imbalance. This boy has a future you have not seen."

"He has no future!" Kellen said. "He is dead!"

The Lama shook his head slightly. "Kellen, you do not understand. Nothing is dead. Everything is pregnant with life. You said I cannot kill you. You, I, and nobody conscious are all that remain in this tank. I am free to do as I wish. Have you not understood the secret of the dried leaves in Autumn?" The mat of hair floated upward and shivered as if caught in a warm breeze.

Tears began to fall from Kellen's eyes. "You are sworn to preserve life, Lama!"

"Oh I am," the Green Lama said. "*Om! Ma-ni pad-me Hum.*"

"You cannot harm me, Lama!" Kellen's mouth frothed. "You can't!"

The Lama nodded. "True. I cannot harm you. I can do nothing not meant to be." He repeated the chant. "*Om! Ma-ni pad-me Hum.*"

Kellen grasped his chest and pulled his hand away. It was covered with blood. "What are you doing?" he asked again.

The Lama shrugged. "I am returning the gift you offered the world. *Om! Ma-ni pad-me Hum.*"

"You are killing me!" Kellen said.

"I am not. I am giving life." The Lama breathed deeply. "*Om! Ma-ni pad-me Hum.*"

Kellen looked to see Ravi's chest raise slightly with breath. The mat of hair slowed in its vibrations and waved as a lily floating in a Monet painting. He touched his chest again and brought away his blood-soaked hand. He tried to arise. "I can't move!"

The Green Lama nodded. "Now you are only beginning to understand. Nothing may move. Om! Ma-ni pad-me Hum."

The hair fluttered wildly again. Kellen was crying profusely now. "Let me live, Lama!"

The Green Lama opened his eyes, glowing with green illumination. "As you said, I cannot stop you. Do you still not see? I am doing nothing to you. You are killing yourself." The Lama's eyes softened. "Truly, I pity you."

Kellen's eyes widened as he let out a desperate, last gasp. The gasp fluttered against the hair floating between the Lama and Kellen. Taking his hand off Kellen's chest, the Lama placed it with his other hand in a crossed position over his own chest. The mat of hair fell to the floor as Kellen slumped against the wall.

Ravi coughed and sat up. He looked about the interior of the small tank, observing Kellen's lifeless body and the Green Lama in a serene pose of meditation.

"Jagmohan!" the boy exclaimed. "What happened?"

The Green Lama opened his eyes and looked at the dead mystic. He shook his head. "Something that should not have happened." Taking the mat from the floor, he began to weave the hair together into its ring shape. "Strength unfailing, I should not cause it to occur again."

Ravi watched the Lama reform the ring. "I have been sleeping."

The Lama nodded. "Indeed, Ravi. What did you dream?"

"I dreamt of a turtle flying through the air," Ravi replied. "I am to help the turtle to find its way."

The Green Lama nodded as he stood and twisted the wheel on the tank. "I saw your dream, Ravi. You have far to travel and will do much good in the turmoil to come. Your mother will tell you more about it."

Ravi and the Lama ducked to avoid the rotatank's still propellers. They climbed out, seeing Pari walking with Twin Eagles toward the Nazi war machine.

"Ravi!" Pari shouted as she ran toward the tank. Ravi ran to his mother. "Mother!"

Pari hugged Ravi. "How is it you are alive?"

Ravi looked over his shoulder at the Lama. "I do not think I know, and I do not believe the Lama will tell us."

The Green Lama smiled broadly. "Ah, yet there you are wrong, Ravi. You are alive because you are meant to be. You are purposed to aid the turtle to fight against injustice."

The End

NOTES

1. During World War II, the British government contracted the M.L. Aviation Company to develop a Rotabuggy and a Rotatank based on designs by Raoul Hafner in 1942. Planning for the project started in 1940, though the conception may have been much earlier. The military tested an operating version of the Rotabuggy, an ordinary jeep converted to fly with an overhead propeller, with limited success. In early flight tests, the wild, rotating motion of the control stick made the pilot's job quite harrowing. Improvements made to the Rotabuggy's controls and tail fins added eventually made operating the odd craft "highly satisfactory", according to official records. Plans for the Hafner Rotatank, an ordinary Valentine tank outfitted similarly to the Rotabuggy, never made it past the concept stage. The V.T.O.L. (Vertical Take-Off and Landing) abilities of the Rotatank made it unique among flying-tank projects, which more often utilized traditional glider or propeller-driven airplane technology.

Here we see an example of German ingenuity beating the British 'to the punch' as it were, based on earlier designs likely stolen from Spanish gyroplane inventor Juan de la Cierva. While the records of this project have yet to surface, it is verified with film footage that the Nazis did manage to launch single-man gyrocopters from the decks of u-boats, planning to insert covert agents into enemy countries. That display of Nazi technical prowess in gyroplane engineering supports the validity of the claim by Jethro Dumont in his private journals, although his word is more than adequate for this commentator.

Paths of Green

Working with a character like the Green Lama is something I've wanted to do for some time. Being a dabbler in religion and philosophy a story about the Buddhist superhero held a natural attraction. How can a man dedicate himself to a non-violent religion and still use violence to fight crime? Certainly, this seems a perennial difficulty with lessons for the adherents of many religions.

Gandhi, perhaps the most recognizable example of one against violence, once said, "Between violence and cowardly flight, I can only prefer violence to cowardice." 1 It is likely that our western culture places values on matters distanced from us by time, culture, and geography. This is not so much a criticism as an observation. In all matters, we make judgments. If I may be so bold, we make prejudgments. This seems to me to be where we come from in our most primal state. As cavemen we see a threat and judge its danger and value. This prejudice causes us to attack, welcome, or flee, or just ignore depending on the prejudgment we arrived at.

It is to be remembered that long before civilized society and those myriad issues that receive so much finger-pointing even existed, homo-sapiens murdered Neanderthal men. That is if the archaeological findings hold true. Violence has been with us since before organized religion. It predates governmental and structured economic systems. It likely arrived before the shaman and holy men first stepped into the paradoxical pool to try to understand and explain the world around them. This was the concurrent birth of magic, religion, and science. Sir James Frazier does a fine job describing this evolution in *The Golden Bough*.

Men use violence for ill-gotten gain and lord over those with limited defense. So how does a man live up to non-violence when faced with the abuse of innocence and freedom by violent men? I really think this is the most important question an individual like Jethro Dumont faces every day. Jethro, as Twin Eagles reminds him in the story, is not from Asia. He is a well-to-do American. Without the background offered a childhood in India, he would be sorely tempted to fall back on the belief that the individual holds power over himself, is a free agent answerable to no man unless he chooses, and is responsible to create an atmosphere where others can be free as well. This would naturally give him an understanding unlike that of a Buddhist raised in India, for example. This is not a comparison of the two culturally-influenced paths or a judgment of one over the other. It offers a window to view into Jethro's very soul.

In writing my story, I wished to remove Dumont from the later stories and see him in his primal state. I therefore started before the beginning to examine an encounter before he began fighting crime in America. In the retold origin story from the *Green Lama #1* comic, creator Kendall Foster Crossen (writing pseudonymously as Richard Foster) says the Green Lama took on the appellation after arriving in America. It seems there is no exclusion of the possibility of the Lama being called the Green Lama before arriving in America, just that he took on the name after. A slight distinction that further material may prove impossible. Until the material presents itself, I took the liberty of making the assumption that he was called such before coming to America. It seems the name could well be a title he earned, and this I suspect is true.

For the story itself, two characters that were back-ups in the Green Lama comics appear; pilot Rick Masters and his Seminole partner Twin Eagles. This is before Masters and Twin Eagles began their air-transport business, and before Masters' injury in WWII caused his honorable discharge. It seemed appropriate that Twin Eagles might object to Jethro's presentation as a Lama; a presentation the Seminole saw as disingenuous and thus preposterously insulting. The two come to an understanding in the story and become friends.

I have little more to say aside from the surprising turns the story took for me as a writer. The Green Lama as a character took on a life all his own, though not to my mind significantly removed from his pulp and comic representations. He is still attempting to discover his place as a Lama and struggling with the non-violent identity which he would like to maintain. Like Gandhi, Jethro abhors cowardice more than violence.

1.) GANDHI LIVES: by Marc Edmund Jones

Author Bio:

KEVIN NOEL OLSON - lives with his wife in Butte, Montana where he serves as Castellain of a Masonic building. He writes children's adventure novels, various articles, and sundry material. He enjoys reading old books and watching old movies. A daily constitutional to retrieve a cup of regular coffee is often a requirement. Perhaps equal to oxygen.

the

in

The Menace of the Black Ring

by Nick Ahlhelm

Mike Washington clutched the two packed paper bags under his arms as he walked away from the local grocers. The early morning air was cool despite it being almost May. The streets were still empty; it was too early for many to even be awake. While the dawn was well under way, the last shadows of night still held on the city.

He started down the six block hike from the grocers to the small apartment he resided in. He was thankful for the small furnished room in a time when many didn't live in more than a shack. His job as a line cook wasn't much to write home about, even if he did have any family, but it paid his bills well. That's all one could hope for in the Depression after all.

Though he was still young, barely into his thirties, he walked with a limp, an old sports injury. It slowed his movement a bit, but allowed him to take in more of the early morning city. He was only a block from his home when he heard it.

The shrill scream cut through the air and stabbed into him like a dagger. Mike raised his head, suddenly attentive of the sound. He wasn't much of a fighter, but someone needed help. Something told him he should be the one to do so.

He glanced down a connecting street and saw the source, three young unkempt men hassling a young well to do woman out far too early in the morning without an escort. She appeared to be Asian, a rarity in this neighborhood, but her clothes marked her as coming from money.

The hooligans tried to get her purse from her shoulder, but she struggled against their attempts. The pushing and pulling had spilled the contents of the bag onto the cement sidewalk. None of the would-be thieves were much over twenty and the youngest looked barely into his teen years. The oldest, a scruffy man in a bowler, pulled his hand back and slapped the woman across the face.

Washington looked down the street toward his apartment building. *It isn't my business*, he reminded himself. *I'm a cripple, not a fighter. I could get hurt if I interfered.*

He gently placed the two bags on the ground. He pulled the glasses off his eyes, tucked them in his shirt pocket. He walked across the street ignoring the limp that slowed his gate.

I cannot let this stand.

He sprung on them with speed well past a normal man, let alone one with a bad knee. He didn't even know how he moved like he did, but it felt right and real. He threw his body at the man pulling at the purse. The ruffian fell down under his weight.

Washington delivered two sharp blows to each of the man's shoulders. The blows were carefully aimed at the nerve cores of both arms, sharp stabs that would disable the hooligan's hands and arms for several minutes. It would cause no lasting damage, Washington knew; though he wasn't sure how he knew that.

He turned as the other man came at him from behind. The glint of metal flashed toward Washington, but he rolled out of the way. It seemed the ruffian was not just the kind of man that would hit a defenseless woman. He was also the kind that would attack an unarmed man with a blade.

The thug leaned in again with a fierce stab. Washington's hand shot out, much to his surprise as well as the hooligan's. It struck the man in the wrist and forced the blade up and away, even as Mike moved in to deliver a blow to the man's forearm. The knife shot up into the air as Washington spun around and delivered a hard kick straight into the hooligan's solar plexus.

The would-be robber stumbled back. Washington's hand shot out in front of him and wrapped around the hilt of the mugger's blade just as it came down out the air. His hand flashed up as he charged the criminal.

He stopped just short of severing the man's head from his shoulders. Washington held the blade to the thief's throat.

In all, his attack on the men lasted only about thirty seconds. Washington didn't quite know how or where he learned to fight like this, he was just glad for his and the young woman's sake that he did.

"Perhaps you should apologize to the young lady, sir?"

The mugger nodded, clearly in fear for his life.

"Say it," Washington demanded.

"I'm sorry! Lady, I'm sorry! I won't never do it again, I promise."

"Good. Get up."

Washington pulled the knife away from the other man's throat. He reached down and yanked the man around. He reached into the back pocket and yanked the man's wallet free.

He flipped it open and was taken aback to see a star inside. The worlds United States Secret Service were emblazoned on the badge.

"I don't understand," he said. "You were robbing the lady, but if you're Secret Service. Is this some kind of test?"

He turned back to the young woman. In her right hand, she held a Colt

.38. The weapon was standard issue for local police agencies, if not the Secret Service. Mike wasn't sure where he gleaned that fact from, but it did little to assuage his confusion about this whole situation.

With her free hand, she pulled her own wallet from her purse. She flipped it open to reveal her own Secret Service badge.

"We are with the Secret Service, Mister Washington. And we think you're a man we've been searching for since February. It's been a long search, but we're not the only ones that want you found."

Washington lowered the knife and looked both ways down the streets. They were empty accept for a few straggling cars driven by workers on their way to an early shift.

"I'm not sure what you're talking about, miss, but I don't like this entire set up. I'm just a cook, a guy working to earn a living in bad times. I'm just a bit luckier than most, especially all the guys with a leg like mine. But if you wanted to talk to me, you could have just come to my house. My shift doesn't start until eleven. We can talk about it over coffee."

The "mugger" met his victim's eyes. "What do you think, Sun?"

She shrugged. "I'm not sure, but we aren't going to find out here. Might as well take Mister Washington up on his offer."

Mike Washington lived in a two room apartment on the second floor of a five story apartment building. The apartment was basically a bedroom connected to a kitchen with a small bathroom off to the side of the bedroom. It wasn't much, but it was more than a broken down box.

The neighborhood outside wasn't the best. A lot of people were out of work and a lot of crime came with that. Gambling was a major problem in this neck of the woods, often housed in old speakeasies the cops either ignored or still didn't know about almost half a decade after Prohibition. Some of the poorer women had turned to prostitution, often using private rooms in apartments like Washington's as makeshift brothels.

The apartment was sparsely decorated, just a twin bed with a throw, a small bed stand and a single chair. A small, partially used bookshelf sat to the opposite end of the bed as the stand. The kitchen seemed bare and almost unused.

Washington watched the two Secret Service agents take in his home as they entered it. He said nothing as he walked past them into the kitchen. He opened up the cabinet and pulled out three mugs and a coffee pot. He set the water to boil on the stove and went to put the groceries away.

He focused on his current task, but he kept his sense tuned to the actions of the two federal police. They both seemed impatient as they waited for him to finish. They wanted to talk to him and didn't want his daily chores to get in the way.

He was more than comfortable making them wait and stew for a bit. He put his life at risk for this woman, only to have her act like he was some criminal on the lam.

The woman, Sun, cleared her throat. "Mister Washington, I know it's an inconvenience to you but we really must talk."

Mike continued to put his groceries away. "Then talk."

The male agent took over. "My name is Perry Turner. This is my partner, Sun…"

"Just Sun will be fine, Perry. Mister Washington doesn't care about our names anyway. He just wants to know why we are here."

"I suppose so," Perry said. "We've come to you with good reason, Mister Washington. We believe that you might be in grave danger.

Mike paused with a can of tuna in hand.

"I doubt that highly, Mister Turner. I'm just a cook. No one is interested in me. And it seems I turned out to be a better fighter than I thought if today was any indication. Do you think I really have anything to worry about?"

Turner stuttered, lost for something to say in response. Sun spoke for him.

"I think you do, Mister Washington. Tell me, does the name Black Ring mean anything to you?"

Washington stopped and stared at Sun. The words Black Ring echoed in his brain as though they were something he should know, something he desperately needed to remember.

"Why are you here? How do you know me?"

"I'm going to give it to you straight," Sun said. "Your name is not Mike Washington, though this is a disguise you have used in the past. Your real name is Jethro Dumont. You come from a wealthy family and after graduating from college, you left the country for a decade to travel to Tibet. You stayed away for a full ten years, studying the path toward enlightenment in the Buddhist tradition. You returned as a Lama and a master of mystic arts that Western America can't even begin to explain. You kept your identity a secret from all but your most trusted confidants, but those men and women have all disappeared with you over the last few weeks. For the first time, you came under attack by someone that knows you, knows how you work and wants you out of the way."

Mike listened intently, still not sure what she was getting at.

"Does any of that strike you as familiar, Mister Washington, or should I say Dumont?"

Mike shook his head. "I've read newspaper stories about the Green Lama and his war on organized crime in the city. But I'm just a cook with an old college football injury. I could never do half the things that fellow does with a leg like this. Besides I'm no fighter, today notwithstanding. I just got lucky against you, Mister Turner."

"That's just what your enemy wants you to believe," Sun said. "He wants you out of the way, so that you cannot interfere with his plans for the city, the plans carried out by his personal army."

"I wish I could help you, but I think you've got the wrong man. I've told you, I'm just a cook. I don't know anything about criminals, let alone about this Black Ring of yours. I wish I could help in some way, but like I said…"

"…you're only a cook," Sun said. "I wish I could just accept that and walk away. But I can't. The Black Ring is a group of killers, murderers and thieves bent on controlling this city through criminal means. Five people are already dead and you may be the only person that can help us stop them, but only if you snap out of these false memories. You're not Mike Washington. There is no Mike Washington."

"I wish I could help. I really do. It sounds like Mister Turner and you have quite a fight ahead of you. But I don't have anything that I can tell you and I'm certainly not the right man to recruit to any fight. Whoever you think I might be, this Dumont fellow, the Green Lama, whatever, I am afraid you will be quite disappointed."

Turner cleared his throat. Sun turned to him and angrily said, "What is it, Perry?"

Turner pointed to the shelf. "Interesting collection you have here, Mister Washington. *Lost Horizon*, *Utopia*, lots of religious tracks from all around the world. Interesting reading for a small time cook."

"I am a very spiritual person," Washington said. "I believe there's a lot more to this world than what we can just see with our eyes. But that doesn't make me some kind of Buddhist Lama, whatever color you choose to make him."

"I'm sorry to interrupt your day to day life," Sun said. "But we've looked long and hard for you. I saw today a man trained in secret fighting arts yet to be seen in this town. You aren't just some cook, I know that. And if I know that and the Black Ring knows that we know that, your life could be in very serious danger."

"I doubt any set up they create will end as positively as ours did," Turner added.

"I'm just a man," Washington said. "I wish I could do more, be more, but I am who I am. And that's Michael Washington."

"But..."

Sun threw up a hand and cut off Turner's argument.

"I understand where you're coming from, Mister Washington. I'm sure our argument sounds crazy to you, but I hope you will come around in time."

She reached into her handbag and withdrew a small rectangle of paper. Washington took her card, a simple form with her name, position with the Secret Service and a local phone number on it.

Washington stared at it a moment, before he took it and slid it in his shirt pocket, next to his glasses. Realizing he hadn't put the twin glass frames back on, he quickly withdrew them from his pocket and put them over his eyes. He stopped short as he realized the lenses did nothing to bring the world any closer in focus. He quickly raised and lowered the glasses as he looked at Sun. Glasses or not, she appeared the same.

He said nothing about the sudden revelation, not sure what it meant. Could it be that they were telling the truth, that he wasn't Mike Washington at all? Or it could just mean his eye doctor was stealing his money, not unheard of in this day and age.

Sun walked back to her partner as Turner held open the door. She turned back to Washington. "If you change your mind, Mister Washington, don't be afraid to call. I have a receiver in my office and that's the direct line. An answering service will pick up if I'm not around and pass the message on to me as soon as possible. If you know anything, remember anything, you can tell us there."

"Thank you," Washington said. "I'm sorry if I wasted either or your time. I wish I could help you find this Green Lama."

Turner started to speak again, but Sun cut him off with another hand gesture. She gave Washington one last smile before she ushered her partner through the door.

Washington closed his eyes. Sun's words echoed through his head, all too familiar. He didn't know why, but he knew he should know this Green Lama, or at least know where to find him. Washington wondered what was wrong with him.

With a rolling sense of uneasy resting deep in the pit of his stomach, he returned to the kitchen to start his breakfast.

Despite the visit from the Secret Service agents and the unease they brought with them, Washington continued his morning ritual as he did every other day. He ate two eggs cooked overhard with a slice of lightly buttered toast and a cup of cool milk. From there he read the morning newspaper from cover to cover. After that, he went to the window and loaded the twin birdfeeders that sat on the sill. He pulled his chair around and in front of the window to see what kind of birds he might attract to the feeder.

After he grew tired of watching his avian friends, he returned to the latest addition to his library, Allan Quatermain's first journal of his adventures, aptly titled *King Solomon's Mines*. He found the account a bit preposterous, but modern biographers were nothing if not overwrought in their prose.

It reminded him a bit of the writing of his old friend Foster, but for the life of him, he couldn't quite recall exactly what old friend his mind might be remembering. He couldn't think of any Fosters at work at the restaurant and he certainly didn't know any authors.

With work looming closer, he rose from his chair and returned to the kitchen to make an early lunch, his last meal before a nearly twelve hour shift. He wiped down the pan on the stove and lathered butter on two slices of bread. Between them, he cut and placed a layer of cheese before he brought the entire sandwich to the stove to cook.

As he flipped the grilled cheese sandwich with a spatula, he heard something from down the hall. Usually his neighbors didn't come around much at this time of day. Most were at work and those who weren't tended to do most of their work at night. They were still asleep in the middle of the morning.

He felt the hair stand up on the back of his neck as an ominous sense of dread fell over him. He knew the sound came from an attacker; just the type of figure that Sun warned him might be coming. He pulled the grilled cheese off the stove, not wanting to let it burn.

If these men were as skilled as the Secret Service agents indicated, he knew they would waste no time now. They wouldn't risk giving him a chance to run. They would come from the door and the window, all poised to strike him down without a second thought.

Despite knowing they were coming, he remained strangely calm. He slid a spatula under the grilled cheese and flipped it onto a plate. He picked up the plate as though he was ready to move to the next room. He bent down and grabbed the frying pan, as if to move it back onto the stove.

Instead he turned in a sudden twist. He hurled the pan straight through the patio door. Glass rained down on his victim before the plate thudded into the skull of an assassin dressed all in black. The strike dropped the attacker off the window sill, tumbling the single story to the ground.

Washington walked to the window, unsure of how he knew the man was there let alone incapacitated him with a common household item. He instead focused on the man's outfit: a tight mask over his face, a loose-fitting *gi* and the *tabi* of the ninja, the silent Japanese assassins. He thought back to the thump in the hall. *If these men are truly ninjas they are surely not making them like they once did.*

He wasn't sure where that thought came from, but Washington realized it wasn't his. It was someone else, lurking in his brain, someone that knew how to fight.

Washington barely avoided the attack by the other ninja that lurked outside. A throwing blade flew toward his skull, but he ducked inside just in time for it to whisk past toward the ground.

He stumbled back into the stove and found the teapot, still warm from earlier in the day. His fingers wrapped around the metal pot as he heard the crash of his door falling inwards. He turned to see three other men, dressed just like the other two assassins, which across his living room.

The other ninja came in through the window and attacked him with a long sword, a Japanese *katana*. Washington barely dove out of the way, striking the ground hard with teapot still in hand. The sword sliced clear through his counter tops like butter, an almost impossibly sharp blade. Washington knew he couldn't survive a strike from it.

Say the words.

The command echoed through Mike Washington's skull, but he didn't know from where. He only knew these men wanted him dead and he wasn't the fighter Sun or Turner claimed. He was just a cook, a normal man thrust into a situation he could never hope to survive. He wasn't something more, wasn't someone that could stand up to injustice.

Say the words.

The command echoed inside him again, spoken in his own words, his own voice. He knew they were true. He knew that they were his only chance for survival, but the very thought of them scared them. To say them out loud invited catastrophe, perhaps even death.

Death by sword or death by action, only you can choose. Say the words.

The ninja loomed large over him, a menacing figure in the black of pure

The sword sliced through his counter top...

evil. No good existed in this man's heart, only a single minded urge to fulfill his master's wishes. He would not stop until Mike was dead.

He just didn't realize that Mike was already dying. With a sob, he closed his eyes, opened his mouth and screamed.

"*Om mani padme hum!*"

His eyes flashed open but gone was the fear of Mike Washington. He leapt to his feet landing on the heels of both legs. The pain in his knee was vanished along with a simple cook. He was not Mike Washington. He had never been Mike Washington. He was something more, something powerful, something good and pure that this city needed.

He was the Green Lama and he would not die this day.

He hurled the pot out and took the ninja by surprise. The blow clubbed the assassin in the skull. The Lama used the momentary distraction to charge forward and deliver a strike to the man's heart. He fell in a heap, instantly paralyzed by the heart punch. With a little bit more applied force, he could very well have died.

Fortunately even against an assassin, the Green Lama was a man of peace, not a killer.

He could hear movement from above. These assassins were not alone. They knew who he was and wanted to offer him no chance at escape. But if they thought to catch him off guard, they would be sadly mistaken.

He slowly bent down and retrieved the beaten assassin's weapon. The Lama recognized it as a *ninjato*, a traditional short sword used by the shadow warriors of feudal Japan. It would serve his purposes in place of his usual gear.

The Green Lama closed his eyes and concentrated. He listened, but more he felt, everything around him. He could feel the gentle flow of wind against the window. He could hear the gentle flow of wind against the windowsill. He felt the reverberations of tiny feet as mice scurried beneath the floor boards. And he could almost see the assassin's movements above, all in his mind's eye.

He drove the blade straight up into the thin ceiling. It passed easily through plaster and week wood. The blade sliced up and through the back of the would-be assassin's foot. It severed the man's posterior tibial artery, a bloody wound but non-fatal if treated quickly.

The Lama left the kitchen and his apartment. He found the single phone in the hallway and quickly dialed the operator.

"We need an ambulance. A man has been stabbed." He gave the address and immediately hung up.

Ninjato still in hand, he climbed the stairs to the next floor. The door to the apartment above was broken, shattered by a sharp kick. The Lama stepped inside and quickly made his way to the back of the apartment, the area he knew was directly above where he struck.

He found the assassin bleeding profusely on the floor of the bedroom. The Green Lama walked toward the injured man. The assassin weakly raised his blade, but the Lama batted it away with his own. He bent over the assassin and held his blade to the killer's throat.

"I know not if a killer like you fears his own death. But I am sure you know that if treated correctly, your wound may not be fatal. I can spare your life, if you answer my questions. Will you help me?"

The assassin said nothing.

The Lama brought the blade lower and grabbed the man's hand. A never pinch on the killer's wrist immobilized the limb, but would leave him with full sensation. The Lama brought the blade down and sliced it into the assassin's pointer finger just above the cuticle. He quickly snapped the nail from the finger.

"I am a man of peace, but I am not a happy man. Your kind have cost me much this day. I will do what is necessary to learn the identity of your master."

The Green Lama moved the finger over to the assassin's middle finger. "It will be your nails first. After that, I will start on each fingertip. I have more than enough medicinal training to keep you from bleeding out. I can make the pain last for hours."

"You're bluffing," the assassin said.

Though he knew the killer to be right, the Lama kept his face impassive. He sliced down into the man's middle finger. The nail popped off even easier than the first.

"I don't bluff," the Green Lama said. "Are you with the Black Ring?"

He brought the blade to the next finger.

"Yes! Yes! I work for the Ring! But I don't know nothing else. They just tell me who I should kill."

"Your weapon says otherwise. No common American thug carries a Japanese short sword. Where did you get it?"

"A warehouse on the pier. Lot 167. But it's nothing, just a place to meet and get the goods. Our boss comes in with a black mask. We don't know his name or nothing, not even what he looks like without that thing. He just pays us, we do the work and it's done."

"What was your mission today? Did you want me dead? Are you here to kill me?"

The assassin shook his head. "The boss wanted you captured, tied and bound and dropped at the warehouse. We was only supposed to off you as a last resort."

"Whoever is your master that was his first mistake."

The Green Lama reached his free hand to the assassin's throat. He raised two fingers to strike, but turned his hands as he quickly drove them down. The blow struck a nerve cluster between collar and shoulder. The assassin's eyes rolled back as he fell instantly unconscious.

He heard the sound of sirens approaching. The first were already stopping in front of the building, police and ambulance. They were finally here, good time for the local constabulary. He used his shirt to wipe the blade free of prints. He dropped it at the assassin's side. The Lama stepped over the killer and walked toward the apartment's rear window.

While a stairwell served as an emergency exit down, the Green Lama knew he would never make it all the way down without the police finding him. He could not afford to be exposed in such a way. He needed another way out.

It was a ten feet leap between this building and the next. For a normal man, the distance might be too great. But for the Green Lama, nothing was insurmountable. It was just another obstacle and far from the longest leap he ever made.

He took just a moment to measure the jump, stepped back several paces and then hurled his body forward as fast as he could run. He threw his body through the open window and out into the open air of the alley. His jump took him straight across to an exterior railing, an emergency staircase designed in case of fire. He landed on it, walked up to the window and tried the latch. It slid open. He heard no sign of anyone inside. The tenants were either at work or out looking for work.

He made his way quickly to the front door, let himself out and started his way down the stairs. He walked out onto the street and walked past his old apartment. He gave the cops on scene only a cursory glance, looking like nothing more than any other spectator as they walked past the scene of the crime.

The police never saw him and would never suspect his presence. After all, the only lead they had was a man named Mike Washington. And Mike Washington was dead, if he every truly was. The Green Lama felt a sense of loss, a ghost of something simple evaporated into the mists of memory. Mike may not have been real, but he was a true soul, something lost to the Lama with the return of his memory.

Mike Washington was gone and whoever created him, whoever took away the Lama's mind in the first place, would pay.

Nestled against his side, Scarlet's long red locks fell over his chest as she slowly ran her hand across his thick, heavily muscled gut. Lei Mei worked higher, rubbing the tight knots from his shoulder. The newest girl, the waifish blond Amber, caressed him in a more intimate manner.

Vong Den, master of the Black Ring, took it all in with detached disinterest. Normally his mind would only be focused on his own pleasure during his afternoon ritual. Instead he waited, anxious for news of the missing Green Lama.

The newest of his lieutenants, a local named Baxter, entered the far end of the chamber. The young man's arrival over his more seasoned commanders bode ill for the results of the hunt. Nor did Baxter's appearance project welcome news; he looked uncomfortable, scared at being in his master's presence.

"Uh, your eminence, er..."

"He escaped your grasp. You sent your incompetent men and he made short work of them. Is this correct?"

"Well, I..."

"Is this correct?"

"Yes, sir."

"I warned you, Mister Baxter. I told you the lowly training of your operatives would make them no match for the Green Lama. But you insisted you could handle him, did you not?"

"He was just one man! Some schmo no one even knew!"

"He is far from just one simple man. He is one of the most highly trained warriors in the world. He possesses more power in one hand than you could even imagine. You have failed and exposed us. Now I will have to handle this matter personally."

"Personally, sir? I thought I could..."

"You have served me for long enough, Mister Baxter. Your services are no longer required."

"No longer needed? Look, I've worked my way up this organization for years! I'll be damned if you think you're just going to throw me by the wayside!"

"I believe you misunderstand me, Mister Baxter."

The girls scattered to the floor as Vong Den shot up out of his lounge. He covered the fifteen feet between him and Baxter in a blink of the eye.

He struck only once, a powerful, graceful thrust to Baxter's throat. By the time, the lieutenant realized his throat was crushed, he was well past saving.

Baxter's corpse fell to the floor, his eyes still wide from the shock of his own death. Vong Den stood over him for just a second. A broad grin crossed his face. It felt good to work again. It seemed far too long since his last kill.

He walked back to the lounge and picked up the phone receiver. Immediately the other end of the line picked up, the direct line always answered by one of his men.

"Yes, my lord?"

"Mister Good, Baxter has failed me in his task. Green Lama is in the city. Mobilize everyone. I want him caught."

"Yes, my lord."

Vong Den hung up the phone. His wishes were clear. Neither he nor Good had any need for pleasantries. He looked down at the three women. He silently beckoned them back to his body.

He hadn't felt this alive in years. Soon his prey would finally be in his grasp.

Still in his street clothes, Jethro Dumont, the Green Lama, felt almost naked on the streets. He walked casually down the street. He had been on foot for nearly an hour now, making his way down the four miles of road between Mike Washington's home and his nearest apartment safe house. He placed a half dozen of the rooms across the city, all in mind for the day he might need a spare costume or a place to hide from overanxious lawmen.

He entered the building, climbed to the second floor and quickly found the spare key hidden in the potted plant across the hall from his door. He entered the apartment and headed to the bedroom.

The tenant wasn't here. He didn't really live here on a regular basis. His job was just to maintain three of the safe houses, stopping in once every few days to make the home seem lived in. In this economy, it wasn't unusual for someone to be working twelve or sixteen hour days to make ends meet, so the other residents wouldn't be too suspicious of an irregular schedule.

The closet was filled with a full wardrobe, from simple overalls and work clothes to three piece suits. Jethro chose a business suit, nothing too expensive, but far past the old, beat up clothes he currently wore. He quickly changed out of the old outfit and into the suit. It was properly sewn for his frame, just one of many outfits replicated by a discreet tailor.

He checked his appearance in the full length mirror just to the left of the closet. He took a moment to properly tie his necktie, and then adjusted his attire until he was satisfied with his appearance. He couldn't let people see Jethro Dumont in anything less than his best.

He reached out to the mirror and found the latch hidden on its side. He clicked it open and the mirror swung out to reveal a second, hidden closet.

Dumont pulled out the familiar green robe inside the secret chamber. He knew he would have great need of it in the days ahead.

He checked the cloak's many pockets and verified his stores of radioactive salts were in place. He picked up the card left for him by Perry Turner and the mysterious Sun. He went to the kitchen phone and dialed the number.

"Treasury Department, may I help you?" The voice was unfamiliar. This man was certainly not Sun and he sounded nothing like Agent Turner.

"Where's Turner?"

"He is out of the office at the moment. May I take your message or be of assistance?"

"I need to meet with him immediately."

"I'm sorry, sir. He is not available. I am Special Agent Wendell Good. Perhaps there is some way I can help you?"

"The pier. Lot 167. It's a warehouse. Tell him to meet Washington there. Do you have that message?"

Good was silent for a moment. "Yeah, sure, buddy. I…"

"Enough chit chat. Tell him. It is of the utmost importance that he meets me there."

Dumont hung up the phone. He would need to move fast if he was to reach the pier by nightfall.

It was well past dusk by the time Dumont exited his taxi at the edge of the city pier. He made his way on foot the last several blocks to Lot 167. He found a broken down old warehouse upon his arrival, its windows shattered and its interior completely black. It matched any number of other storage areas on the pier, all left with nothing to hold in the wake of the Depression. He donned his cloak as he reached the outskirts of the lot.

The Green Lama snuck through the shadows of the warehouse, invisible to all but the most trained of his eyes. The green of his robes were just dark enough to meld with the darkness and his training taught him any number of stealth techniques to move him through the shadows.

He found the front gates locked, secured by heavy chains and padlocks. He could pick them, but just removing them would make more noise than he would like. He moved around the building to find another point of entry.

He found a side door to the building unlocked and leaning slightly open. He thought it strange to see any lot in the area left unsecured. It invited squatters in a city with so many homeless men and women just fighting to stay alive. The Lama could only guess that the Black Ring's presence was known here and the threat of their actions was enough to keep all but the least intelligent away from Lot 167.

The building was dark and empty. Even with his highly trained senses, the Green Lama couldn't see through the blackness. He worked his way toward the front of the building and the secured doors. Once he reached them, it took only seconds to find the switch for the main lights near them.

Power flowed into the room with a low hum. Light flooded the dirty empty room. Much to the Lama's dismay, it also exposed the body in the center of the large open warehouse.

The Lama ran to the still form, but he already suspected there was no hope for the man. The body lay on his stomach and the Lama carefully rolled him over. He was fair skinned and dark haired. His eyes sat open and vacant, all life gone from them.

The Lama quickly checked the man's pockets, in search of any form of identification or any clue of the man's identity whatsoever. He found nothing save a single piece of jewelry, a thick band carved from the darkest obsidian. A Black Ring, clearly a mark left by the man's killers.

"Stop where you are! Raise your hands above your head or we will shoot!"

The Lama turned toward the side door from which he entered. Three plain clothed federal agents held their sidearms on him. He recognized the voice of the speaker almost instantly; this was the Treasury Department man that answered his call earlier. But why would he follow the call, instead of passing the message to Turner?

Clearly these men didn't know who he was or why he was here. They were armed and saw him standing over a dead body as they entered. The Green Lama knew when he faced trouble, but this was all too pat. All too easily set up.

"Agent Good, I told you to send Turner, not come yourself."

"I don't know who the hell you are, but I told you he wasn't around. I just thought it would be a good idea to check out a call from a mystery man. Looks like I managed to walk in at just the right moment."

"You can't honestly think I would call you here and then kill a man? I'm no fool. No, I don't think that is what is happening here at all. I think I have been set up."

"It doesn't matter," Good said. "You need to raise your hands above your head and surrender or we will shoot."

"I cannot do that. I am afraid I cannot remain. I have too much to do if I am to stop the Black Ring. Do you know of them, Agent Good?"

"I-I don't know what you're talking about!" Good's gun lowered slightly. The Lama could see the sweat bead on his head. He was nervous, scared of something.

Good quickly strengthened his grip on his gun. "Stay there and raise your hands or I will shoot! You're not leaving the scene of this crime, guilty or innocent."

"I did not kill this man." The Green Lama rose to his feet. His right hand slipped into his robe, found the pocket hidden inside. "But I may know who did."

"You can tell us all about it at police headquarters," Good said.

"Alas, that is not what will happen today."

The Green Lama opened his hand and slammed the vial of radioactive salts down hard on the ground. The salts exploded into a flash of dazzling light, one of Tsarong's latest creations for his crime fighting endeavors. The Lama closed his own eyes just before the vial shattered, but even through his eyelids, he could see the blinding white light.

He kept his eyes closed as he charged forward, straight toward the Treasury agents and his only path to escape. He heard them yell, felt the shift in air currents as they waved their weapons wildly in hope of finding their green-cloaked target.

The Lama leapt into the air as he reached the agents, splitting his legs and driving each one into the chest of an agent. The two men sprawled to the ground, but before Lama even landed, he knew neither was Good.

Good had gone quiet, probably dropped to the ground. He knew the defenses against blind fighting, an interesting bit of knowledge for a simple Treasury agent. The Lama would have to keep a close eye on this one, but not now. He still needed to find Turner and the woman that called herself Sun.

The salts exploded into a flash of dazzling light...

The Lama ran out into the night and let the shadows cloak his trail.

He fought the fury rising inside him, silently chanted mantras of serenity. Too much was outside his control. It was not a feeling he liked.

He would need to take the initiative and for that he would need new allies.

Perry Turner and Sun stood outside the apartment building of Mike Washington. Thy conferred with the remaining uniformed officers. The police seemed rather annoyed at their continued presence at the crime scene; so many hours after the agents of the Black Ring were carted away.

The Green Lama waited in the shadows as Turner finished with them. When the last officer climbed into his car and pulled away, the Lama swooped down from his hiding place, a fire escape on the building directly across from his, Mike's, old apartment. He landed just inches in front of Turner and Sun's car as they approached it.

The Treasury agent and the mystery woman stopped short. Turner's hand flashed to his side, wrapping around the handle of his gun.

The Green Lama rose to his full height. His face was cloaked by his heavy hood despite these two individuals clearly knowing his true identity.

"We need to speak, Agent Turner. And you have been less than truthful with me, young lady. Your name is not Sun, just as mine was not truly Mike Washington. Nor do I think you are now or have ever been employed by the Secret Service or the Department of the Treasury."

"I see your memory has returned, my Lama." Sun dropped to one knee and bowed her head, a mark of supplication the Green Lama knew well. The villagers below the monastery used it in the presence of a learned monk, a holy man. It was the bow of those that knew the ancient order of monks he trained under in Tibet, the bow of the people that the missing Tsarong called his own.

"Who are you?"

"My name is Tsarong Sun. My brother is your sworn ally. He asked me to visit in his last letter home, many months ago, but after all the traveling I have done; I came to a city where he seems to never have existed. I feared he rested in the hands of the Black Ring, so I contacted the man that helped me get into your country, Agent Turner."

"Helped you get into the country?" the Lama said.

"I was not a legal immigrant and knew nothing about papers when I boarded the boat that took me from China to the city of Los Angeles. I was lucky enough to meet Agent Turner aboard the boat and he helped me file the right paperwork while aboard and well…"

"What Sun is trying to say is that we fell in love," Turner said. "We wait only to find her brother before we set the date for our marriage."

The Lama looked between the man and woman in front of him.

"I see. This is not what I expected. I supposed something more nefarious may be at work, but no matter. If this is truly the case, I wish you both the best. But first, we have more pressing matters to attend."

"Like finding my brother and destroying the Black Ring," Sun said. "We must make them pay for kidnapping my brother."

"I'm not so sure they kidnapped your brother in the first place," the Green Lama said. "The men that came for Mike Washington were clearly agents of the Black Ring, but they had no idea of my location until they tracked you to his home."

"His?" Turner said.

The Green Lama ignored the lingering question. "The Black Ring are a foul lot. Their origins rest in the South China Sea, a band of pirates and brigands that date back a hundred years, though they did not gain a formal name until they were organized by their latest leader. I fought them in Hong Kong before I ever made my return to America. I thought I destroyed them, but it seems they have followed be back to these shores. I fear this crime wave may be my fault."

"How so?"

The Lama did not meet Turner's eyes as the question lingered in the air.

"I knew their leader, a man named Vong Den. Both Tsarong and I did."

"You knew him," Sun said. "How?"

"He was a member of the order until he killed one of our brothers. I had been there only a few weeks at the time, but I watched as he was expelled from our ranks. He fought like a mad man, but even his skills were not enough to defeat all the masters. They branded him with a mark of shame; a black circle burnt into his chest and expelled him from Tibet forever."

The Lama shook his head. "He was on the path to becoming a true lama. He could have been in my stead had he not walked the dark path he chose."

"If my brother knew this, could he have altered your memory, perhaps as a way to hide you from this Vong Den? Could he be responsible for your Mike Washington alias?"

"I think not," the Green Lama said. "He has the needed skills in hypnosis to perform such a feat, but I am not sure if he could work their power on me. More importantly, I do not think he would commit such a heinous act, even to protect me."

"Heinous," Turner said. "I'm not sure I understand."

"In order to submerge my identity under that of another, the hypnotist needed to create another person, a wholly generated human over my own psyche. Mike Washington was as real as you or I. When my mind returned and I escaped the Black Ring's assassins, he died, lost forever. His memories remain, but they are only a phantom of the man. Mike Washington is a dead man, whether or not a body remains."

Turner said nothing. Sun reached out a hand, rested it on the Lama's shoulder.

"I am sorry. I feel your pain, great lama. If only I could ease it."

The Green Lama nodded his head. "Your concern is enough. Thank you, Tsarong Sun."

"I'm sorry for your…" Turner paused, chewing his lip. "…loss, I suppose is the best word. But it doesn't change the fact the Black Ring is out there and they want you dead, at least if Mike's apartment is any sign."

"That much is clear," the Green Lama said. "And they seem more than willing to use the city's police to accomplish that goal. They abandoned their warehouse meeting place and left one of their own dead on the site. They did all of this to set me up, to make the Green Lama appear to be a murderer. I suspect the murdered man most likely was the one behind the failed attack, if Vong Den's past treatment of his lieutenants is any sign. But even if the police do learn his identity, the Black Ring covers their tracks well enough to keep his name off any wanted lists."

Turner shook his head. "But if the dead man has no ties and the people you cut down here know nothing, we're back at square one. How do we find the Black Ring and this Vong Den?"

"You know much about me, Agent Turner, more than even some of my agents are aware. I will find this Vong Den and destroy him, but before I accept the assistance from you I must know this. I must have an answer if you are willing to give me what is necessary to trust you. Will you sit in my service, answer to my needs, as long as you are needed?"

"Service? What do you…?"

"Will you aid me or will you not?"

Turner glanced to Sun. His fiancée nodded only once.

"I will work for you," Turner said.

"Excellent. Then you can help me uncover my only lead. He played his cards far too close to the table. In doing so, he exposed himself as an enemy to me and to all mankind. Tell me what you know of your colleague, Agent Good?"

It was another full day before they made their move. Jethro Dumont spent the time in the city, never far from the local headquarters of the United States Department of the Treasury. Their base of operations was anything but spectacular, just a small office front in a multistory building a block down from the downtown police plaza. Turner gave him the details of the location. About twelve agents worked out of the building at any time, split evenly between basic Treasury investigators tasked with fraud issues and full Secret Service agents working against organized crime in the city. The agents currently operated without a senior officer in charge after the previous chief moved back to Washington to accept a higher post in Roosevelt's administration. This left the agents all on equal footing. Their case load was a mess according to Turner with no one assigned officially to anything. It was the kind of situation that would allow an agent with criminal ties to flourish.

It seemed Good was anything but his namesake. Turner filled the Lama in on the details of his fellow agent. John Good was a former leg breaker operating out of Chicago; he was famous for his tough guy image. But even then, it seemed he used his talents to help the rise of the Capone mob while helping local law enforcement corner any rising opposition. His commanding officer, probably as corrupt as he was, gave him the recommendation that brought Good to the federal level. Now he served an organized crime ring while working as an agent to bring organized crime down in the city.

Good left the building multiple times over the course of the day and Jethro Dumont discreetly followed him to each of his meetings.

His first stop was a local opium den. Jethro watched Good collect the profits there in an unmarked paper bag. Good casually threw it in the seat of his car before moving on to his next stop: a brothel near the pier. Again he received an unmarked paper bag, but this time he disappeared into a room for nearly a half hour with one of the madam's ladies.

He climbed back into his car and started back through the city. Over the course of the next several hours, he visited a pair of brothels, one in the less savory part of the city, one of the high rent district. He also stopped at the pier to meet what looked like the local opium distributors. At each stop, he picked up another bag almost certainly stuffed with American currency.

It seemed all too clear that Good was the money man for the Black Ring. His position in the Treasury Department gave him air air of legitimacy. He used it to walk in and out of these dens of iniquity with few questions asked. Of course, someone investigating the mob might need to visit less savory locations. Few individuals in his own department would question a Treasury man, and no police officer would bat his eye at a Treasury agent carrying a bit too much money should they stop him. It was a nearly perfect con.

At least to anyone other than the Green Lama.

Good wasn't just dirty. He was far more than a simple stooge. Jethro knew one of Vong Den's lieutenants when he saw them. Good was of great importance to the Black Ring and therefore the perfect target for tracking down their leader. He made a clear mistake targeting the Lama back at the warehouse. He tipped his hand far too early.

Now the Lama had his way in.

They made their move, as planned, in the evening. Turner left with Good, both men exiting the building within seconds of one another. Turner chatted harmlessly with his corrupt coworker.

The Green Lama watched from the shadows of a nearby alleyway and waited as they moved the several yards down the street to their cars. Sun sprang out from behind Good's car as they approached. She held a gun in her hand and waved it wildly at Good.

"Where is he? Where is my brother?"

Good didn't even bat an eye at the sight of the weapon.

"You are making a mistake, miss," Good said.

"Am I? I think you know all about the Black Ring! Now tell me where my brother is!"

Good smiled. He turned away from Sun and looked at Turner before he turned back to the woman. "You misunderstand me, Tsarong Sun. Your mistake is thinking that you and Perry here have the drop on me. In truth, you've walked into *my* trap."

Still in the shadows, the Green Lama saw them coming. At least a dozen figures emerged from all around them, as if out of nowhere. These were not the simpletons in warrior's clothing that he defeated at Mike Washington's home. These were the true acolytes of the Black Ring, the most trusted soldiers of Vong Den. These were Chinese warriors trained from childhood at the arts or death, raised to strike a kill from the shadows. Turner and Sun would be slaughtered.

The Green Lama sprung from his hiding place, but it proved to be just another error in his plan. The Black Ring were already all around him, dropping down to surround him. They struck with cold, calculated fury. Within a second, they had him trapped, surrounded by the deadly blades of their ninjato.

He could only hope they still underestimated him. Their ninjato were held with the skills of a true shadow warrior. These men knew how to use them, but they may not know who they used them against and the powers that he held.

The Green Lama dodged a swing from the deadly blade of one assassin only to walk into another's path. He threw a hand up as the ninjato silently swiped through the air. The back of his hand struck the flat of the blade and forced the deadly blow away.

The Green Lama rolled back and away from that killer, but the move brought him near two more shadow warriors. His hands disappeared into the pockets of his cloak. They each wrapped around very specific bottles of his radioactive salts. He clutched both tightly as the assassins once again closed on him.

He flicked the stopper off each vial as he let them slowly encircle them. This time the shadow warriors did not attack wildly. They closed slowly, each ready to strike him down as he fought one of their brothers. He could feel their confidence. They thought they had him, even as he splashed the salt onto the skin of his hands.

They came at him at once. He rose up and roared for all of them to hear.

"*Om mani padme hum!*"

He lashed out with the roar of thunder. When he struck, his hand exploded like a burst of lightning. Electricity struck his foe and instantly the would-be assassin flew into the air. He struck the wall of the alleyway and slumped down, not moving.

The Green Lama's hand ached but nowhere near how bad his broken enemy would when he awoke.

He wasted not a second in contemplation of his beaten foe, as he had three more to stop. He turned and blasted another shadow warrior with a swift salt-powered strike to the solar plexus. He could already tell though that he would not escape unscathed.

Two more warriors emerged to strike him from behind, faster than even he could react. He rolled forward with the blows, but still their *ninjatos* cut deep into his back, even as he found himself face to face with another shadow warrior.

Blood flowed freely from his back and caked into his cloak as the Green Lama brought his hands up and blasted away the man in front of him before the shadow warrior could strike.

He turned and blasted the two shadow warriors that struck him before with twin lightning fists, even as they closed to attack again. But the shadow warriors knew they faced a master and four more moved to close on him. They pummeled and slashed and the Lama could do nothing but fall to his knees, unable to strike back.

The Green Lama reached again into his cloak and found another bottle of the salts. He hurled it to the ground as far in front of him as he could. The blast rang through the alleyway as the vial exploded with a burst of pure green fire. The shadow warriors and the Lama were all hurled into the air. As he was ready for the force of the explosion and shielded from its flames by the assassins, the Lama was able to land on his feet and roll with the force of the blast. The Black Ring's soldiers were not so lucky.

The Green Lama stood alone, but the warriors were not all defeated, he realized, as he looked toward Good, Turner and Sun.

His two allies were each flanked by a pair of the shadow warriors. Turner and Sun each had a ninjato held to their throat. Good stood between them, his hands calmly held behind him as he looked at the Green Lama.

"You could very well survive this fight," Good said. "You might even beat me and all these men. But your friends will die if you do not surrender right now."

"You monster! You will pay for this!"

"Will I?" Good said. "I'm not so sure. Whatever the case, I will only extend my offer once more. Do you surrender? My master would have a word with you before you die."

The Green Lama knew he was outmaneuvered; for now. Again things were far from his control. But his goal had always been locating and beating Vong Den. If surrender would save his allies and take him to the Ring's leader, it seemed his choice was all too simple.

"I surrender. Take me to Vong Den."

***

They transported Jethro Dumont—ßsans his ceremonial robes—Perry Turner and Sun by car, but Good and his companions blindfolded them before throwing them in the back of a freight truck. The route was long and circuitous, far more than necessary, Jethro guessed. He knew that this was for his sake. They did not want him retracing his steps here easily should he escape their clutches.

Caution was always Vong Den's trademark. The criminal leader clearly had not changed since their last meeting in Hong Kong.

After nearly an hour on the road, ticked off by Jethro one second at a time in his mind, they finally came to a stop. Still blindfolded, they were escorted on foot through the cool night air into a much warmer room.

The heat here was almost furnace-like. It was a moist heat though, much like the natural steam rooms under the monastery in Tibet. The humidity in the air reminded him of the tropics on a hot summer day.

Jethro heard the shuffling of feet across the rocks beneath their feet, the sound of creatures far from human. The pad was rough and low to the ground, perhaps a crocodile or alligator, but the creatures seemed far more massive.

A hand to his back shoved Jethro Dumont to the ground. As he fell to his knees, the blindfold was yanked from his eyes.

He stared up into the face of a massive beast, a dragon come alive.

"Impressive, are they not?"

The animal was a komodo dragon. Jethro recognized them from an encyclopedia only, as even in his travels he never encountered such a beast. It was almost as tall as him and nearly twenty feet in length from head to tail. The dragon was far larger than his near perfect memory could recall the beasts growing. And it was not alone. A second dragon growled in the distance.

The dragon was pulled back toward the wall by a chain around its throat. Jethro could now see he was in a large antechamber. To each side of him, the great komodo dragons were chained to the side walls. In front of him sat a large throne. A familiar green robe sat across it, clearly delivered to Vong Den before the removal of his blindfold. Three young women were chained to it, almost certainly the concubines of Vong Den. His lascivious nature had been legendary in Hong Kong and it seemed little had changed about that since his arrival in the United States.

Vong Den stood in front of his throne, alongside a figure dressed in heavy robes, ordained with the circle of the Black Ring. Vong Den was naked from the waist up. With no shirt, the mark that gave his organization its name was all too clear. A burnt ring of flesh formed a perfect circle around his heart, an old scar left there, the punishment placed on him upon his exile from the Tibetan lamasery.

"My pets are quite rare creatures. They live only in the most remote of

"Impressive, are they not?"

locations and these two specimens are the largest ever recorded. They were too beautiful for me to leave behind when I traveled from Hong Kong, where you and your man left me for dead all those years ago. And since I came here to see you killed, it seems apt to let my pets pick your bones."

"You always were melodramatic, Vong Den. You swore you would destroy Tsarong and me back in Hong Kong. Instead we left you floating face down in the Pacific. Clearly you survived, but your luck won't hold a second time. This time you will end up in jail or dead, mark my words."

Vong Den's gut shook as he chuckled. "On this we can agree. One of us dies today. But it will not be me. I will enjoy watching your demise, Jethro Dumont."

"We will see," Jethro simply said.

The shadow warriors came in from behind him. Before he could move, he felt the salts forced into the wounds on his back. The pain was massive, but he knew the purpose of the radioactive salts. They would heal him, staunch the remaining flow of blood and leave him a fighting chance in the coming battle. It was an almost honorable move on Vong Den's part.

Turner and Sun were pulled to the side of the room, near one of the komodo dragons. A pair of shadow warriors flanked each of them. Their *ninjatos* were out and ready to strike down either of the pair should Jethro not cooperate with Vong Den's plans. A single command would mean his allies' deaths, of this Jethro had no doubt.

"Strike them down and you will be next," Jethro said to Vong Den and his men. "No one will stop my fury should another innocent die this day. Now face me, Vong Den. Let us end this."

"Fight you? I have no interest in fighting you. The last time I made that mistake, you soundly beat me. I do not make the same mistake twice. No, I have chosen someone quite special to face you.

The robed man stepped forward. He grabbed the front of his white robes and pulled them slowly down and off of him. Bare chested, dressed in a simple *gi* and painted with the Black Ring around his heart, he was still instantly recognizable without his usual accoutrements. Jethro stood across from his old friend Tsarong.

His friend's eyes were glassy, clearly muddled by some drug or dark power.

"You fiend! What have you done to him?"

"It was quite fascinating, actually," Vong Den said. "My men found him working in a simple ethnic store, working as a fishmonger. He was completely unaware of his history and answered only to the name Ping.

But he was so poor, he was more than willing to speak with me and hear the offer of the Black Ring. It proved quite easy from that point to dose him with the correct mix of drugs to make him my loyal servant. From there, it seemed more than fitting that you die at the hands of your best friend!"

Without another word from Vong Den, Tsarong lunged toward Jethro Dumont. Jethro ducked out of the way of the deadly blow; the shot had been aimed at his jaw and certainly would have snapped his neck. It was quite clear Vong Den did not exaggerate. Tsarong would not hesitate to kill him.

Jethro rose up and struck his friend with a forearm to the sternum. It was a move designed to cause pain and momentarily disable his foe without any permanent damage. Tsarong took the blow without even a grimace.

Tsarong delivered a spinning strike in return. The blow sent Jethro tumbling to the ground.

He was in trouble. He could not kill his oldest ally, even with his mind subsumed by Vong Den's drugs. But Tsarong would kill him if he could not get through to his friend.

"Tsarong, you don't have to do this. You don't have to fight me!"

Tsarong said nothing. He just closed with Jethro and threw a hard punch toward Jethro's head. Jethro twisted his neck to avoid it. He rolled across the ground.

His former friend did not let up for a second, striking again and again as Jethro dodged his way back. He struck the side of Vong Den's throne. Jethro knew he was cornered, unable to escape his friend's deadly strikes.

"Tsarong, please remember!"

He loomed over Jethro, his hand raised and ready to deliver the final killing blow. Jethro knew this was it. He had no escape and his friend would not listen to him, would not remember.

"Tsarong, stop!"

Sun's words cut through the air. Tsarong hesitated, his hand shook, but did not strike. He looked across the room and met Sun's eyes.

"Tsarong, he is your friend. You must remember!"

Tsarong's fist continued to shake. Jethro reached up and grabbed his friend's arm, clenched it tightly in his grip. "You don't have to do this, brother. We can fight together. You must only remember. And perhaps I can help you with that. Perhaps...."

Jethro's hand closed tightly around his friend's arm. He clenched his eyes shut and centered his *chi*. With one perfect breath, he found his inner calm and felt the words rise on his lips.

"Om! Ma-ni pad-me Hum!"

Tsarong's body shook as if struck by lightning. His eyes grew wide as he threw his head back and screamed.

The komodo dragons joined his roar a moment later.

"Release them," Vong Den said. The panic was evident in his voice. "Release the dragons and kill them all!"

The dragon's chains slackened and the two massive lizards rushed forward. An unfortunate shadow warrior stood in the path of one and was quickly trampled and skewered by the dragon's claws.

It was clear the beasts were trained only to kill, not to discern ally from enemy. Nothing would stand in their path of destruction. Nothing but the Green Lama.

Jethro charged the nearest beast as it finished tearing the shadow warrior to pieces. He drove one fist hard into the dragon's snout. The blow was enough to stun the massive beast, but would only give it pause momentarily.

He hoped that was all the time he needed. He grabbed the side of the beast's head and used its loose skin to flip up and onto the monster's back. As it recovered, the Komodo dragon realized where he was and fought to shake him off. He clenched his thighs around the beast and struggled to hold on. He raised his fists above his head and drove them down hard into the dragon's spine. He struck again and again and again until he heard a sharp crack. The beast collapsed under him, suddenly crippled and dying.

Across the room, the other dragon roared as it charged Turner, now suddenly alone but for his guards. Sun was gone, clearly hiding somewhere in the room. Good unfortunately stood between the beast and his fellow Secret Service agent. With one great massive claw, the beast sliced him from sternum to hip. Good's blood flew into the air as the dragon rose over him and ripped a chunk of flesh from his neck.

Sun rushed suddenly across the room and pulled the stunned Turner away from the beast as it continued toward him. The two shadow warriors raised their weapons to strike at the rampaging monster. The *ninjatos* proved little more than a nuisance to the dragon's claws and teeth. It made short work of the two soldiers of the Black Ring, just two more men ripped to shreds by the horrible beast.

"My Lama!"

Tsarong's voice rang across the room. Jethro turned as his greatest ally, his mind once again his own, hurled a ball of green cloth across the room. Jethro leaped into the air, hurled his form up to meet the precious package. He snatched the robe from midair. It flashed around him as he fell. When he landed on the ground, he was dressed in the tattered cloak of the Green Lama.

He charged the surviving komodo, his hands disappearing into his cloak. The beast's attention was back on Perry Turner. Turner was at the body of Good and he rummaged through his fellow agent's remains. Turner came up with both his and Good's firearms. He turned to face the dragon as it charged toward him. The bullets hit the great Komodo dragon, each blast a flash of red mist across the dragon's massive form. But the bullets failed to slow the massive beast one bit.

The Lama struck the beast from the side. The radioactive salts once again coated his hands. The burst of lightning knocked the dragon off his feet. It fell to its side, dazed by the blow. Blood flowed freely from where Turner's bullets struck. The Komodo dragon moaned and tried to stand, but it was far too late for the massive animal. It was not long for this world.

The Green Lama's attention turned toward Vong Den. Turner walked up to stand at his left, guns still in hand. Tsarong joined them to the Lama's right. They all stared down the leader of the Black Ring.

"It is over, Vong Den. You have lost. Give up now."

"Never," Vong Den cried from across the room. He pulled a device from his pants, some kind of radio transmitter. "If I die today, it will not be alone. This room is wired with explosives. With just a press of a button, they will ignite. It seems we will all meet our fate this day."

"Do not be a fool, Vong Den! It need not end this way!"

Vong Den shook his head. "It was always going to end this way, Dumont." He raised the transmitter, his eyes on the trigger. "Good…"

His final word was cut off by a low gurgle from deep in his chest. The tip of a *ninjato* blade sprouted from his chest. It turned the black ring around his heart into a perfect bull's-eye. Blood gushed from the wound as the transmitter toppled from his hand. It shattered as it struck the floor.

The *ninjato* was pulled free and Vong Den toppled forward, already dead. Sun stood behind him, gazing coldly down at her victim, the bloody blade still in her hand.

"Sun, thank god," Turner said. "I lost you in the mêlée."

"You didn't lose me, Perry. After I saved you, I left your side on purpose." She dropped the weapon on Vong Den's still body. "I had work to do."

"What? I don't understand. We came here to save your brother, not kill his kidnapper. I thought we were here to save Tsarong."

Tsarong turned to Turner and spoke with calm, quiet words. "I am sorry, friend, you must be mistaken. I am quite certain I have no sister. I have never met this woman."

"Then who is she?" Turner said.

"Magga."

The Green Lama's word seemed to echo through the chamber.

"You continue to be wise beyond your years," the woman said with a nod. "Even now, I see you putting the pieces together."

"It was you that supplanted our minds. You created the identities of Mike Washington and Ping to hide us from Vong Den and the Black Ring. Vong Den brought the Black Ring here with the goal of killing us both and you knew he would do anything to find us. But his cautious nature meant he would be wary of exposing himself without good reason. So you went and found Agent Turner, convinced him of your love and used him to expose me and, I assume, Tsarong. You knew that Vong Den would not resist the chance to pit the two of us against one another, knowing all the time that you could break us from the spell with just a few words."

"Quite close, my Lama. I hadn't taken into account the full strength of Vong Den's brainwashing. Tsarong may not have broken his control fully if not for your aid. But otherwise, you are quite correct. You have again shown you possess faculties far beyond mortal ken. But, alas, the time for discussion has come to an end."

"Not quite yet," the Green Lama said. "You knew what you were doing when you created the identities of Mike Washington and Ping. You killed a monster this day, but you are also responsible for the death of two innocent men. You must answer for those sins."

"We must all come to answer for our crimes at some point," Magga said. "But my reckoning will not come today."

Her hand flew out and smoke seemed to pour from her very palm. Within a moment, she was blanketed in a thick cloud that obscured all vision.

The Green Lama rushed forward but he knew it was already too late. He found nothing in the smoke and, as it cleared, no sign of Magga remained but for one. A wig of long, flowing black hair lay on the ground.

It seemed Sun was gone as well, vanished into the ether with Mike Washington. But his date with Magga would come.

The Green Lama would see to that.

Jethro Dumont and Tsarong met with Perry Turner late the next day. While Dumont and Tsarong needed to recover from their ordeal, not just physically, but mentally and spiritually, Agent Turner found himself at the center of a major investigation. Vong Den's three concubines proved more than willing to expose every aspect of his operations with only the promise of amnesty.

They sat once again in the apartment of Mike Washington, one last visit to the scene of the man's death.

"It is done then," Turner said. "The Black Ring is done, dismantled throughout the city. The police and the Secret Service have rounded up dozens of men and women from all walks of life. We've got more than enough to prosecute even the richest and most powerful members."

"If only it was that easy to stamp all crime from the city," Jethro said. "But it always remains. Others will rise to take back their place. The Italians already have made moves back into the city."

"The Secret Service will be ready for them," Turner said.

"As will the Green Lama," Jethro said. "And I expect you will remember your promise to me."

"Call on me whenever you have need, Dumont. But I'll warn you. I doubt I will be in the city much longer. It sounds like Washington already has plans for me. This kind of bust always seems to be rewarded with a boring desk job, but after Sun…Magga's…betrayal, maybe riding a desk will be all right for a few months."

"I understand," Jethro said as he rose and took in the apartment.

"I spent weeks here, but that life is gone, as dead as Mike Washington. It sits on me like a phantom. Mike had a good life here, a simple life, to be sure, but a good one. For all I have seen in the world, for all the good I have done, I wonder if his life would be more fulfilling than my own."

Tsarong rose and rested a hand on his friend's shoulder. "My lama, a simple life was never our path."

"I suppose you are right, my friend. Come, I've seen enough of this place."

The three men exited the apartment. Jethro Dumont turned and took in the door. He drew the key from his pocket and placed it in the lock. After he pulled it free, he checked to make sure it was secure.

That door was closed. Mike Washington was gone.

The Green Lama lived on.

The End

Changing Things Up

I came to a realization as I wrote this story. I'm terrible at emulating classic pulp writers' styles. As much as I enjoy the work of Kendell Foster Crossen, his style was not meant for me. I had to come at the Green Lama in a very different way.

The first thing I decided to do was drop much of his recurring cast. As I first came to the character through his later radio adventures, characters like Gary Brown, Evangl Stewart and the like just didn't hold my interest in the way the simple team of the Green Lama and Tsarong did. With a set-up that involves so many assumed identities I could establish a situation where those other players would not be needed and even set up a new ally for the Green Lama in the process.

Perry Turner is the character I wished I had more room to flesh out in my tale as the 1930s Secret Service agent had so much room to grow. The Service was an interesting place to work in that period before the rise of the FBI, and Turner has a lot more personality than made it onto the pages of this story as he was pushed to the side by its other players. Should I return to the Green Lama, expect Turner to be in tow. (And the answer is yes to any "Phineas & Ferb" fans that might wonder about the origins of his first name, much to the chagrin I'm sure of any Erle Stanley Gardner fans.)

Magga will almost certainly make an appearance in any future tales as well, as she proved the most interesting and elusive character from the original pulps. I knew from the get go that I would have to use her as the exception to my removal of most of the original pulp's characters. She is a character whose motivations and goals I would love to explore more deeply, even as I question whether those motivations and goals should ever really be explored. So much of what makes her great is the mystery, and I've seen far too many characters ruined when their mystique is ripped away.

"The Menace of the Black Ring" is anything but a traditional Green Lama tale, but, at the same time, I think it stays true to the character and his Buddhist underpinnings. Much like the interpretations of the character changed a bit from medium to medium, I hope Green Lama fans can find something to love in my twisted mind games and rotund villain from Jethro Dumont's past.

Author Bio:

NICHOLAS AHLHELM was born and raised in Iowa where he still lives. He founded the publishing venture Metahuman Press (http://www.metahumanpress.com) and continues to run it. His short work has appeared in anthologies from Pro Se Press, Metahuman Press and Pulp Empire, including *The New Adventures of Thunder Jim Wade*, *Horror Heroes*, *Modern Pulp Heroes* and *Blood-Price of the Missionary's Gold*. "The Menace of the Black Ring" is the first of several projects upcoming with Airship 27.

His novels, *Living Legends* and *Freedom Patton,* remain available at most online retailers.

He lives and writes in the city of Cedar Rapids, alongside his wife and two children. He has no cats and often wonders why everyone talks about cats in these short biographies.

the

in

The Studio Specter

by W. Peter Miller

Chapter 1
The Mayan Mummy

The stone walls of the tomb drip with dew and are draped with spider-webs and fear. The dim light reveals little save the slow crawl of a tarantula. The creature reaches a carved stone sarcophagus in the center of the room.

The scraping of boots disturbs the ancient silence. The hairy spider scurries out of view. Light appears in the entryway, torchlight dancing through the eons of cobwebs blocking the entrance. A bold silhouette follows the torch: a woman's form with a torch in one hand and a high caliber revolver in the other. The shadow pauses behind the webs.

The chamber walls are carved with the smooth art deco-esque stonework of the Mayan people. The intruder throws her torch through the webs. The strands spark and sizzle.

The woman steps through the sparkling portal, pausing in the dramatic flickering light from the torch at her feet. Her shapely figure wears tight khaki pants ending in black leather boots. Her white blouse is snug in all the right places and her short blonde haircut is tucked under a pith helmet.

She turns to look at the intricate carvings on the stone casket and smiles a perfect smile. She runs her hands over the carvings.

"You are finally mine," she says, looking into the eyes of the sarcophagus. "The Queen of the Mayan Empire is mine."

A low moan seems to emanate from the very rock. The woman's smile cracks and her eyes dart around the room. The moan gets louder, more shrill. Then it suddenly stops. The woman calms slightly. Then there is a sound like a low wind. The adventuress' hair blows back and she screams, suddenly spinning about. She fires the gun wildly, emptying the cylinder.

"CUT!" a man yells.

The woman explorer screams angrily. She whirls around, violently throwing the gun at the faux stone wall. "Where are you?" she shrieks. Her expression is wild, out of control.

"I SAID CUT!" the director yells, pushing the cameraman aside and running onto the temple set. He is a smartly dressed, handsome man in his early thirties. He holds a script in his hands. He runs up to the woman and puts his hands on her shoulders. She jumps away. He looks into her wild eyes and says, "Fay… It's okay. Really. There's nothing here."

She looks at him as if he had just slapped her. After a moment, she runs through the cobwebs and off the set, sobbing.

The man throws his script to the ground in frustration and chases after her. "Fay! Fay!" he yells.

He follows her through the cobwebbed opening and out of sight. The film crew just stands there, dumbfounded.

A man with a clipboard steps into the tomb and turns to the film crew, "That's a wrap, everybody. Call is 8 a.m. tomorrow, rushes will be at lunch."

Fay Reynolds, the actress in the explorer's costume, is sobbing with her head on the mak-eup table. Fay is the biggest thing in Hollywood right now. The tabloids call her, "This season's 'It Girl.'" Fay hit the big-time fast and hasn't had time to look back. But something is troubling her now. Something dark and strange that has shaken her deep in her soul.

There is a light knock and she looks up. Even in tears she is a knockout. "Go away," she says softly.

The door opens. The director peeks into the door. "Can I come in?"

Fay looks at him. Her face softens a little. "Alright," she says.

The Mayan Mummy director, Freddy Dmytryk, smiles and enters Fay's dressing room. Dmytryk pulls up a chair and sits next to her. He takes her hand in his and says, "I don't know what is happening, but I promise you that I will keep you safe. There is nothing to fear…"

"Nothing to fear!" Fay shrieks. "You can't tell me it's nothing because it's real. You've heard the rumors. There is something… wrong here. There's a presence. I felt it."

He looks deep into her eyes and that's when it hits him like a ton of bricks. He's never felt this way before. He has dated a long series of starlets and made many of their careers. He has helped actress after actress get lead roles in his films and in his bed, but he never felt anything but longing for the next one. He didn't notice, but he sighed deeply at the realization. He loves her. He smiles and speaks with an unfamiliar sincerity.

"Fay. We've all been working too hard. Let me take you home. You can have a hot bath and get some rest. I'll pick up some soup at Canter's. You must be dog tired."

Fay looks at him. She softens a little more. "Okay," she says. "You can take me home. But there was something there. Really. I swear I felt something."

"I'm sure you did, Honey," the director says. He stands and takes her hand. She smiles and feels a little bit of a flutter. Not from fear this time.

Ice-cold air freezes an exhaled breath into a soft fog as it exits the dark green folds of the hood of the Green Lama. He is perched on a ledge overlooking a man walking down Wall Street. It is dark and the street is empty, not surprising considering the hour of the night and the light snow that is falling. The Lama has tracked this prey for 2 days, hoping to get a look at the man's boss: the chief of the Tong, the Chinese Mob. They are in the business of trafficking opium and selling companionship. The man stops on the corner of Front and Wall to fish a deck of Luckies out of his pocket. When his coat briefly opens the Green Lama sees a revolver parked in a shoulder holster. The man lights up. He lingers at the corner.

The Green Lama senses the man is waiting and starts to click a prayer wheel inside his robe. He speaks a quiet chant.

"Salutation to the Buddha.

"In the language of the gods and in that of the *lus*,

"In the language of the demons and in that of men,

"In all the languages which exist,

"I proclaim the Doctrine.

"*Om! Ma-ni pad-me Hum*!"

The Green Lama is not cold. Ten years spent in a mountaintop Buddhist monastery taught him to master his body's temperature.

After the man finishes half his Lucky, a large expensive black sedan pulls up. A chauffeur steps out of the car. He is dressed in a smart black suit and leather cap. The Green Lama surmises that the owner of the car would be riding in the cavernous rear compartment. Wanting a better look, the Green Lama silently slides down a storm drain to the street and makes his way through the shadows toward the imposing sedan.

From his new vantage point, the Lama sees through the back window that the car is unoccupied. The Green Lama expertly picks the lock on the trunk. The driver lets the waiting man into the car but doesn't see the Green Lama slip into the large boot of the car. The Green Lama timed this action to be simultaneous with the waiting man getting into the car. The car drives off.

After a short time, the car rolls to a stop. The Green Lama hears two doors open and shut. Footsteps walk away. The trunk opens and the green hooded figure slips into the shadows of a deserted back alley. The air smells of cooked duck and rotted octopus. A light shines ahead, illuminating Chinese calligraphy above a doorway. "Mandarin Cuisine – The World's Finest" the Lama reads. He slips the red *kata* out from around his neck. It is his only weapon on this night. His supply of radioactive salts would not be replenished until the morning. He enters the door without fear.

The kitchen is empty, but the Lama hears voices having an argument in the restaurant beyond. The green-cloaked figure silently reaches the door. The argument reaches its zenith. Kyu Lee, the man with the gun and the cigarettes holds one in each hand. He gestures with the lit nail at a balding, older Chinese man in a chair. The driver stands off to the side. The Lama feels he should not underestimate this man. Lee is shouting in Cantonese but the Green Lama understands him fine.

"Where is the money?" Lee screams.

"We have no money. It was stolen," the restaurant owner says. "Please, give me more time."

"Mr. Fong says you are out of time. But I will go easy on you," Lee says and jams the smoldering cigarette into the man's eye. The man screams. Lee nods to the driver and the driver grabs the screaming man's head to steady it. Lee holsters his pistol and lights another Lucky.

Lee blows smoke in the sobbing restaurant owner's face. "Tonight, I will let you live." He moves to jab his fresh cigarette into the man's good eye, but his arm won't move. The crimson *kata* has wrapped around his wrist.

"Men who walk in darkness must expect to stumble on a rock," the Green Lama says in Cantonese. The strength of his voice startles all in the room.

Mr. Fong's enforcer, Lee, whirls to draw and fire the gun. The Lama ducks under the Colt's blast and turns gracefully, the *kata* twisting the man around. The Lama raises his arm in a wide circle and the Tong enforcer is spun over crashing to the floor.

"I am that rock," the Green Lama says, and renders the man unconscious with a sharp blow to the back of his neck.

The chauffeur steps forward, throwing off his cap. The man adopts a *Xíng Yì Quán* Steel stance. The Green Lama bows in respect and adopts the first stance of the Earth form. The chauffeur nods his head in respect, acknowledging the Green Lama's obvious training.

Then the chauffeur closes in. He rushes the Lama, snapping his arms and launching into a tornado force spin kick. The Lama avoids the brunt of the attack, but still takes quite a wallop. He flies back toward the bar. The chauffeur pursues, arms whirling in a ballet of battle.

The Lama uses his momentum to flip over the bar. He sees the chauffeur in the mirror and grabs a pair of liquor bottles and hurls them hard over his shoulders. The chauffeur avoids one, but the other smashes on his temple, halting his momentum. The Green Lama vaults back over the bar, driving his feet into the driver's solar plexus and knocking him to the ground. The Lama pursues, striking a vicious blow to the man's neck, stunning him. Without his radioactive salts the Lama is required to apply more force to do the job, but the chauffeur is finally subdued.

The Green Lama turns back to Kyu Lee. He shakes him awake.

"Where is Mr. Fong?" the Green Lama asks in Cantonese.

"You or I will die before I answer," the Tong enforcer answers.

"It shall not be I," the Lama says. He makes a vicious fingertip strike at a certain nerve bundle at the base of the man's neck, regretting the force necessary without the salts. The man's body is paralyzed. The Lama uses simple fear to extract the information he needs.

Twenty minutes later Lt. John Caraway of the NYPD Special Crime Squad and his men are cleaning up the mess. Caraway says, "You couldn't have waited until morning?"

"What is written, will be. We cannot choose the time. The time chooses us," the Lama says, "Your man's name is Mr. Fong and you will find him in a warehouse at the corner of Hester and 16th in Brooklyn. There should be enough opium there to put him away for a long time." The Green Lama heads for the door, "Farewell, Lieutenant Caraway," he says.

Caraway chuckles and shakes his head. "Let's get this mess cleaned up," he says to his team.

"It's another gorgeous Hollywood day and the sun is already out. Despite what the calendar says, this January morning is looking to be another scorcher – eighty-five degrees and it's only 10 a.m. In the news this morning are reports of more troubles in Europe with that reprehensible..."

Freddy Dmytryk snaps off the radio as his car pulls up to the main gate at Triumph Pictures. The driver waves to the guard and the car pulls in. In the back seat, Fay Reynolds looks into the director's eyes.

"Freddy, I'm a little scared, you know, about coming back here. That stuff yesterday just gives me the creeps about coming back to this place. I think it's haunted," she says.

The director takes her hand. "Fay. I will never let anything happen to you. We need to go in there and look at the rushes and you will see what I saw. I was standing just off the set. There was nothing there. A bit of wind from a fan. That's all."

Fay sighs, "You're probably right. It's probably nothing."

Dmytryk smiles and says, "Atta girl."

Most of the crew has already arrived at the small screening room. There is the murmur of gossiping going on in the jammed theater. The whole crew is curious to see if Fay Reynolds is going to show. The cameraman, Linn Edwards, is talking to Triumph Pictures President Samuel Blintz and Herman K. Herman, the Producer of *The Mayan Mummy*. Fay Reynolds and Freddy Dmytryk walk in and suddenly, the room is silent.

Fay steps up and addresses Mr. Blintz and the crowd. "I know I caused a bit of a scene yesterday, and I'm terribly sorry," Fay says.

Mr. Blintz says, "That's alright Miss Reynolds. You're here and that's what matters. We are all thrilled to have you back."

The room erupts in applause. Fay smiles in embarrassment. Freddy Dmytryk grins. As the applause dies down, Mr. Blintz grabs Dmytryk by the arm and pulls him off to the side.

The Mogul speaks in a harsh whisper, "Well, that was one of her better performances. Did you rehearse that in the car? You better keep her under control. We need that dame. You need that dame. Your last 3 pictures sank like the *Titanic,* and if this one goes down then you're gonna be lucky to find space on a lifeboat. Nobody will hire you."

"Yes, sir," Dmytryk manages to squeeze in, but the Mogul steamrollers on.

"You'll be lucky to direct traffic. Fix this. The Studio can't afford to lose that dame."

The Director looks at the Studio Chief and says, "She's here, isn't she? She's gonna be fine."

"She better be." Blintz turns away.

Freddy Dmytryk returns to his leading lady and says, "You ready?"

"Ready, Freddy," she says with a grin. They sit.

Dmytryk says, "Roll 'em!" and the projectionist starts the film. The reel unwinds into the projector and the dailies start.

A clap board fills the screen and we hear the clapper/loader shout, "*Mayan Mummy* Scene 35 Apple, Take 2." He steps out of view. A passageway in the temple ruins fills the screen.

"Action!" Dmytryk shouts. Fay, in expedition attire, finally enters the Mayan ruins carrying a torch. She pushes her way through the dimly lit tunnel. She comes to an abrupt stop. The temple is full of dust and cobwebs, skeletons and rats. As she looks ahead into the dark tunnel, something catches her eye. She looks genuinely scared. She pushes the torch forward a bit.

In her seat, Fay isn't scared. In fact, the corners of her perfect mouth are starting to turn up with the beginnings of a grin. She lightly elbows Dmytryk. He looks at her and smiles.

On screen, a skeleton suddenly shoots out of a side passage and flies right past Fay. The skeleton is followed by a lanky grip, who trips over his own feet and flies past the stunned starlet.

The screening room erupts with laughter and applause. "Good one, Hess!" somebody shouts.

Up on the silver screen, we hear a crash off screen and Fay is again alone on the set of the ancient Mayan pyramid. Somehow she has maintained her composure, though we hear the film crew laughing. Then she breaks and turns to camera laughing. The crew in the screening room is laughing, too. In the dailies Dmytryk yells, "Cut!" and at that moment on the screen a strange shape starts coming through the stone wall behind Fay. An arm reaches out for her. The image only lasts a moment, but Fay sees it and goes cold. Then the screen flashes white and another slate appears.

Fay isn't laughing anymore. She jabs Dmytryk. He doesn't react.

Fay elbows him again, "Did you see that?"

"See what?" Dmytryk answers.

"It looked like a ghost or something."

"I didn't see anything," he says. She looks at him in dismay.

Scene 35 Apple Take 3 goes off without a hitch. The skeleton falls at Fay's feet, just as it should, she jumps back and yelps, and the grip even manages to stay out of the shot.

Two more scenes spool through the projector without incident. Fay however is getting more and more nervous. She is on the verge of a total panic attack.

While the projectionist changes reels, Dmytryk calms her down.

The next reel of dailies starts. This is the one. Fay squirms in her seat and Dmytryk holds her hand.

The whole theater is hushed in anticipation. On the screen, explorer Fay appears at the cobwebbed door and throws the torch through. Then she approaches the carved stone tomb and says, "You are finally mine. The Queen of the Mayan Empire is mine." On screen Fay starts to look around nervously. After a moment, she seems to calm down.

Dmytryk looks at her and says, "See, honey. Nothing. No sounds. Nothing."

Fay smiles faintly at him and then looks back to the screen. Her face goes white. Dmytryk's too. There is a gasp behind her. Everyone in the screening room is transfixed by what they are seeing onscreen.

In the movie, Fay's hair is blown around by a mysterious wind. Behind her an apparition floats through the wall and into the chamber. The ghostly shape approaches Fay with its arms out and a horrific maw opening up in a low groan.

Fay suddenly screams and spins around firing the blanks in her Colt wildly until it clicks again and again against the spent ammo. She screams frantically, the spectral shape stalking her.

On screen, Dmytryk yells "CUT!" Fay is shrieking and out of control. Dmytryk screams, "I SAID CUT!" The camera is jolted and the film runs out. The theater lights come up.

Fay is sobbing and enraged. Dmytryk is just staring at the blank screen. Fay slaps him and it jars him out of his fog. She stamps to her feet and storms out of the screening room with Freddy Dmytryk and Herman K. Herman chasing after her. Dmytryk finally catches her and grabs her arm.

"Stop, Fay…" he says.

She stares him right in the eye and says through gritted teeth, "Let me go."

"C'mon Fay…" Dmytryk says.

Herman is winded but finally catches up. "Miss Reynolds, please don't be hasty. Let's all calm down and I'm sure there is a good explanation for all this," the Mogul says.

Fay is not having it. She has not shifted her gaze off of the director's eyes. In fact, she hasn't blinked.

"Let go of my arm, Freddy," Fay says in a monotone.

Dmytryk flashes her that patented Freddy Dmytryk smile that has worked so well on so many young starlets. Fay provides a different response.

"Go suck an egg," she says coldly and socks him square in the jaw. The playboy director drops like a stone. Fay storms off and the Mogul is torn between his star and his sense of self-preservation. He ends up helping Dmytryk to his feet.

Jethro Dumont sits at the desk in his library reading the afternoon newspaper. A light snow is falling outside. Each day he clips the stories that catch his eye, or provide clues to cases in which he or the Green Lama are involved.

At one time, Dumont was a young Harvard graduate looking for adventure. He spent his youth satisfying the ambitions of his parents and one day he decided he needed something more, something for himself. He travelled the world, finally ending up in the mountains of Tibet. The place seemed to call to him. He climbed the Himalayas and found a monastery perched among the clouds. Dumont met a Buddhist Lama there and found the place compelling. He didn't want to leave. He felt that this was the place where he would find his purpose. He stayed there searching for peace within his mind and in his life. He spent ten years in Tibet studying, eventually uncovering secrets hidden in the temple for centuries. Secrets that revealed even greater powers, secrets that surpassed even the powers gained as he became a Buddhist Lama, secrets that took a great effort to hide. But hide them he did. Or so he thought.

Shortly after entering the monastery, Dumont met a wise Tibetan monk named Tsarong and they became fast friends. When the time came to leave Tibet and return to New York, Dumont asked Tsarong if he would join him. Tsarong agreed.

While Dumont pays Tsarong a salary, Dumont considers the Tibetan a friend and colleague. Tsarong is the only one who knows the full story of Jethro Dumont and how his time in Tibet changed him forever.

Tsarong enters the library and plugs a portable phone into a socket on the wall. "Sir, it is a Mr. Herman."

Dumont looks intrigued and picks up the line. "Herman! This is a surprise. Are you in the Big Apple?" Herman K. Herman had attended Harvard with Dumont and they are old friends.

"I wish, Jethro. Unfortunately this isn't a social call. I've got trouble and I'm hoping you can help."

"What's the problem, Herman? Wait, don't tell me. It's a dame, isn't it?"

"Sort of, but more like the trouble we had on *The Last Dinosaur*. You remember that picture, don't you, Jethro?" Herman says.

This gets Dumont's attention. The last time Dumont was in Los Angeles, Herman's picture, *The Last Dinosaur*, was about to premiere when the starlet was murdered, seemingly by a dinosaur. Dumont and the Green Lama captured the real killer and saved Herman's career.

"I remember," Dumont says. "What's the trouble this time?"

Herman proceeds to tell Dumont about Fay Reynolds' antics on the set and the bizarre ghostly images on the film this morning. "So, what do you think?"

Dumont picks up a framed photo on his desk. "The film was tampered with."

"We thought of that, but the film goes straight from the camera to the lab right here on the lot. It's developed and printed and then we screen it the very next day. There's no time for someone to create optical effects."

"That's strange, alright...What about a motive?" Dumont says.

"That's easier. There are a lot of people that would want to scare Fay Reynolds."

"Like who?"

Herman pauses a moment. "Well, the other studios for one. That girl is the hottest thing in tinsel-town right now. They would love to scare her away from her 5-year contract with Triumph Pictures."

"Who else?" Dumont asks.

"Jealous actresses, bitter writers, crazy ex-wives. Hollywood is full of people that would love to see her fail."

Dumont thinks a moment and then says, "I think I've been needing some sunshine."

"So you'll come?" Herman asks.

"I'll head out tomorrow."

"What about your… friend?" the producer adds hesitantly.

"I'll see if I can locate him."

Dumont hangs up the phone. "Pack our bags, Tsarong. We are flying to Los Angeles."

Late that evening, the Buddhist monk, Dr. Charles Pali is in his laboratory, hunched over a delicate instrument, carefully measuring out doses of radiation from his newest batch of salts. Satisfied, he puts the correct dosage into a series of small vials and closes each with a stopper. He puts the vials in a small velvet-lined steel case.

Then Pali presses a concealed button beneath the edge of his work-bench. There is a small click then a section of the bench slides back and a microphone rises up. Some switches are thrown and the hum of a transformer fills the air.

At precisely ten o'clock the Green Lama tunes his radio transmitter to a particular frequency and speaks into the microphone.

"Calling Jean Farrell; calling Jean Farrell. *Nimitta; Nibána, lobha, dosa, moha*. Calling Jean Farrell…."

This mantra is repeated every two minutes for ten minutes. At last the microphone is set down and the Green Lama sits quietly in front of his small shrine, clicking his prayer wheel.

A few minutes later, the telephone rings. The Lama answers, "Hello?"

"Hello Dr. Pali, it's Jean Farrell."

"Greetings, *Né-tso-hbum*," Dr. Pali says.

Jean smiles. "*Tulku.*"

"How is your acting career going?"

Jean sits in the parlor of her flat at the actor's rooming house. She says, "I don't have anything at the moment."

"Maybe that is for the best. I need your help, Miss Farrell. It seems there is some trouble in Tinseltown. Make a reservation at the Hollywood Roosevelt. Check in the day after tomorrow. I will leave word there. *Tashi shog*."

"Pack our bags, Tsarong. We are flying to Los Angeles."

Jethro Dumont and Tsarong arrive at New York Municipal Airport, eager to catch their early morning flight. Tsarong checks their bags with a skycap and Dumont pays the taxi driver. They walk into the brand new terminal together.

"I hope this place was worth all that taxpayer money," Dumont says.

"You should visit the LaGuardia Admirals Club," Tsarong says.

Dumont laughs, "It's a bit early for that. Perhaps next time; we've got a flight to catch."

They hurry to the gate and board the mighty DC-3, a state of the art aircraft that can reach an altitude of over 20,000 feet and cruise at over 150 miles per hour!

A mere 15 hours later they are pulling up to the Chateau Marmont Hotel. Dumont gets out of the cab stretching his legs. Tsarong follows. A concierge approaches.

"Welcome to the Marmont, Mr. Dumont. Your bungalow is this way," the young man gestures and escorts Dumont to the private, 2-bedroom hillside bungalow, leaving Tsarong to handle the luggage. Dumont enters the bungalow and retires for the night.

Chapter 2
Triumph and Tragedy

Hot coffee and the morning newspaper get Dumont's attention.

"Tsarong!" Dumont says.

The man appears from the second bedroom. "Yes, Jethro, what is it?"

"I think that our little favor just got a lot more complicated," Dumont says, pointing at a headline screaming in massive type.

'STARLET DEAD ON MUMMY SET – Police Baffled' the type shouts.

Dumont reads, "Last evening actress Janet Leary was killed when a giant column collapsed on the set of *The Mayan Mummy*, the new Fay Reynolds picture. Miss Reynolds and dozens of other actors barely escaped being horribly crushed to death. Two crew members were injured. A studio spokesman called it an accident that happened during rehearsal. Studio Police are investigating."

"My word. I'll call you a car," Tsarong says.

Dumont's car is waved through the Triumph Pictures gate after passing a police inspection. A junior V.P. escorts Dumont to a small screening room in the basement of the executive building. Dumont's Harvard classmate meets him at the door.

"Jethro, I'm so glad you've come," Herman K. Herman says, "even if it is under such awful circumstances."

The men shake hands. Dumont notices his friend's hands are clammy and cold. Dumont says, "Well, hopefully I can help you out."

"Yes. Come inside," Herman says. The men enter the screening room and Dumont is surprised that the two men are the only ones there. Herman and Dumont sit down next to a wooden console with a button on it.

Dumont says, "Where's the crew? What's going on, Herman?"

"I didn't want anyone else to see this... You see, we lied to the press – it wasn't a rehearsal – we have it on film. Janet's death," Herman says. "No one has seen this film. Not even me. I've been up all night. I oversaw it through the lab myself. I didn't want any copies made. The original negative is in the safe in my office."

Dumont looks into his friend's eyes. Herman is near tears.

"She's a lovely girl, Jethro. Has... had a real spark," Herman says, choking back tears. He pushes the button on the console. "Go ahead, Guy."

The lights go down and the projector's carbon arc lamp sparks to life. A thin spiral of history uncoils into the machine. On the screen, the scene is slated.

A beautiful Mayan temple fills the screen. A crowd of Mayan extras worthy of an epic line the steps and the stone platform at the summit of the temple. Vines twist around 20 foot tall square pillars at the top of the stairs.

Our view moves in on Janet Leary, playing a Mayan maiden. She is dressed in revealing, exotic Mayan garb. She is lashed to a pole, her chest heaving with excitement. A Mayan Priest wearing a Quetzacóatyl headpiece is screaming up to the gods and speaking a Hollywood version of the Mayan language. He looking skyward. He draws a huge ceremonial knife and moves it to threaten Janet. A bowl is carved in the platform at the base of the pole to capture her blood.

Dumont realizes that the camera must be on a crane because it swoops down to reveal Fay Reynolds racing up the steps. A Mayan warrior steps out to stop her, but she pistol-whips him and he tumbles down. Fay keeps going. She is almost at the summit, almost to the priest.

Just as the priest's ceremony reaches a crescendo there is an inhuman scream and a bizarre spectral shape flies into view and crashes into one of the huge columns. The column starts tipping and Fay has stopped dead in her tracks. The column is headed right for her, but she is frozen in fear.

Dumont can't believe what he is seeing. "Run! Run!" he says.

But Fay doesn't run. The pillar is past the point of no return and the spectral shape shrieks again and flies off screen.

Fay is frozen, the priest runs into the temple behind him, and the extras scramble.

The huge pillar is almost on Fay when the Mayan Maiden, Janet Leary, pulls free of the pillar and dives forward, pushing the star out of the way. Unfortunately, Janet is not so lucky. The huge blocks come down on her, crushing her athletic form.

The film flashes white and then stops.

"The poor girl," Dumont says. He sits quietly for a moment and then says, "I need to see it again."

"Four times. I watched that girl die four times. I needed to have each detail in my head. I needed to absorb everything in an attempt to discern what transpired," Dr. Charles Pali says. He is sitting in the lounge of the Hollywood Roosevelt with Jean Farrell.

Jean puts her hand on his arm in support and says, "That's awful." She thinks a moment, and has a realization. "But you had already called me here before that poor girl was killed. I must have been on the plane by then. Her death isn't the reason you contacted me." Jean looks him in the eye. "Why are we here?"

Dr. Pali sits for a long moment before he answers. Just as Jean wonders if he will speak he says, "There once was a song bird that stopped singing. Many wise men were brought to the palace to make it sing, but they all failed. The Emperor was terribly saddened because the bird had been a gift from his beloved wife. When she died the bird stopped singing. Finally, a young girl walked by outside the Palace walls playing a cheap bamboo flute and the bird began to sing again."

"What does this have to do with me?" Jean asks.

Dr. Pali smiles and points at her, "You are the flute player."

Jean says, "I'm not sure I follow."

Dr. Pali nods. "Someone is trying to scare off Fay Reynolds. We need to find out who or why, because one will lead to the other," Pali says. "The suspects are many, but at this time I think we can be assured that it is someone at Triumph Pictures. They may not be working alone, but they need access and the whole picture is being filmed on the lot. Well, it was. The production is shut down for now."

Jean says, "Put me in with the cast. I'll see what I can find out."

"That's why you're here. To play a little bamboo flute – metaphorically speaking, of course. Triumph has already invested a bundle on this picture, so I'm sure they'll resume production soon. See the producer, Herman K. Herman, and he'll get you a job on the show."

Jean Farrell is escorted into Herman K. Herman's office. The door shuts.

"So, Miss Farrell, you're interested in acting for Triumph, eh? A friend recommended you," Herman says with a bit of a wink in his voice.

Jean is curious about the friend. "I needed a break from New York. Too cold."

"Wonderful. Our friend said I should put you in the cast of *The Mayan Mummy*, so I will. It's a small part, but you're pretty enough, you should be fine." Herman hands her a contract. "Just sign this and you'll be on the payroll."

Jean looks it over and signs.

Herman stands up and says, "Why don't I show you to your dressing room?"

"I'll be fine," Jean says and stands up.

"I insist," Herman says, putting his arm around her shoulders. "This lot can get very confusing."

Jean looks away and rolls her eyes, but plays along. "Alright. Lead the way."

Tsarong sits in a shadow behind a curtain in a small screening room. He has a good angle on the seats as the people come in. After they are seated, Jethro Dumont walks up to the front of the theater.

"My name is Jethro Dumont," he says. "I recognize a few of you from when I was here last summer. Mr. Herman has asked me to look into the events of the past few days. In order to do that, all of you will need to watch a few particular scenes of the picture. Some of what we will see here is difficult to watch, but we need to find out what has been happening and why. If you could, please introduce yourselves."

Dumont listens carefully as the Set Designer, Cameraman, Editor, and their assistants introduced themselves. One gentleman is of particular interest to Dumont. His name is Raymond O'Brien and he is the optical camera supervisor.

Dumont asks for the film to roll. The first reel shows the scene of Fay Reynolds entering the tomb through the cobwebbed door. She gets nervous and then the mysterious specter appears and she runs off, terrified. The take plays three times in a row and then the projector stops. The lights come up.

Dumont says to the cameraman, "Mr. Edwards, how'd they do it? It looks pretty real to me, but personally, I don't think you happened to be lucky enough to catch a real ghost on film."

Linn Edwards says, "I don't know, it must have been added to the shot afterwards."

"That is the obvious answer," Dumont says, "but is it possible? Mr. O'Brien, could this be done?"

The shy special effects man looks nervous as he is put on the spot. "Yes. It is possible to achieve that look on film. However, there is no way that this shot could have had the ghost added to it and been done in time for the rushes the next day."

"Thank you," Dumont says. "Does anyone have a different opinion?"

The room is silent.

Dumont asks for the second roll of film. This time the epic Mayan Temple scene plays out. After the third viewing, Dumont asks the same questions, but no one has an answer. Dumont thanks the crew for coming and lets them go.

Tsarong comes out from behind the curtain. Dumont asks him, "Well, what do you think?"

Tsarong says, "I think that there were a few particular people that looked very uncomfortable watching that film."

Dumont agrees, "That's what I thought, too. Both Linn Edwards, the Cameraman, and his assistant both looked like they wanted to be anywhere but here."

"I would agree with that," Tsarong says. "And the young man sitting in the back, something was worrying him, too."

Dumont thinks a moment, "I'm not sure who that was."

Tsarong says, "I didn't see the film, I was watching the audience."

"Let's run it again," Dumont says.

They head to the exit of the screening room where an assistant editor is leaving with the film. Dumont calls to him, "Hey! Hold up. I want to see that again."

The kid stops. When he turns back Dumont and Tsarong realize that he was the kid sitting in the back of the screening room. He comes back carrying a couple of cans of film.

"What's your name?" Dumont asks.

"Marcus Phillips," the kid says nervously.

They run the film again. The exterior scene of the Mayan temple is running when Dumont says, "Did you see that?"

"What?" Tsarong says.

"I'm not sure, but I thought I saw a flash of something above the specter,"

Dumont says as the lights come up.

"Like what?" Phillips asks.

Dumont grabs the kid's shoulders. Not hard, but with a solid strength. He looks the kid right in the eye and says, "You have been acting unusually. Like you have something to hide or you have something to say, but are afraid to say it. Spill it."

Phillips takes a deep breath and says, "The scene where the girl, Janet, you know…." He looks down. "My friend is one of the camera assistants and he was running a second camera. He…he missed the beginning of the take and then the film ran out and the pillar fell and he'd rather no one knew about this. He asked me not to tell anyone, but there is more film."

Phillips runs back with another can of film and hands it to the projectionist.

The film starts. This camera is filming a very wide view of the scene. So wide, in fact, that the other camera crew can be seen in the shot. Just as the pillar starts to move, the scene goes white and the film runs out.

"Oh, well, not much to see there," Phillips says. "My friend got the 'A' camera crew in the shot. No wonder he didn't want anyone to see it. That could ruin his career."

"I saw enough," Dumont says. "Thanks, kid. Keep this under your hat, would ya?"

He grins, "Sure thing, Mr. Dumont."

"What was your friend's name?"

Phillips pauses a moment. "Alright. You seem like a good egg. His name is Dave Huey. Please don't get him in trouble."

"Trouble comes to those that look for it. I seek only answers."

Phillips looks relieved.

"Oh, and I'll hang onto the film for a bit," Dumont says. The assistant editor leaves.

Dumont gives some instructions to Tsarong and then says, "I'm going back to Herman's office to get the negatives. I'll meet you at the bungalow after dinner."

Jean Farrell is walking across the Triumph Pictures lot toward the Sunset Boulevard gate when she hears an argument flare up. She peeks around the corner and sees two men arguing in the doorway of Stage 7.

"You're fired! You have messed up every step of the way! Get off this lot and never come back!" Jean recognizes the screamer as Linn Edwards, the *Mayan Mummy* cinematographer.

"What did I ever do to you?" the other man, Linn's assistant Dave Huey says.

"Do? You are incompetent! Worse," Linn says, flashing a look into the dark stage, "you are meddling in places where you have no business."

Dave Huey's eyes look into the darkness of Stage 7. "And you are a control freak. I've seen what's in there. Believe me, Mr. Herman and Mr. Dumont will be hearing about that!" Dave says.

"Shut up!" Linn says. "Shut up!" He slams Dave Huey against the huge stage door. The young man tries to squirm loose, but isn't succeeding. Linn throws him through the door into the darkness beyond.

Jean looks around, but no one else is in sight. She creeps up to the edge of the open door. Silence. She waits and after a few minutes steels herself to go in. She takes a step and Linn Edwards strolls out of the door, right in front of her. Jean jumps back, startled. "Oh! Mr. Edwards..." she says.

He pushes past her and heads off with determination. When he has rounded a corner, she steps into the stage.

It is dark and quiet inside. Jean can make out the outline of a doorway on the opposite side of the stage. Jean waits a moment for her eyes to adjust. She looks around the stage. There is a bit of lumber laying on the floor and a huge piece of black duvetyn covering one wall, but otherwise the place seems empty. Then Jean notices a large lump on the concrete floor next to the black fabric.

She creeps up to it and pokes it with her toe. It is solid. Jean carefully lifts the black fabric. Hidden underneath are cases of fresh Kodak movie film. Jean pulls back the black duvetyn a little farther and gasps when she sees a large tin of gunpowder.

A scuffle startles Jean. She looks up and sees the door open on the other side of the stage. A shadow crosses the shaft of light from the open door. Huey must have left, Jean thinks and decides she better follow the cinematographer. She runs out of the same stage door she came in and heads for the studio gate.

Jean sees Linn get into his car and start it. He exits the gates of Triumph Studios in his tan sedan. Jean breaks into a run, hailing a cab as she rushes past the protesting guard at the gate. A hack pulls up and Jean jumps in.

"Follow that car!" she says and the cab pulls away.

It is just a few miles down Western when the tan sedan pulls into the El Cholo Restaurant parking lot. Linn leaves his car with the valet and enters the restaurant. A few minutes later, Jean Farrell climbs out of the cab and steps into the Mexican eatery.

Jethro Dumont returns to his bungalow at the Chateau Marmont. Orange evening sunlight streams in, reflecting off the private pool. A patio is next to the pool and can be seen from the living room through a long wall of glass. Tsarong meets Dumont at the door. Dumont says, "Did you get it?"

"Yes, sir. I've got it set up in the smaller bath," Tsarong says.

Dumont gets two cans of film from the safe in the living room and joins Tsarong in the small bathroom.

There is a table over the tub, and centered on the table is a photographic enlarger. A pair of film rewinds are fixed to the ends of the table. Dumont dons a pair of white cotton gloves and laces the film between the rewinds. He starts winding film. After a moment he stops and looks at the film through a magnifier. He inches along the negative for a few moments. Then he stops and puts the film into the enlarger. He clicks on the lamp and focuses the frame. He clicks the enlarger off again.

Tsarong switches off the overhead light, leaving the room bathed in the strange amber glow of a photo-safe light.

Dumont pulls a large sheet of paper out of a box and places it under the enlarger. He clicks on the lamp and counts to five. The light clicks out. Dumont and Tsarong repeat the process several more times and then put the prints in developing solution and finally, hang them to dry.

"Let's get a bite of dinner," Dumont says.

The beautiful, rustic interior of El Cholo is one of the most welcoming in Los Angeles. Jean sits at the bar, slowly nursing a margarita. She has her back to Linn who is sitting on a cozy couch, his feet up on a leather coffee table. A mirror behind the bar allows Jean an easy view of Linn behind her. Jean wonders how long she can make her drink last, but it turns out to be long enough.

A black-haired woman comes into the restaurant. She enters the bar and spies Linn. She slides onto the couch next to him. Jean peers over her drink. The attractive black-haired woman puts her arm around the cameraman and they kiss. It is a passionate, deep kiss that goes on and on. Jean looks down at her drink feeling very alone.

The smooch session continues for a few more minutes, then the couple talks quietly. Jean tries, but she is unable to hear them across the room. Fresh drinks arrive and Linn and the black-haired woman sit back to enjoy an appetizer. Linn tells a joke and the black-haired woman laughs loudly, throwing her head back revealing a flash of blonde hair. Jean looks at her again, realizing the woman is wearing a wig. Then it clicks. The woman is

Fay Reynolds. Jean tosses back her drink and leaves a dollar on the bar. She leaves carefully, unwilling to risk being seen.

Dumont and Tsarong are hunched over a large coffee table that is littered with black and white photos. Dumont has two pictures of the Mayan temple scene where Janet Leary was killed lined up side-by-side on the table. He is looking through a powerful magnifying glass. One picture is a blow up from the 'A' camera. There is the wisp of the specter near the top of the column as it falls. Dumont moves to the other picture. It shows the same scene from the other camera angle, the 'B' camera – the one that ran out of film – at the same moment. The column is in mid-topple. Dumont moves from one picture to the other. He looks at the actors, the extras, and every detail until he is sure that they show the exact same moment.

"Look at this, Tsarong," Dumont says, handing the other man the magnifier. "We did it; captured the same moment in time from each camera."

The Tibetan takes the glass and looks at the picture. "This was the last frame before the film ran out…."

"It is conclusive, isn't it?" Dumont asks.

Tsarong stares through the large magnifying glass a moment longer. "Yes, it really couldn't be clearer."

"The Specter is a fake and Miss Leary was murdered," Dumont says.

The phone rings, interrupting the moment.

Jean sits in her room at the Hollywood Roosevelt. Grauman's Chinese Theater is lit up in Klieg lights across Hollywood Boulevard from her. She holds a telephone handset up to her ear. "Hello? Dr. Pali? It's Jean Farrell."

Tsarong answers, listens briefly and hands Dumont the phone saying, "Dr. Pali, it's Miss Farrell."

"Yes, Miss Farrell?" Pali says.

"I ran into Mr. Edwards on the lot today. He was pushing around that kid… his assistant…"

"Dave Huey?" Dr. Pali says before he can stop himself.

"You know him?" Jean asks.

"I know who he is. Go on."

Jean pauses, about to say something. She is bothered by Dr. Pali's answer, but she lets it go. "Well, he shoved Dave Huey into Stage 7. It's an empty stage. I could hear a bit of a scuffle, so I walked over for a better look, but Mr. Edwards came marching out – nearly ran me over – and then he drove off in a hurry. I poked my head in the stage, but it was empty, well almost empty. There were some cases of movie film and a can of gunpowder."

"This was the last frame before the film ran out..."

"I am sure you are going somewhere, Miss Farrell…" Dr. Pali says.

"All right. After seeing that, I grabbed a cab and followed Mr. Edwards. He stopped at El Cholo Restaurant and met up with a young lady. They got quite friendly. Frankly, the necking went on and on. Finally, I got uncomfortable staring at them and left. The woman was Fay Reynolds in disguise."

"And you are certain that it was her?" Dr. Pali asks.

Jean says, "Yes. I saw her blond hair beneath a black wig. It was her."

Dr. Pali says, "Thank you, Jean. Are you at the studio tomorrow?"

"Yes, we're rehearsing a few scenes in the morning. I think they are going back into production soon."

Chapter 3 The Specter Lives

The following morning is the start of one of those oppressively hot Los Angeles days. The air doesn't move and by 10:00 a.m. you just want to crawl into a freezer somewhere. Jethro Dumont doesn't have time for that, however. Today he needs to catch a killer.

The rented car speeds east on Sunset Boulevard. There is a briefcase on the seat next to Dumont. He looks down and the inventory of the case goes through his mind. Radioactive salts are the last item on the list. They are secured in the small steel container lined with velvet. The car passes Vine and then Western. Dumont makes a right, pulling onto the Triumph Pictures lot.

"Jethro Dumont to see Mr. Herman," Dumont says to the guard. The man checks a list.

"Have a good day, Mr. Dumont," the guard says and lifts the gate arm. The car pulls in and parks. Dumont gets out of the car and in no time is in the opulent executive offices of the studio head.

Dumont carefully removes the two pictures from his briefcase and lays them out on Herman K. Herman's desk.

"Have a look at these."

Herman glances at the pictures and points to the print from the 'B' camera. "Where did you get this?" he demands.

"That's not important," Dumont says, surprised by Herman's reaction.

"Oh, yes it is. Someone is going to catch Hell for hiding that! Why wasn't I informed there was film in another camera? I'll have their hide!" Herman raves, hot with anger.

"Look at the pictures again," Dumont urges.

After a moment Herman's mood cools slightly, but he is still mad. He looks at one picture and then the other. He looks much closer at the 'B' camera photo. A thin smile crosses his face. "There is no specter in that picture," he says.

Dumont felt like he is now getting somewhere. At least he is confident that the specter isn't real. Someone created it to scare Fay Reynolds right off the Triumph Pictures lot. There are a number of suspects and no easy answers.

Dumont decides to start in the camera department. After asking around, he tracks down Dave Huey, finding him in the commissary. Dumont buys a grilled cheese sandwich and coffee and approaches Huey at a table. The young man looks very nervous.

"Do you mind?" Dumont asks, gesturing at a chair at the table.

Dave Huey couldn't look more nervous. "…No… problem… sir."

Dumont parks himself in a seat across the table from the twenty-year-old Huey. He takes a bite of the sandwich. Dumont says, "I guess you remember me from the screening?"

The young man nods and mumbles, "Uh huh."

Dumont casually looks around and is confident no one is listening. He continues in a subdued voice. "I spoke with your friend, Phillips, a few minutes ago."

Huey takes a panicked look around the place. "Look – I can explain…"

Dumont cuts him off, "No need. I saw your footage and it was very helpful." Huey relaxes a small amount. Dumont continues, "But I had a few questions."

"Alright… Go ahead," the assistant cameraman says.

"Tell me about Linn Edwards. How long have you worked for him?" Dumont asks.

Dave says, "About two years, although sometimes I'm with one of the other camera men."

Dumont looks at him intensely. "Was everything okay between you two?"

Dave looks down. "I thought so…."

Dumont presses him further, "Well, was there anything unusual happening before the accident," Dumont asks.

"Not really. Well, I misloaded a magazine about a week ago…."

Dumont looks confused. "Magazine?" he asks.

"That's the container that holds the film when you put it on the camera.

So about a week later Linn gives me a nasty dressing down and says that I won't be loading the film anymore."

"So you didn't load the film I saw yesterday."

"No. Not yesterday or the day before. Linn insisted on loading all the film personally. I was afraid that I would be blamed for missing that expensive sequence. I started running the camera late, but it ran out of film anyway."

Dumont smiles. "But you didn't miss it completely. In fact, you got the only part that really mattered."

"Which part was that?" Huey asks.

Dumont smiles, "That would be telling."

Dumont leaves the interview with the young camera assistant with a few ideas, but no proof of anything. He is pretty sure that Linn Edwards is responsible for the Specter. But why would he want to terrify Fay Reynolds, especially if they were having an affair?

Dumont finds himself wandering the backlot, walking down New York Street. He feels at home here, even if the Big Apple feel is just a façade. He finds himself back on Wall Street at a fake version of the corner where he climbed into the trunk of Tong gangster Kyu Lee's car. The whole thing overwhelms him for a minute.

He sits on the steps of the fake New York Stock Exchange to sort things out. A few minutes pass. A strange feeling creeps over him. He looks up and sees an attractive young woman standing in front of him. She seems familiar. Dumont remembers that his adventure in Florida was the last time he saw this particular woman.

"Magga…"

"*Tulku*, the chronology of the world does not always follow man's vision of it," the black haired beauty says.

BANG! Dumont whirls and looks behind him. *BANG*, a Stock Exchange door slams in the wind. He looks back to the street, but Magga is gone.

Dumont ponders what Magga meant on the way to the hotel. He meets with Tsarong at the Chateau Marmont and together they think about it.

Tsarong says, "You say that it is impossible for the film to have been tampered with after the accident. What if it wasn't an accident? What if this was carefully planned?"

"Could they have tampered with the film before?" Dumont wonders. "The film could have been exposed first with the image of the Specter and then with the scenes from the movie. And there is only one person that could have planned that!"

Dumont grabs the phone and calls his friend, Herman K. Herman, to get an address.

After giving Dumont the address Herman asks, "What's cooking, Jethro? You think he is our man?"

"I'm not sure, but it sure looks bad for him. I'll explain everything later," Dumont says. He hangs up the receiver and pauses in front of the small Buddha. He says a prayer and leaves.

Dumont arrives at a beautiful Beverly Hills home. He parks his rented convertible roadster in the drive along with a several other cars. Dumont knocks at the front door. A middle-aged woman in a crisp, white uniform answers.

"The others have already started, this way please," she says and heads into the house. Dumont is slightly confused by this reaction, but plays along. The domestic looks back and asks, "Your name, sir?"

"Dumont," Jethro Dumont says as he walks toward the back of the house. He passes through several rooms containing souvenirs of Linn's travels. Greek pottery, Chinese inlaid furniture, and a stuffed lion catch his attention. As does a room containing several cherry wood gun cabinets. Dumont notes a classic Winchester rifle and a pair of Colt .45 revolvers. There are also flintlocks and even a blunderbuss. A brightly lit enclosed porch lies ahead.

The housekeeper says, "Mr. Edwards, your friend Mr. Dumont has arrived."

Linn turns suddenly; holding a hand of cards. Dumont thinks he sees a bit of panic in Linn's eyes, but if he did, the moment passes quickly.

"Care to join us?" Linn says. "There's one seat left." He gesture across a table strewn with poker chips and playing cards. Three other men dressed in expensive casual look on.

"Maybe later."

"As you wish. We're in the middle of a game here," Linn says turning back to the cards. He picks up a stack of chips and says, "I'll see you and raise you four hundred."

Dumont looks on. He can tell Linn is bluffing, but the other men don't see it. They fold and Linn takes the pot. Linn stands up and walks Dumont to the gunroom.

"What do you want, Mr. Dumont?"

"That was a nice bit of bluffing back there, very smooth," Dumont says.

Linn smiles and laughs a little. "Clever. Have you ever been hunting, Mr. Dumont?"

"Sort of...."

Linn turns to a cabinet full of rifles. "Sort of? Either you have stalked and killed an animal or you haven't."

"If that's your definition, then no. I am a vegetarian."

The cinematographer opens the cabinet and pulls out a Winchester Model 70 with a black scope on it and extracts a cartridge.

"Thirty-ought-six," Linn says. "Accurate to a thousand yards, although I was only about two hundred yards when I bagged that fellow." He gestures to the stuffed and mounted grizzly bear. He puts the cartridge back in the rifle and snaps the action closed, lining the bear up in his sights. "Why are you here, Dumont?"

"I think you know."

"Enlighten me," Linn says.

"I am here at Mr. Herman's request to assist in locating Janet Leary's killer."

Linn is surprised at this. "Killer? That was an accident. A horrible accident."

Dumont comes on strong, "That was no accident. It was an attempt on Fay Reynolds' life! And I aim to find who, or what, was responsible!" Dumont is right in Linn's face.

Linn looks a little spooked. "There are those that believe that the studio is haunted. They believe there is a Studio Specter."

"Now we're talking. What about the Studio Specter?" Dumont says. "I was hoping that you could tell me about that. How'd you do it?"

"How did I do it? Are you mad!" Linn yells. "That is outrageous."

Dumont smiles. "Really? You were the only one with access to the film. I talked to Dave Huey."

"That boy is a liar!"

Dumont shakes his head. "He told me that you loaded both cameras the day that pillar crushed the life out of poor Janet Leary."

"Lies!"

"Why did you load a short end into the 'B' camera?"

"A short end? Why would I do that? I didn't, Huey loaded that film," Linn Edwards says, his mind racing. "But if he didn't load that camera...." He thinks a moment. His expression softens. "Did you see anything on that film?"

"Nothing," Dumont says.

"That's too bad," Linn says. He looks up at Dumont, his expression brightening, "But surely you must know that I was not the only cameraman on the set that day."

This time it is Dumont that is surprised. "No. I did not know that."

"Freddy Dmytryk started his career in Germany as a cinematographer," Linn says. "*Kaiser's Ghosts* was his last film before coming to America. Quite spooky, I've heard."

Dumont's mind is spinning. Could Dmytryk have done it? Why would Dmytryk want to destroy Fay Reynolds? Does Dmytryk know about Linn and Fay? Could this all be about jealousy and revenge?

Dumont apologizes to Linn for disturbing his afternoon and excuses himself. The housekeeper lets him out.

On his way back to Triumph Pictures, Dumont stops at Hollywood Book and Poster. A clerk helps him navigate the massive collection and locates a one-sheet of *Kaiser's Ghosts*. There, staring at him from the poster, is a dead ringer for the Studio Specter. Dumont wonders what could turn a man to murder.

Stage 7 isn't the biggest stage on the lot, but it is the tallest. The massive stage door is closed when Dumont reaches it. Dumont looks around, but there is no one in sight. He pulls the stage door, but it doesn't budge. Locked. Dumont reaches in his pocket and pulls out a small leather wallet. He extracts a pair of thin, hooked metal shims. He looks around one last time before inserting the picks into the lock. A moment later and the hasp falls open. Dumont pulls the door open just enough to step in.

The massive stage is silent, save for Dumont's footfalls echoing off the cement floor. He looks around in the dim light. One wall is lined floor to ceiling with black cloth. Dumont looks closer and sees that the wall has a number of black panels of different sizes leaning up against it. These have hinged wooden stands folded behind them.

A coil of rope lies in a corner with some scrap lumber. Another rope hangs down in the corner, next to the black wall. Dumont tugs on it and realizes that it isn't rope at all. It is an electrical cord that is looped through a pulley. The pulley is rigged to a series of metal arms high above the floor. Dumont plugs the electrical cord into a socket, but nothing seems to happen.

Dumont's eyes adjust to the dim light. He sees a ladder bolted to the wall opposite to where he came in. He crosses the floor and scales the ladder. About sixty feet above the floor the ladder reaches a catwalk that runs along the wall and then crosses the stage suspended from the ceiling.

Dumont notices a black object in the corner of the stage next to the black wall. He walks the catwalk to the corner. Something large is wrapped in black cloth with a coil of wire lying next to it. One end of the wire runs underneath the black cloth. The other end runs through the pulley that is hanging from the metal rails.

Dumont pulls the fabric off the shape in the corner and a glowing light shines from under the fabric. A luminescent figure is revealed.

"The Specter!" Dumont exclaims, his eyes widening. The spectral apparition looks just like the one from *Kaiser's Ghosts*.

In the quiet corner of the empty Stage 7, glowing brightly, is the Studio Spectre. Dumont inspects it. The wire attaches to the Specter and runs through the pulley and down to the ground below. There are strings running off the arms and head like a giant marionette.

Dumont softly chuckles, "It's a puppet." His expression darkens, "A big puppet that helped commit murder...."

Dumont rewraps the Specter, unplugs it, and exits the stage. He goes off in search of a phone.

A gorilla nods a friendly hello as Dumont crosses the Triumph lot heading for the commissary. A group of Mayan girls is waiting in line. Jean is laughing and chatting with the group. He sees her, but it is too late to evade her glance. Her eye catches Dumont for a moment.

Jean eyes him, flashes a bright smile, "Jethro Dumont, how interesting to find you here."

Dumont plays it strong. "I'm helping a friend out," he says, leaning in close to whisper, "with this nasty business. You know, the murder."

"How is that coming along?" Jean asks, returning the lean.

"How about I tell you over lunch? I'm buying," Dumont says, looking to the cashier. He points at their two trays and pays.

Jean excuses herself from her Mayan costumed friends. They give Dumont a once over and give Jean their seal of approval. The pair finds some seats at an empty table in a shaded courtyard.

"So who's your friend?" Jean asks, taking a bite of her grilled fish.

Dumont laughs, a little taken aback by Jean's directness. On the other hand, it is one of the things he likes most about her. The directness, and the red hair, and the green eyes, and her perfect skin. Tan and flawless under the strapless Mayan get-up she is wearing. Jean blushes, and Dumont realizes he's staring. "Herman," He says. "Herman K. Herman is an old Harvard classmate."

"Really? He offered me a part in the *Mayan Mummy*."

"I'm sure you'll be great. How's the director?" Dumont asks, diverting attention off Herman.

Jean looks up past her fork. "He seems distracted. He's dating the star, you know, Fay Reynolds." Jean leans in and whispers, "But I hear that she is two-timing him with the cinematographer."

"Are they serious?" Dumont asks.

"I don't know. Some of the other gals think that she is playing them both."

Dumont lets that sink in. He is lost in thought for a moment.

"Have you figured out who the Specter is yet?" Jean asks.

Dumont looks at her. She has caught him completely off guard.

"Well?" she says.

He flashes a look around, but there is no one else within earshot. "No. Well, yes. Sort of." He stammers. "I'm pretty sure, I think."

Jean smiles, "Mr. Dumont, are you nervous?"

"No. Well, I, uh. Look. I found the Specter in Stage 7. The whole thing is a fake. Movie magic. I don't know exactly how it was pulled off or who is responsible, but I am certain that the Studio Specter is a crock of bull conjured up to scare Miss Reynolds off the lot."

"Really? And what makes you so sure I can be scared off?" a familiar voice says.

Jean and Dumont whirl around, startled to see Fay Reynolds standing by their table. She's got her hands on her hips and is looking feisty.

Dumont is knocked further off balance. He stumbles to his feet and says, "Miss Reynolds! I, uh, I'm surprised to meet you here. So the Specter doesn't have you scared?"

"Me? Heavens no! That was acting!" she says with a forced laugh. "They're begging me to stay. Jean, you haven't introduced me to your friend."

Jean stands and says, "Fay Reynolds, meet Jethro Dumont."

Fay says, "Mr. Dumont, it is my pleasure," and holds out her hand.

Dumont takes it and she guides her hand up to his lips. He kisses it without thinking. He glances at Jean. She looks jealous. Fay sees this, too. Fay extracts her fingers, turns, and walks away. Dumont watches her. Fay looks every bit the movie star in her tight skirt and high heels.

Jean is watching Dumont watch Fay. She walks over to him and pushes his jaw shut. "Back to business, tiger," she says, throwing a nasty look at Fay.

Dumont turns sheepishly back to Jean. "Sorry. Now the question is, when was she acting? On the set, or right here?"

Jean laughs. "I'm not sure. And I'm not sure knowing would help us find out who is behind the Specter."

"I'm quite sure it is either Freddy Dmytryk, or Linn Edwards," Dumont says. "But which one? Unless it is Fay Reynolds…"

Jean says, "Oh, she's good, she's very good. One look and you are loopy."

"Perhaps if we find the motive we will find the man," Jean says.

"Now you're sounding like Maga," Dumont says.

"What?" Jean says.

Dumont says, "Never mind. You follow Edwards and I'll follow Dmytryk. One of them is bound to show their cards sooner or later." Dumont says, but he thinks to himself, "I hope sooner."

Jean visits the guard shack and the studio gate. She talks up the security captain about Linn Edwards, trying to get some useful information. Jean pretends to be romantically interested in Linn, and asks the guard some questions.

Chapter 4 The Dream Factory

Dumont heads to Freddy Dmytryk's office. When he gets there the office door is open a crack and the secretary is away. Dmytryk is in the inner office, screaming on the phone. "No! He can't have her. I don't care who he is, I'm Freddy Dmytryk for Pete's sake." Dumont silently steps into the outer office. Dmytryk continues his rant, "Look, I am paying you a lot of money and I want that bitch all to myself."

Dumont watches from the shadows, stunned. Dmytryk paces all over the office. He listens on the phone for a moment and is getting worked up again. "No. No. NO! He is not getting her. There is no sharing. I'll kill her before I will let him have her." Dmytryk slams down the phone.

Dumont eases his way out of the office, unnoticed. Herman K. Herman has an office in the same building. That is Dumont's destination.

In the meantime, Jean has caught up to Fay. Jean sees the starlet sneak in the back door of Stage 7. After a moment, Jean peeks in. She sees Fay Reynolds and Linn Edwards talking.

Fay says, "You've got to do something. That friend of the producer's – the guy that fixed *The Last Dinosaur* problem – he's getting too close. And his little friend Jean Farrell, too. She's in on the fix with Dumont."

Linn says, "I think it's time the Studio Specter disappears once and for all." He crosses the stage and climbs the ladder up to the catwalk sixty feet above the stage floor. He reaches the catwalk and approaches the hidden form of the Specter.

Suddenly, the shape under the black cloth moves. Linn Edwards screams, "The Specter!" and jumps back, nearly falling off the high catwalk. The black shape rises and sloughs off the black cloth, its brightly glowing form revealed. The Specter starts moaning. It shuffles toward Linn. He screams again.

"What the blazes is going on up there?" Fay shrieks.

"It's the Specter. It's alive!" he says.

"You're scaring me, Linney. Get that thing down here!"

The glowing Specter moans louder and shambles toward Linn. The frightened cameraman crosses the catwalk. He trips on a cable and almost falls seventy feet to the cement floor. He hooks his arm on the catwalk railing and hangs tight. The Specter shambles across the catwalk approaching the dangling cameraman. The Specter claws at Linn. The man screams and fights his way back onto the catwalk. The Specter keeps coming.

Down below, Fay looks up in horror as the Specter is relentlessly pursuing Linn. Then she notices that a cable is trailing behind the Specter; the cable that loops over the pulley and trails down to the floor. She races to the wall and unties the cable from a cleat bolted to the wall. Fay looks up. The Specter is bearing down on her man, tearing and pulling on his arms and legs. Linn desperately hangs onto the railing.

Fay pulls the black cable with all her might. "Hang on, Linnie!" she yells. The spunky starlet yanks again and the Specter lifts up off the catwalk.

"Keep at it Fay!" Linn yells encouragingly.

The Specter has been lifted just far enough away from Linn for him to get on the catwalk and make a run for the ladder. Linn scrambles down the ladder – sliding half the time – and lands on the stage floor.

Fay has the Specter swinging out over the open air. She runs to the middle of the stage to keep him away from the catwalk and the ladder.

Suddenly, Fay trips over a piece of lumber and falls to the ground, the cable slipping out of her hands. The Specter plummets toward the floor, the cable trailing up. Twenty feet... thirty feet... fifty feet the Specter falls. Then he stops, having grabbed the cable in his own arms. He now descends – hand over hand – down the cable.

Linn is sliding down the ladder, panic in his eyes. He reaches the stage floor. "We better get out of here, Fay!" Linn says. He grabs her around the waist. Fay is just staring at the Specter. Linn bodily grabs her and drags her out of the main door of Stage 7.

Jean rushes in the back door of the stage as the Specter is reaching the floor. She pulls her gun on the strange form. "Hold it right there," she says.

"Please. It is I," the Specter says in a voice that surprises Jean with its softness and strange phrasing. Jean keeps the gun trained on the glowing form.

The Specter reaches its arms up and pulls off its luminescent head.

"Miss Farrell, we really should be chasing after the killers," Tsarong says. He shucks off the rest of the Specter costume and they race out the airplane hanger-sized door of Stage 7. Linn and Fay are a hundred yards ahead. Tsarong and Jean pour on the speed.

Freddy Dmytryk is putting a beautiful black Labrador into the back seat of his car. An angry man runs toward the car. His name is James Harold and he is the animal wrangler on *The Mayan Mummy*.

"Mr. Dmytryk! Wait!" Harold says.

Dmytryk looks up and sees the man coming. Dmytryk slams the door as Harold approaches. The director gives the man the stink eye. "Stay away from my dog!" Dmytryk says. "I told you on the phone that she is mine, there is no way DeMille is getting this dog."

Dumont bursts into Herman's office suite, racing right past his stunned secretary. She stammers, but doesn't quite get the "Wait" past her beautiful lips before Dumont is in Herman's private office. The Mogul has a gorgeous office; all oak and glass and modern art on the walls. Paperwork covers Herman's desk and large windows show off the studio gates behind him.

Herman has the phone up to his ear. He looks up from some contracts, startled. "Jeez, Jethro, what's the hurry?" he says.

"How much longer does Fay Reynolds have on her contract?" Dumont asks.

"Two years and seven months. Why?"

"I have a feeling that she is trying to shorten that!" Dumont says.

Two figures get Dumont's attention. Through the window he sees Linn and Fay race into the parking lot. Moments later Tsarong and Jean follow.

"If you'll excuse me, Herman," Dumont says and rushes out the door, nearly bowling over the drop-dead secretary.

"Sure. I'll be fine," Herman K. Herman says, looking back to his paperwork. "No problems here. Stop by any time...."

Dumont throws open the door to a stairwell and starts to go down. He quickly changes his mind and heads up. Dumont opens his briefcase on the run and pulls out a vial. He downs the salts within and lets the vial drop. He continues his frantic climb. He pulls the green robe out of the briefcase and throws it on. He paws the *kata* free, slamming the case shut. There is no time to apply the make-up that transforms him into Dr. Pali.

"That's just it. That is not your dog. She belongs to the studio," Harold says.

Dmytryk moves to the driver's door and opens it. "She was in my movie and she is mine. I cast her. She would be nowhere without me." Dmytryk gets in the car. Harold tries opening the back door, but it is locked.

"Aw, c'mon, Mr. Dmytryk. If that dog goes missing, I'll lose my job," Harold says as he moves around to stand in front of the car.

Dmytryk starts the engine, revs it a few times. Harold stays put.

Another quick flight up and the Green Lama crashes out the fire exit onto the roof. He dashes across the roof and sees the starlet and the cameraman clawing their way into a tan sedan. The Green Lama takes aim and hurls the briefcase off the roof.

Linn Edwards jams the key into the ignition of the tan sedan and the starter cranks away. "C'mon!" he shouts.

"Get us out of here!" Fay cries.

The engine catches and Linn throws the car in reverse. At that moment, the briefcase hits, the windshield smashes, and shattered glass showers the occupants of the car.

Fay screams. Linn squeals the tires and the car lurches forward.

"Give me the dog. She belongs to Triumph," Harold yells.

Dmytryk couldn't be angrier. "This bitch is mine!" Dmytryk throws the car in gear and hits the gas yelling, "Get out of the way!"

Harold dives out of the way. Dmytryk's car misses him by scant inches. Harold gets up and watches the car race off the lot. Suddenly, a blaring horn gets his attention. A tan sedan burns rubber through the parking lot and heads straight for him. The animal wrangler barely avoids the sedan as Linn Edwards and Fay Reynolds race by. Harold shakes his fist in frustration.

On the roof, the Green Lama watches the sedan holding Fay and Linn. The car tries to leave, but its path is blocked by a large studio fire truck. Jean and Tsarong rush across the parking lot toward the sedan. The Green Lama takes a few steps back away from the edge of the roof and hopes that the salts have had time to work.

After a few softly spoken words and few clicks of the prayer wheel around his neck, the Green Lama runs full speed toward the edge of the five story building and launches himself into the air. While his body is active, he has calmed his mind and he soars through the air, the radioactive salts doing their work, temporarily giving him mild levitation powers. He floats slowly toward the ground but the speed of his jump takes him toward the gate as well.

Linn Edwards is wearing out the sedan's tires as he screeches around the ladder truck. He shoots out the entrance ignoring a shouting guard. The car hurtles down the street.

Jean Farrell leaps up to the open air cab of the fire truck and says, "Excuse me, I need to borrow your truck."

The Green Lama takes aim and hurls the briefcase off the roof.

She pulls a burly fireman out of the driver's seat. He tumbles to the pavement. Jean hops in, jams the truck into gear, and floors the gas pedal.

The Green Lama floats down and just manages to grab the last rung of the ladder on the back of the fire truck as it speeds away.

Jean sees the sedan make a hard right onto Western Avenue and guns the motor. At the back of the truck, the Green Lama climbs up onto the ladder and crawls along it toward the front of the truck.

Jean sees him in the rearview mirror and smiles. "I've been waiting for you to show up," she shouts while he scrambles along the ladder toward her. She flicks a switch and the siren starts wailing.

In the sedan, Linn shoves the briefcase back out through the hole in the windshield. It slides off the hood and clatters onto the street, bouncing its way across traffic. The case is crushed by an oncoming car. The Green Lama winces, hoping that he won't need any more radioactive salts. He has only a few precious minutes left.

Fay looks back and sees the truck coming. "Would you lose them already?" she yells.

Linn pushes pieces of the broken windshield glass out of the way. His eyes go wide. "Red light! Hang on!" he shouts, twisting the steering wheel to avoid the Sunset Boulevard cross traffic. A car clips the driver's side rear fender and wheel, sending the sedan into a slide. Linn somehow manages to clear the intersection and straighten the wheels. His foot tromps the accelerator and the sedan rockets toward Griffith Park, the left rear tire a bit wobbly in the crushed fender.

The Green Lama scrambles along the ladder, finally arriving at its front, perched above Jean. She looks up and shouts above the siren, "Hang on!"

A car runs the red at Sunset, darting out in front of her. Jean jams on the brakes. The Green Lama barely manages to hook his arm in the rungs as the force of the brakes sends the extension ladder slamming out. It hammers to a stop ten feet past the front of the truck. The force of the stop jars the Green Lama loose and he flips off the end, hanging by the last rung out in front of the racing fire truck. He dangles there with the roadway rushing under his feet, facing Jean in the open cab of the truck. He looks at her and says, "Don't lose them."

Jean determinedly guns the engine and the big truck gains speed. She spots the sedan heading up the hill toward the park.

The Green Lama climbs hand over hand like a kid on monkey bars and reaches the cab. He launches himself over the short windshield and into the passenger seat. He throws a lever and the ladder retracts.

Jean pushes the truck as fast as it can go and flies through a green light at Hollywood Boulevard and up the hill toward the park. Griffith Park and the Hollywood Hills lie immediately ahead.

The sedan races into the park, passes a creek, and reaches a sharp turn. Linn hits the turn too hard and fishtails to a stop in the dirt on the side of the road. Fay is clenching the dashboard with an iron grip. Her knuckles are white as a sheet. Her eyes meet Linn's and they sit in the car breathing heavily. After a moment, the blare of the siren reaches them and Linn jolts back into action, sending the car hurtling forward. The rear wheel is wobbling badly.

Jean fights the wheel of the fire truck as she makes the turn into the park. She only drives on the sidewalk briefly and no one is injured as they dive out of the way. Jean drives past the creek and slows to make the sharp turn. As the truck ascends the winding grade, the Green Lama sees that Jean is really struggling with the steering wheel of the large truck. The sedan gains ground as wrestling with the wheel wears Jean out. After a particularly slow turn, Jean looks at the Green Lama and says, "Sorry...."

The Green Lama makes a decision. "Let's switch!" he says, gesturing to Jean.

"Great idea," she says.

The Lama slides over and puts his foot on the gas. Jean stands up in the open cab of the truck. The wind lashes her red hair around. The Green Lama grabs the wheel and slides into the driver's seat. The truck hits a bump and Jean bounces into his lap. The Green Lama holds her with one arm and the wheel with the other as they power through a turn.

The road straightens out and Jean pauses a moment longer than necessary before extracting herself from the Green Lama's lap.

"Jeee... that was fun," she says. "We should do it again sometime."

Another turn is coming up. The Green Lama says, "You flatter me, Miss Farrell," and the truck's tires scream through the turn.

The wheel of the sedan is really wobbly, throwing the passengers around. Fay Reynolds bangs her head on the window and screams, "What's wrong with the car?"

Linn keeps his eyes straight ahead and says, "I don't know! It feels like one of the wheels is gonna come off." The tires complain around a turn and the sedan rockets into Griffith Observatory's small parking lot. Linn slams the brakes and turns to avoid a car backing out of a spot. He blares the horn to stop anyone else from doing the same.

Fay reacts like a caged animal; her eyes are wild, frantic. She whirls around looking for a way out. She spots a road behind them and points, "There! There's another road back there."

Linn hits the brakes as the siren gets louder. He jams the car in reverse and slams the gas. The car zooms backward for the other gate. When he is clear of other cars, Linn twists the wheel hard, spinning the sedan around. He throws the car into second gear and floors it. The sedan straightens out as it races ahead.

Fay looks at him with a new hunger. "Where'd you learn how to do that?"

Linn grins. "Stuntman buddy. Classic Bootlegger Reverse."

The sedan speeds down the other road just as the fire truck appears. The sedan veers left, narrowly avoiding an open bus full of tourists headed for the Observatory, and races into a short tunnel.

Jean's gorgeous green eyes frantically scan the parking lot. She spots the escaping sedan darting into the tunnel. "Over there!" she exclaims.

The Green Lama throws the truck into a hard right turn, the rear skidding wildly, smashing into four parked cars. The Lama downshifts and powers through; metal parts complaining, shredding, and finally giving way to the powerful truck.

The sedan is near the summit of the Hollywood hills, shaking wildly from the loose wheel. Linn soon pulls the car off on a fire road and pulls to a stop behind some scrubby brush.

"What are you doing? We have to get away!" Fay says hysterically.

The fire truck roars through the tunnel, the siren echoing off the tile walls of the tunnel.

Linn cocks his head. The siren is getting louder. "Just wait."

Fay is about out of her mind. "But they're almost here!"

"Trust me," Linn says.

The siren gets louder and louder, finally deploying by the hidden sedan. The sound gets quieter and quieter.

Linn says, "There they go...."

Fay grabs him and pull herself close, kissing him hungrily. They kiss a moment and then Linn extracts himself from her grasp.

"I need to have a look at that wheel," he says and gets out of the car. Fay follows.

The wheel is hanging on by only one lug nut. The rest are ripped out.

Fay says, "That doesn't look too good."

Linn scowls at the wheel. Then he turns his head to look back to the main road. Deep concern crosses his features. "Do you hear that, Fay?"

"No.... You're scaring me Linney."

"It's a truck… GET IN THE CAR, FAY!" he shouts. "Get in the car and go!"

The fire truck screeches around the corner onto the dirt fire road just as Fay Reynolds, the hottest starlet in Hollywood, jumps behind the wheel of the sedan. She looks back at Linn and sees the big red engine bearing down on him with the Green Lama at the wheel. Fay jams the car in gear and dirt showers over Linn. The car shoots forward, leaving a plume of dust that enshrouds the cameraman.

The Green Lama blindly propels the truck forward into the cloud of dust. There is a sickening thud and Jean and the Lama look at each other. Linn's limp form bounces off the side of the truck into the brush.

The thick dust is choking, and nearly impenetrable. The Green Lama slows down and wraps the *kata* over his mouth to ward off the dust.

Jean jams one of the levers in front of her. Motors whir. The Lama looks over at her. "What are you doing?" he says.

She flashes a quick smile, then quickly coughs. "Just trying to get a better view!" she says looking back at the ladder that is extending straight up. She jumps up on her seat and climbs onto the back of the truck.

"Well, hang on!" the Green Lama yells, trying to follow the sedan and avoid driving off the cliff.

Jean Farrell grew up on the range and she is used to horses trying to throw her off, so she will have none of that. She gets on the back of the truck and finds her way to the ladder. She grabs it and starts climbing up. After a few feet the dust begins to clear a bit.

Jean can see the sedan just twenty yards ahead fishtailing wildly around a tight right turn, open sky straight ahead.

"Hard right coming up!" she shouts, waits a beat, "NOW!"

The Green Lama steers hard and makes the turn. "Great going, Jean."

The sedan struggles with Fay behind the wheel. She is not the driver that Linn was. Fear and self-preservation are overtaking her desperation to escape, just as the truck is beginning to overtake the car. She sees the Green Lama gaining and pushes aside her fear and then floors the accelerator.

Jean guides the Lama through another turn and yells, "Gun it! You've got a straight shot for a hundred yards."

"Speaking of straight shots," the Green Lama shouts, "are you still armed?"

Jean rolls her eyes, thinking herself the fool. "Of course I am! Good idea!" She pulls out her revolver, nearly drops it, and tries to get a bead on the car. *Don't kill her,* she thinks to herself and aims for the back wheels of the car. She fires twice in quick succession. The truck is shaking wildly and the shots are not true. The slugs slam into the fender and trunk, doing no harm.

The bullets beating on the metal may have missed, but they do a number on Fay. She panics, mashing down the accelerator. A turn comes up and she is going too fast. The car slides wide, but fortunately it's an inside turn and the hillside serves as a guardrail. The paint is sandblasted off the passenger side, but Fay manages to keep the gas pedal pressed to the floor.

Jean talks the Green Lama through the turn, but sees Fay is going too fast for the next turn. "She's going too fast! She won't make it!" Jean tries to shoot out Fay's tires, but the range is too great. She misses four times, but still squeezes the trigger hoping for a live round, but the gun just clicks over and over again on empty chambers.

Fay Reynolds realizes too late that she is going too fast and, when she hits the turn, the bum wheel finally twists loose and the sedan spins wildly, careening off the dirt road into open air.

Fay sees flashes of something white as the car spins and spins in mid-air. For a moment, she wonders what it is. Then realization hits her and the starlet smiles as the sedan crashes into wood and steel. The car is torn open like a cracker box and Fay is thrown from the tumbling wreckage and smashes into earth and rock. She hears the car explode but cannot see it.

Fay Reynolds lays on her side, battered and bloody, facing the massive white letters that lured her and thousands of others to the dream factory. The former real estate advertisement now shouts out just the name, "HOLLYWOOD." The remaining letters of the sign were obliterated in the crash. Fay lies with a peaceful expression on her face looking up at the sign. Her eyes stare at the letters long after life has left her body.

The fire truck stops at the turn and the Green Lama and Jean look down past the twisted guard rail onto the tragic scene. The sedan is in a fiery heap with the giant letters of the word "LAND," and movie starlet turned killer Fay Reynolds lays bloody and still on the rocky hillside in the shadow of "HOLLYWOOD."

The Green Lama descends the slope and tries to save her, but she is gone. This reminds him that not everyone can be saved. Standing on the mountainside reminds Jethro Dumont of another mountain—a snow-covered one that started this journey of his—that held the source of his unique powers.

The Green Lama and Jean Farrell watch the tragic scene for a long moment. Jean takes his hand. He wipes her tears with the red *kata*, and lets her hold his hand.

Linn Edwards runs up the road, sees the smoke, and releases an anguished cry, "FAY! FAYYY!"

He reaches the edge of the road and looks down at the wreckage. He sees Fay's twisted form. He cries to her and scrambles down the sandy hillside. Somehow he keeps his footing until he reaches her side. He collapses to his knees. He takes her hand and brushes the hair from her face. He gives her one last kiss and then, sobbing, looks at her lifeless shell.

"Oh, Fay. Why, Fay, why?" he cries. He looks up at the Green Lama. "She could have had it all. She should have had it all. But she wanted it too fast, too soon, and I let her push me around. I put up with her romancing that pig," he spits, "that *schweinhund*. He never loved her like I love her, he only loves himself."

Linn holds her hand for a long time.

Epilogue

Herman K. Herman's office is quiet as a tomb. Herman sits at his desk staring straight ahead. Dr. Pali stands behind him, facing the window where a gorgeous sunset paints the sky with orange, red and purple.

Jean Farrell sits on a corner of the desk facing the two men.

Finally, Herman says, "So, it was Fay Reynolds all along?"

The Green Lama doesn't turn from the window. He says, "Yes. With Linn Edwards' help. She was the mastermind and he was her pawn."

"Why did she do it? How did they do it?" Herman asks.

"She wanted out of her contract," Jean says, "but it was more than that. She had caught Freddy Dmytryk cheating on her. She wanted to ruin his career in the process."

"Nasty girl," Herman says.

Dr. Pali continues, "Linn thought up the Specter idea after seeing a poster for *The Kaiser's Ghost* in Dmytryk's office. With access to all the production's unexposed film he realized that he could photograph the ghost first and still be sure that the production photography would match."

Herman's mind reels. "But why? She could have gotten anything she wanted here. She never asked for a raise, not one."

Dr. Pali says, "She wanted freedom. Either Linn had convinced her or Fay had convinced herself that she was trapped by her contract and that the only was out was through a single clause in her contract."

"Emotional distress," Herman says.

Dr. Pali turns from the window. "Exactly. If she could show that the

Triumph Pictures lot itself was the cause of her distress, then she knew you could never hold her to the contract."

Herman says, "But why risk her own life with the collapse of that Mayan temple? The death of Janet Leary? Surely that was an accident?"

Jean stands next to Dr. Pali and looks out at the sunset. "Punishment," she says, "Janet Leary was Freddy Dmytryk's latest conquest."

The End

Notes:

Xing Yi Quán – an aggressive, Shaolin style that uses rapid movements to simultaneously attack and defend.

Né-tso-hbum – A thousand parrots.

The Green Lama & Me

Puerto Rico. That's where my experience with the Green Lama began. My wife and I travelled there to celebrate our 25th anniversary. I had a week on the beach at a beautiful resort with a bag of books and magazines to read. I had picked up a bunch of pulp reprints from Adventure House's holiday sale and brought two of them with me—the single issue of the original *Captain Hazzard* and the fifth Green Lama novel, *The Man Who Wasn't There*. I had also decided to reread the Doc Savage series from the beginning and in the original order, so I brought "The Land of Terror" as well.

Back from vacation, I wrote Ron Fortier regarding his experiences with Captain Hazzard to include with the Hazzard review I was writing for my blog (www.docsavagetales.blogspot.com). Ron gave me lots of info and I hyped his new Captain Hazzard stuff. At the same time, I was finishing up writing a pulp flavored short story. Throwing caution to the wind I asked Ron if he would read it. He did and liked it enough to offer me a spot in this very book.

At that time, the only Green Lama story I had read didn't even include Jethro Dumont, the main character. So I ordered more Lama reprints. I read those in very short order and set to work.

In my online research, I found old radio show episodes of the Green Lama. One of the episodes was entitled, "The Last Dinosaur." I thought it was fun and since several of the pulp novels take place in Hollywood, I thought that it might serve me well to keep the locale close to home.

I outlined several story ideas for the Lama and sent the proposal for "The Studio Specter" to Ron. He liked it and I was off writing.

The short story I sent Ron was about 2300 words. Now I had to write 15,000 words. That was a little scary, but having written 6 unproduced feature-length screenplays, I knew I could do it. But 15,000 words is a lot of writing.

In school, I struggled with writing term papers and ended up either not writing them at all, or having a ton of pages of handwritten scrawls. Pages that went here and there, all out of order and incomprehensible to anyone but me. My mother started her career as a secretary and she would type them out for me. I wrote science fiction and the teachers hated it, even the teacher of a class on science fiction.

I have been editing film starting with super-8 in 7th grade. You shoot the stuff you want in any order and then assemble it into a movie. In college my roommate had an Apple II computer. That changed everything. The computer let me do with the same thing with words that I was already doing with film. Cut. Paste. Restructure. Delete. I could write in any order and make a story out of it.

To create "The Studio Specter," I started with the basic idea of an actress being terrified by a ghost that no one else could see until the film was developed. I knew the opening scene and the scene with the crew watching the dailies right away.

Researching the Hollywood sign I read about the sign's caretaker drunk driving off the road into the sign. I now had my ending. Then I just had to work out who was responsible for the Specter and why. Those elements grew organically from the characters. I worked on the scene where Dumont watches the film with the crew. At some point I was inspired to write the scene with the Green Lama and the Tong enforcer in New York. The story grew and I think the last scene I wrote was when Jethro visits Linn Edward's house.

Once my first draft was complete all the way through I rewrote, added, deleted and polished until I showed the story to Ron Kevin Noel Olson and Adam Garcia. I took their feedback and tweaked until I arrived at the final draft. I hope you enjoyed Jethro Dumont and Jean Farrell's latest adventure in Hollywood.

This story is dedicated to Anne Miller for paying for all those comic books, science fiction novels, and Doc Savage books when I was a kid. Thanks, Mom.

Author Bio:

W. PETER MILLER has spent his adult life in the motion picture industry editing feature films and trailers. He has written for adventure gaming magazines and for Steve Jackson Games. He lives in the Los Angeles area with his wife of 25 years and 3 children.

Mr. Miller is active in the adventure and board gaming hobbies where he is known online on many sites as "Doc Savage," a nod to his favorite pulp character, though he enjoys the Green Lama, G-8, and others. You can find his custom gaming creations as well as pulp reviews and news on his blog at www.DocSavageTales.blogspot.com.

the

in

The Case of the Hairless Ones

by Robert Craig

The fist slammed once into Tsarong's cheek.

His head recoiled from the blow.

Fresh blood slowly trickled from the Tibetan's mouth. He was on his knees, hands secured behind his back, arms held at a painful angle.

He drew up his head and spat blood on the hard wood floor. The beating had been without mercy.

Regaining his focus, the same question was asked of him.

"Where is Jethro Dumont?" the voice hissed. "I know that he is the one known as the Green Lama. Tell us where he hides."

Tsarong's answer was only muted silence.

His head was suddenly twisted to the side and pressed firmly against a rough, wooden table. Shards of wood splinters dug into his cheeks, deep enough to allow for his blood to flow along the long grooves of the table's surface.

As a swollen eye strained to look forward, his focus fell upon a pair of strong, raw-boned hands grasping the handle of a weathered axe, its massive, chipped blade stained dark.

"His commitment is to be admired," the dark voice remarked to another. "I suspect that he will tell us nothing, as his loyalty is too great.

"Be done with him."

At that, Tsarong watched the axe blade move away from his vision, rising upward, moving to a destination he assumed to be suspended above his strained neck.

Tsarong's reaction was immediate. A look of quiet serenity fell upon his dark features as a quiet Tibetan prayer escaped from bloodied lips.

And the axe fell.

TWO NIGHTS EARLIER...

No. 240 Centre Street housed the New York City Police Department. Located between Broome and Grand in Manhattan, the impressive structure was firmly located in the city's Little Italy.

Sergeant Moore worked the third shift and the department's front desk. He loved third shift, knowing that whatever entered through the department's front door tended to have merit at this late hour, rather than the trivial walk-ins that filled the hours of the day shifts.

While double-checking the desk logs to ensure that previous shifts had been properly recorded, a strange sound broke Moore's concentration.

It was soft; a sobbing just barely there.

Suddenly Moore knew that another had joined him. He looked up from the desk and was taken back by what he saw.

A nude woman stood there, head hung low, shoulders hunched, a burlap sack held in trembling arms.

Her body was a vivid red, as if she suffered from too many hours in the sun. But the most distinguishing thing about the woman was her hair, or lack thereof, for the woman standing in front of Sgt. Moore was totally bald.

"Miss, are you okay?" he asked, concerned about both the woman's disturbing appearance and state of mind.

The woman looked up at Sergeant Moore with bloodshot eyes, a small gasp escaping from raw, chapped lips.

And she dropped the burlap sack in her arms.

It hit the station's battered tile floor with a dull thud.

The bag came open and its cargo spilled forth.

Staring at Sgt. Moore were the open, pleading eyes of a severed head.

Jethro Dumont lay awake. He did not move, remaining utterly still upon his mattress. Sleep eluded him during the wee hours of this morning.

Quite different from the floor mat that was my bed in Tibet, Dumont thought. Silk sheets now covered his naked form while a mattress with plush, quilted padding supported his lean, muscled frame. Remaining in corpse pose, he brought in a deep breath through his mouth, held it in his diaphragm, and with a deep sound, slowly let it escape from the back of his throat. He did this several more times, allowing his body to be brought into balance with the calm of his surroundings.

Once he attained inner balance, Dumont rose from the bed and walked across the bedroom of his cosmopolitan apartment with a quiet grace.

Pulling back the shades covering his bedroom window, he gazed out at the sleeping city. The light of the pale moon provided him a point of focus, bringing clarity to the space around him as he used even breathing to drop his heart rate to a serene pace.

Donning a golden *namsa* robe that covered his wiry muscles, he questioned what troubled him. It was odd for him to be stricken with random thoughts while he slumbered; normally, his training allowed him nights of utter stillness.

Perhaps what he desired was focus.

Walking to a spacious library, he paused beneath a Buddha shrine to light a small butter candle.

As the soft glow illuminated the room and its impressive wall-to-wall bookcases, Dumont eased himself into a leather-upholstered chair and prepared his mind to learn.

As the emerging light of day fell upon the Buddha shrine, a door to its side quietly opened. A man, slight of frame, stepped through; he carried in his hands a silver tray adorned by a cast-iron teapot, matching iron cup, and folded newspaper.

"Good morning, *Tulka*," the newcomer said in perfect English, addressing Dumont as one who possessed the reborn spirit of a holy practitioner. "I see that the day arrived early for you."

Dumont, seated at his desk with one of the seven books of the *Abhidhamma Pitaka* opened in front of him, turned and a slight smile broke across his angular features. "Slumber seemed to elude me, Tsarong. I was visited by a sense of unease during the night."

A native of Tibet, Tsarong had studied at the Tibetan monastery alongside Dumont. When Dumont decided to return to the United States to share the teachings of Siddhartha, he asked Tsarong to accompany him as his personal aid and valet. By offering him a position of employment, Dumont hoped that he could secure the valued wisdom of his closest friend.

Allowing himself to reflect on what Dumont had told him, Tsarong opened the folded copy of the Daily Sentinel that sat alongside the tea service.

"Perhaps your mind is attuned to duress in the universe," he said, placing an article in front of Dumont.

DECAPITATION! SAVAGE MURDER STUNS POLICE.

Police reported a savage murder after a nude woman appeared at 240 Centre Street in the early hours of the morning, carrying with her a man's decapitated head in a burlap sack.

Sources say that the woman is in a state of shock and has not revealed what transpired. Unconfirmed reports also state that the woman appears to be devoid of hair on her entire body, though signs of chemical burns on her skin indicate that she may have been subjected to some form of chemical depilatory.

No official statement has been issued, but a formal police investigation is expected to be announced.

Dumont's steely eyes looked up at Tsarong.

"When a dark wind comes, the learned one has foretold its arrival," Tsarong said, taking the article to store it away in Dumont's extensive system of crime reference files.

Dumont allowed himself a sip of the tea, musing on the foreboding nature of what he just read.

Jethro Dumont drew in a deep breath and then alighted from the elevator.

The charade begins once again, he thought, stepping onto the tiled floors of New York's Museum of Modern Art's fifth floor, and its current home for special exhibits.

As no more news had arrived in regards to the murder of the previous evening, he now tended to the social affairs of Jethro Dumont.

Dressed in a black doubled-breasted suit, he walked into the main exhibition room, already bustling with attendees in fine suits and beaded chiffon dresses. The bold colors of the chiffon proved a perfect compliment to the watercolor and oil paintings that adorned the walls and easels throughout the room, forming guided pathways that cut gently through the room.

Dumont was here at the invitation of Monroe Warner, retired Vice Consul to the US Consulate in Shenyang. Warner, who had met Dumont deep along the winding rivers of southern Manchuria during the younger man's search for enlightenment, was hosting a reception for the Republic of China's newly appointed ambassador to the United States.

After making his way to the bar for an old-fashioned Dutch with gin, Dumont brought himself into the main hall, only to be greeted immediately by the evening's host.

"Jethro Dumont!" boomed the deep, hickory-tinged voice of former Vice Consul Monroe Warner. "It's a far more civilized world we find ourselves in tonight!"

"I do agree," Dumont said with a warm smile and friendly clasp of his host's arm.

"Come, my friend," Warner laughed, wrapping his arm over his old friend's shoulder and moving him deeper into the room. "I want you to meet our guests of honor."

As Warner led Dumont deeper through the crowd of partygoers,

Dumont chuckled at his old friend's enthusiasm, and then had his attention directed to three intriguing individuals standing before him.

The guests of honor, Dumont realized, as Warner stepped forward to greet the smiling Asian.

"A wonderful evening, a wonderful setting," the man said in perfect English while extending a hand to Warner. "Your Museum of Modern Art holds many treasures for both the eye and the soul."

The man turned from Monroe to Jethro, who immediately took the opportunity to introduce himself, "Jethro Dumont. I'm an old friend of Monroe's, and I'm pleased to make your acquaintance."

A slight bow of the head was the response, followed by a warm handshake. "And I, too, am pleased to make yours. I am Cheng Yi-chuan, newly appointed ambassador of the Republic of China to your nation."

Though Dumont was impressed with the natural ease of Cheng, it was his companions that captured his attention.

Standing to Cheng's rear was a tall, broad man in an ill-fitting suit, intense eyes surveying all of Dumont in a single glance. This was obviously Cheng's personal bodyguard. Thick features topped a wide frame, indicative of the strong people bred by the harsh lands of Mongolia.

And though the man was intriguing, it was the woman at Cheng's side who truly fascinated Jethro Dumont.

A tall, graceful beauty, the Asian woman was taller than most women who hailed from the same region. She was dressed beautifully in a black and scarlet floral silk dress with a slight keyhole opening below the neckline showcasing perfect alabaster skin. The bias cut of the dress, though technically covering most of her skin, still clung tightly to its wearer, allowing for her lean curves to be displayed in a slinky, sensuous way.

Long, raven-black hair cascaded over her shoulders, and thick, blunt bangs, very much influenced by Western style, accented highly arched brows and large, gorgeous brown eyes.

As Dumont paused to admire the exotic beauty in front of him, he noticed a slight twitch to her ruby lips that yielded to a slightly playful smile.

"And let me introduce you to the one who provides me with all of the art that I truly need, Mr. Dumont," Cheng said, noticing Jethro's eyes on the woman at his side. "This is my wife, Mei-feng."

Dumont turned toward Mei and was pleasantly surprised to have her outstretch a slender hand with ruby nails, palm facing downward.

Dumont took the offered hand and symbolically brought her knuckles near his lips.

Her smile widened as Dumont stepped back, a glimmer of intrigue shining in her dark eyes.

"I hope that your stay in my country has been a pleasant one, Mrs. Cheng," Dumont said.

"Oh, it truly has been," Mei said. "It does not take long to become accustomed to your opportunities and amenities. I find it amazing that a country so young, especially in comparison to the empires of the East, can still provide a culture and traditions so truly its own."

Dumont was taken back by the woman's response to his simple question. Whereas Dumont had expected little more than a nod and smile, he had received an intelligent observation. He would not underestimate this woman, as most Chinese women—subservient to their male counterparts—rarely voiced an opinion in public.

This is a woman who may have much to do with her husband's success, Dumont mused to himself.

Warner, always the politician, found the opportunity to insert himself into the exchange. "Dumont knows a bit about your country as well."

"I must admit," Jethro said, "I have been won over by the true magic of your land. Its wise spirit offers a learned path for the truly misguided."

Both Mei and Cheng seemed intrigued by the direction of the conversation, but Warner took the opportunity to return to his wheelhouse.

"Jethro, let's save your spiritual talk for later in the night. I see dear Mrs. Rockefeller with some of the museum board signaling us over for a chat."

Cheng and Mei nodded their heads in farewell and followed Warner across the room. Their bodyguard, though, paused for a moment, staring hard into the eyes of Dumont as if establishing his dominance with a mere glance. Then, after a long blink of his eyes, he followed his wards toward the next conversation.

"Well, well, Mr. Dumont, it has not been that long since our paths last crossed," said a husky voice containing a bit of twang and a whole lot of sultry.

Dumont turned to find yet another gorgeous woman. Long scarlet tendrils fell in finger waves along her alabaster face. A light green jersey knit suit, neatly trimmed by glossy Lucite buttons, proved the perfect compliment to her shimmering green eyes, almost feline in shape; eyes that could be both seductive and sweet at the same time.

"It's always my pleasure to land in your path," Dumont said to Jean Farrell, the young actress with whom the Green Lama had recently worked within Hollywood to solve the case of a supposed studio specter.

And though Jean and Jethro were social acquaintances, she was unaware that the man to whom she had pledged an allegiance to his war on crime, the mystic warrior known as the Green Lama, was the very same man now standing in front of her.

"May I ask what brings you to tonight's affair?" Dumont said, moving closer to Jean in a conspiratorial yet flirtatious manner.

"Mrs. Rockefeller took in a showing of 'Of Mice and Men' that I'm currently in over at the Music Box . She so enjoyed my depiction of Curly's wife that she was kind enough to send along her regards and invite me here as her personal guest," Jean answered proudly.

Before Dumont could continue his conversation with the spunky young actress, the windows to the museum exploded.

* * *

The siege came from above.

The small group of men dropped silently from the concrete architectural treatments around the perimeter of the museum's rooftop. Dark rope had been secured to venting, heating units, and exhaust fans. As the descent to the fifth story was only slightly below the roofline, the men worked quickly.

Garbed entirely in black, little was visible as the attackers dropped like ebony spiders alongside one another, arriving in unison outside the windows of the gala, their feet coming to rest on a slight ledge.

A small explosive charge composed of Amatol, a substance comprised of both TNT and ammonium nitrate, was placed at the base of each picture window. Each charge had been bound in a tight paper wrap, much like that of a common Chinese firecracker, and was attached to the glass with a chunk of modeling clay. A small one inch fuse extended from the top of each charge, providing for a three second burn per inch.

That was all the attackers needed.

With military precision, the raiding party lit each fuse. When the first spark appeared, each man began a silent countdown from three. When they arrived at the number one, the men bent their knees and kicked back, hands still secured to their ropes from above.

Like acrobats, they arched up into the night and then swiftly descended as the Amatol charges blew. Most of the windows exploded in their entirety, the lower glass blowing inward and showering the party guests, while portions of the upper glass detached in larger shards, only to crash hard to the sidewalks of 53rd street waiting below.

Any remaining glass, held precariously by the sills of the windows, was easily knocked aside as the attackers hurled through the wreckage of the picture windows to breach the reception.

The partygoers were in a state of shock. Near the windows, some cried out, some wept, their bodies crisscrossed with shallow cuts from the imploded glass.

But most of the attendees found little ability to focus on the wounds, their attention solely placed on the men who had seemingly invaded from the night sky.

The raiders wore black from head to toe, rough cloth held tight to their forms by tattered dark ties. Heads were covered almost entirely by black hoods, only fierce eyes showing through rough-cut openings.

A number of these men carried firearms, both bolt action rifles and broom-handle Mauser pistols, which they had pulled off their backs or drawn from holsters upon gaining their footing. All of these weapons were well worn, appearing as if they had spent a good deal of time on some war-torn battlefield.

A few attendees had the good sense to try to escape the reception by way of the elevator lobby. Their intentions were cut short as elevator doors opened to reveal several more black-clad warriors. They boldly stepped forward, blocking the escape path, and forcing the intended escapees back into the mass of people now held hostage.

Every nerve in Jethro Dumont's body seemed to explode, throwing him into overdrive, his senses cranked up, his awareness on high.

He instantly calculated the enemies around the room.

Everything was scarlet. Everything was madness. He was ready to move.

But he suddenly stopped.

His training took over, and he allowed himself one breath, one sharp intake of the pungent air of the room, and that was all that he needed.

That single breath slowed him and provided a clear vision of what he now faced.

This was the way of the enlightened.

And this was the way of the Lama.

His base instinct was that of man the killer, the hunter, the slayer of his fellow man. But Jethro Dumont had spent years training himself to rise above his own baser beast, to confront these dark days as a beacon of justice, not a deliverer of death.

Another breath came, and then another. Each one deeper than the last, each expanding into his chest, moving through his blood stream, and opening up his consciousness to the spirit of a shared world.

He was ready, and Jethro Dumont focused his attention on the armed invaders.

Though black hoods hid their faces, Dumont could see just enough of their eyes to recognize that these men hailed from the East, either Chinese or Manchurian in origin.

This assumption was confirmed as one of the men moved forward to address the crowd before him.

"Silence!" he demanded, his English heavily accented. "You can give us what we demand, or you can die. It's a simple proposition."

As the raiders spread through the room, Dumont used their movement as a counter to his own movements. Moving one arm to the side, he gently took Jean's hand and moved themboth back against a wall.

His other hand slid into the inner pocket of his jacket, gently taking hold of a small glass vial. Holding the cylinder tightly in his hand, Dumont used his thumb to quickly unscrew its tin cap, which fell to the museum floor with nary a sound.

"My men will now move through the room. Give them all your valuables, both currency and jewelry."

Several of the dark men pulled canvas satchels from within the folds of their pants pockets. They moved menacingly into the personal space of each partygoer, sometimes shoving a chest, other times harshly gripping a bare arm, collecting any valuables for their sacks.

Dumont and Jean slid along the wall, moving near a swinging door service entry, a large decorative planting to their side.

And then he noticed something; several of the raiding party had closed in on Cheng and Mei, taking each by an arm, and then pulling them toward the elevator lobby.

But their bodyguard wasn't going along with the plan. As soon as Mei and Cheng were pulled away, he moved in to protect them. The towering Asian seemed to grow several inches as he reared back to strike, but it proved futile. For all his intensity, he was no match for a man who quickly moved up behind him and slammed the small of his back with the wooden butt of his bolt-action rifle.

Dumont heard a loud crack, not sure if it was the sound of the wood splitting or the bodyguard's spine. The man dropped to his knees, his head falling either in pain or disgrace.

Another blow from the rifle butt struck the back of the man's head and he was down.

And though the bodyguard had failed, he had provided Jethro Dumont with the opportunity he needed to make a move of his own.

As the room's attention was focused on the struggle around Mei and Cheng, Dumont pushed Jean toward the service door.

"Go," he whispered. "Look for an escape or find a place to hide. Now!"

Jean hesitated for a moment, the former Montana farm girl turned big city actress always wanted be in the center of the action, not running from it. But seeing the intensity on Dumont's face, she decided to take his advice in light of their dire circumstances.

As the vibrant redhead quickly slid past the swinging door, Dumont brought the glass vial to his lips. He quickly downed its bitter contents, a queer brew of radioactive salts developed by his ally, the esteemed radiologist Dr. Harrison Valco.

These strange salts provided him with the rare ability to physically embody his own powers of concentration. Though both fleeting and exhausting in their use, he had found their near-instantaneous enhancements invaluable.

One of the hooded thugs saw Dumont's movements and moved on him threateningly, pressing his bolt action rifle up to the playboy's chin.

"What did you do? What is that?" he demanded in broken English, savage eyes looking at the test tube in Dumont's hand.

"Just taking my medicine," he replied, slowly raising the small tube, his assailant's eye following the reflections within the moving glass. Dumont's fingers suddenly opened, allowing the fragile glass to fall to the floor where it shattered upon impact.

That was all the distraction that Dumont needed.

He brought his hand to the bicep of the hooded gunman, delivering a powerful electrical pulse to the man's body.

With the aid of the radioactive salts, Dumont had become an electrical conductor; able to focus the static electricity within his own body, and then pass it through as pulses to anyone he touched.

The delivery of these pulses had an immediate effect, overwhelming the man's normal nerve traffic, throwing the body into spasms as the brain's communications with the muscles was interrupted.

Dumont immediately grasped the man's rifle before trembling hands dropped it to the floor. With his other arm, he twisted the man to deposit

...his attacker was Asian...

him out of view behind a large, potted monsterio delicio plant.

Kneeling over his attacker, Dumont pulled his black hood away. As he suspected, his attacker was Asian in origin, appearing to be Chinese.

But his appearance was odd. Looking more closely, Dumont saw that the man was entirely hairless, his head completely bald, but he was also bare of any eyebrows or lashes.

Looking down at the hands which had borne the rifle, Dumont saw that they too were devoid of any type of body hair.

A curiosity for a later time, Dumont thought. It was time to live in the moment in which he had control; it was time to take the now.

First, he stripped the hood from his disabled enemy and then drew it over his own head. Accompanied by the dark suit he wore, he hoped that the hood would provide him an extra moment or two to move amongst the enemy before they realized that he was an impostor.

Next, he brought up the man's rifle, though choosing to hold it by the barrel, its scratched wooden butt facing outward.

Life would not be intentionally taken this night. The principles of humanity and justice could coexist.

But though he held the life force as being sacred, he would still move like water through his enemies. Savage and swift.

Dumont found Cheng and Mei being hustled toward the elevator lobby.

This was the reason for the attack. Jewelry or cash were merely spoils of war. The true prize was the diplomat and his wife.

Dumont started to make his way toward the kidnappers.

The room was in chaos. People were charging toward the elevators, trying to escape the bloodshed and gunfire. Their panic only led to death and injury, as the black-hooded assailants let loose a round of bullets at the massing crowd.

Several people fell to the ground, victims of the cruel act, while the remaining people cowered from the gunfire and turned to run back into the exhibition room.

Now was the time for his attack, to protect the innocents around him, no matter at what risk to himself.

Dumont moved, and he moved decisively.

Taking a few running strides toward the crowd of terrified partygoers, he leaped up and atop a serving table. His feet barely touched the tabletop as he used the surface to propel himself up and over the crowd streaming around him.

His body sailed through the air, almost stalling in flight as his eyes aligned on the kidnappers holding Mei and Cheng, waiting for one of the elevator doors to open.

Dumont hit the floor in an arched swan dive roll, his head tucked, the floor abruptly meeting his hands and shoulders. He rode the momentum down his back to his tailbone and then ending the roll by coming to his feet.

He was in the very midst of the kidnappers, men shocked to see one of their fellow hooded attackers suddenly among them with unclear intent. A swift forward snap kick sent the Mauser flying free from the hand of their supposed leader. Dumont's leg, never returning to the floor, delivered several, rapid kicks to the man's hooded head, knocking the mask off and the man to the floor.

Without hesitation, Dumont spun to the men holding Mei. Dumont immediately executed a hard snap punch. His arm straightened, his wrist twisting, as the blow fell alongside Mei's head and directly into the face of the man holding the beautiful woman from behind.

Dumont both felt and heard the resounding crunch of bone through the fabric of the mask. The man lost his grip on Mei as he fell to the floor.

At the same time, Mei lurched forward, falling into Dumont's arm, dark hair brushing the rough material of his mask. He never slowed, though focusing on the final target in front of him. One hand pulled Mei's form tightly against him, both to protect her and swing her out of his way.

Dumont instantly struck the man holding Cheng.

Since the hooded assailant held a gun to Cheng's head, Dumont's strike was much less overt. With Mei pulled to the side, Dumont simply slid an arm around Cheng and gripped slightly above the outer hip of his captor. His fingers quickly dug deep into the pressure point around the body's liver meridian as he let loose one final directed burst of static electricity.

Though the offensive benefits of the radioactive salts were quickly depleted, Dumont prayed to Buddha that he had one last vestige of power left.

And he did.

As if standing in a pool of water that was electrified, the hooded captor was frozen in place, his body stiff as the electrical charge took control of his muscles. Combined with the intensity of a charge being delivered directly to his liver's pressure point, the man was helpless, his gun falling from his hand, his hold on Cheng loosened.

And as Dumont drew his hand away, Cheng simply stepped free.

Mei's hand suddenly shot forward and pulled the mask from Dumont's head. She was shocked to see the socialite that she had just met standing in front of her. Her alabaster eyes were a mixture of both surprise at what she just witnessed and admiration for the fighting skills presented to her.

But Dumont had little time to savor her admiration.

From his peripheral vision, he picked up one last remaining gunman, now targeting him with his pistol. Based on a rapid assessment of his surroundings, Dumont saw little opportunity for cover; his best chance lay in continual movement. His hopes were not high, but his options were slim to none.

A single shot suddenly rang out and Jethro braced for impact. None came.

Instead a fatal bullet felled his stalker. Like a marionette cut from his strings, he dropped to the ground.

Dumont turned to see Jean Farrell, her auburn curls brushed back off her right shoulder, holding a battered bolt-action rifle in a bladed shooting stance.

Dumont was not surprised. He had told her to hide, but his fiery friend from Oklahoma must have liberated a rifle from one of the downed men and decided to take action into her own hands.

Through their past adventures, he could think of very few times that she had ever listened to any advice he had imparted.

"One cannot change the course of the roaring river," he thought, *"One can only decide on how far they choose to follow it."*

Dumont's eyes met Jean's. She simply raised a beautifully arched brow to him and nodded her head, both of them then surveying the room to assure that the danger had been eliminated.

It took some time for the calm to be restored to the Museum of Modern Art. Soon after Jean Farrell had dispatched the last of the raiders, New York City's finest had arrived on the scene, responding to a call of shots fired.

It was disorder at first, the police attempting to comprehend the horrendous nature of the attack, separating the victims from the attackers, the wounded from the dead.

It was only when Lt. John Caraway, head of the New York Police Department's Special Crime Squad, took control of the scene that the crime scene was properly secured.

Dumont stayed on a bit longer than most of the guests, as Caraway had become sociable with the well-traveled playboy since his return to the city.

As the NYPD's Special Crime Squad gathered the raiders, they unmasked each of them unceremoniously. Dumont expected to find that the unmasked attackers were of Chinese origin, but he was surprised to find out that they all shared the same, off-putting characteristic of utter hairlessness.

Each was bald, but their lack of hair extended over the remainder of their bodies as well. Each man shared an odd, waxy appearance, though their hard looks made clear that these were men accustomed to blood and the battlefield.

Why such as a queer, shared characteristic as total hairlessness? This was a peculiar occurrence, one best suited to the tradecraft of the Green Lama.

Prior to Cheng and Mei leaving with their bodyguard, Dumont presented them with a request: would they entertain a visit from his friend, Rev. Dr. Pali, an ordained priest in the Lamaist sect of Buddhism?

He felt that Pali would be a spiritual reprieve for the couple, a holy man able to bring great comfort in times of trial, but also one who had proven valuable as a consultant to the New York Police Force in exotic and esoteric criminal investigations.

Cheng easily agreed to seeing Pali first thing in the morning, believing that the visit would bring great support to his wife, while helping them both come to terms with the evening's misfortunes.

In the late pre-dawn hours of a new day, a small butter candle illuminated a Buddhist shine in an uptown apartment house. Jethro Dumont sat in front of a mirror, but the man gazing back at him was no longer the Manhattan socialite.

His skin was now a ruddy shade of brown, his face fuller. Arched brows, one a bit higher and somewhat inquisitive in its positioning, framed warm eyes. A touch of gray ran through his temples, enhancing the trustworthiness of his features.

Jethro Dumont was gone, replaced by Buddhist priest and revered teacher Rev. Dr. Pali.

The transformation into Dr. Pali was more than assuming a false identity for Dumont. Certainly his make-up was flawless, having trained under the tutelage of Marcel du Plessis, one of the greatest make-up artists of the time.

No, taking on the role of the wise Buddhist touched Dumont deeply.

Dr. Pali was the man that Jethro Dumont wished to be; strong, wise, and compassionate, easily in control of his emotions and existing purely within the flow of the universe.

The man now known as Dr. Pali stood up from his dressing table and walked along a wall of bookshelves, rows and rows of everything from obscure Buddhist texts to modern scientific journals. Stopping at a long bench, he pressed a concealed button hidden in its edge. A microphone rose up from its interior as Pali leaned forward. Hesitating for the sending antenna to click into place on his apartment rooftop, he then proceeded to speak with a firm voice into the microphone.

"Calling Jean Farrell. Calling Jean Farrell. *Nimitta, Nibbána; lobba, dosa, moha*. Calling Jean Farrell...."

It didn't take long. Soon, a salty voice descended from a ceiling-mounted speaker system.

"Jean Farrell coming in. How can I be of service?"

"Justice and truth seek your assistance," Pali stated in the strong voice of the Green Lama. "A woman recently came to Police Headquarters at 240 Centre Street, hairless and carrying the severed head of her boyfriend. Little is known of the events surrounding her plight."

"I saw the story in yesterday's Sentinel. Quite disturbing," Jean replied.

"Find the woman and ascertain the details of her situation." The Green Lama commanded. "My best guess would be that the police have her under observation at New York Hospital-Cornell Medical Center."

"I'll see what I can find out," Jean responded, her voice far more enthusiastic than it had a right to be.

Without a goodby, he terminated their connection. It was nearing sunrise, and the Green Lama had much work to do.

The holy man arrived at the brownstone as the pale morning sunlight cast vertical bands of light across the shadows of Lafayette Street.

He was wearing a deep green business suit, almost black when not being touched by the rays of the sun. Under the suit, he wore a light green ecclesiastical shirt and collar, the sacred symbol of Om engraved in black on the clergyman's collar. A silk scarf of brilliant red hung down over his shoulders, bringing a flash of style to the otherwise orthodox clergy garb.

In his hand, he carried a weathered black briefcase, one obviously used for bringing various religious readings and curios to both believers and the uninformed.

After a few firm knocks, the door was opened by the bodyguard who had been so viciously assaulted the night before. The robust strength of the man was evident; he stood straight and firm, ready to greet the visitor, yet at the same time, coiled and ready to protect the occupants within.

"My name is the Reverend Dr. Charles Pali. I believe that I am expected by Cheng Yi-chuan."

The Mongolian's face softened ever so slightly in the presence of the holy man. "Please, follow me," he said slowly in heavily accented English. "Mr. Cheng and his wife Mei are waiting for you in the drawing room."

Pali realized that it took real work for the man to speak in a foreign language, and he appreciated this attempt to show him respect.

They arrived at a finely appointed drawing room, decorated in very traditional American style. Other than a few rare Asian decorative pieces sprinkled about, little was evident of the Chengs' Chinese origin.

Already a trained diplomat, Pali thought, *ready to make his many callers feel as if he were one of them.*

Cheng was seated in an easy chair, pouring over the morning newspaper, when Dr. Pali entered the room. The diplomat came quickly to his feet and extended a friendly handshake. His eyes dropped to their clasped hands in order to admire Dr. Pali's ring, one made of woven hair in the six sacred Tibetan colors.

"Reverend, thank you for visiting me this morning," he said. "When Mr. Dumont mentioned that you might be available, I wanted to take advantage of the opportunity.

"As foreign diplomats attacked in your country, we are in a unique position. With your position as both a religious man and a conduit to the authorities, I hope that you can assist us in keeping the communications clear with your local police."

Pali looked at Cheng with compassion. He intimately understood what it was like to be a stranger in a foreign land; no matter the level of training or experience, danger had a way of bringing out any feelings of vulnerability.

"I will do my best to be of assistance," Pali responded with sincerity.

His attention was suddenly diverted as Mei entered the room from a side door. She was as magnificent as she had been the evening before. Her art deco patterned cardigan sweater was snug on her figure, falling to a black pencil skirt which revealed smooth, toned legs.

Her snug sweater would have been scandalous just a few years ago, but now the wardrobe of actresses like Lana Turner on the silver screen had made it acceptable. Mei's raven hair hung loose, her make-up toned down from the night before, simple black eyeliner over lush lashes.

"Dr. Pali, I am Mei, the bride of Yi-chuan," she said immediately, once again surprising Dumont/Pali with her liberated ways. It was a tradition, in both the east and the west, for a woman to wait to be introduced by the man of the house. It was obvious that Mei found these traditions outdated. "My husband told me that Mr. Dumont was having you call on us."

"Yes, Jethro is one of my students in the teachings of the East," Pali said, "and he felt that my presence may bring some peace following last night's events. I hope that I can present the noble gifts of clean, clear, and calm."

"Thank you," Mei replied warmly. "Though I must admit that Mr. Dumont is a most unique man. He single-handedly rescued us from our captors, and from what my husband and our security chief have surmised, he may have dealt with the other raiders as well."

Pali was quick to respond, "Perhaps, though Jethro bragged little to me. I hope that I have helped him to see that the defeat of others is merely a starting point to hatred."

At Cheng's direction, Pali took a seat on a finely upholstered chair across from the couple who both sat upon a scarlet leather sofa. Pali declined the offer for refreshment, and instead pursued any knowledge that they may have of their attempted abductors.

"I spoke with Jethro prior to coming here," he said, "and he told me that none of the surviving raiders have spoken with the police. Do you have any insight into the identity of the fallen countrymen who might be of threat to you?"

Mei spoke up. "I fear that we may be dealing with relocated members of a warlord's clan," she said. "For years, many of the bandit armies of China felt no hindrance in sating their own selfish desires, whether for their own benefit or to bring tribute to their warlord commanders.

"Yet this difficult time led to today's rule. It was under the dark oppression of the warlords that men began to strive for intellectual diversity and experimentation. Without suffering, I fear that the minds of my countrymen would not have been ready for the intellectual revolution that is driving our nation today.

"But now the warlords and their bandit armies are scattered, seeking new opportunities," Mei added. "And in this time of great industrialism, with the world getting smaller, my husband and I fear that they look for new opportunity in your country."

Cheng broke in with his thoughts. "I believe our attempted abduction last night was a crime of opportunity and a bold message to both your country and mine. We would have been held for a king's ransom by a group who wanted it known that the bandit armies of China are here."

Pali continued to chat with his hosts for several more minutes, moving away from the dire events of the past evening and exchanging pleasantries about their homeland of China and Pali's visits to the East.

The ringing of the phone interrupted their discussion. Cheng excused himself to take the call, predicting a call from official channels to discuss the failed kidnapping.

Mei rose to her feet.

"Come, Dr. Pali, let us not waste any more of your time. Let me walk you to the door."

A sweet scent of jasmine escaped from Mei as she passed Dr. Pali, leading him to the foyer of the townhouse. Their security chief stood vigilant at his post, as if waiting for another attack to come at any moment.

Mei took the opportunity to lay a hand of Pali's arm and to lean close to him, talking in little more of a whisper.

"I fear that we may know the band that is behind all of this," she said. "My husband fears talking of it, knowing of the prejudice that many American citizens have against the Chinese. We hear the talk of the Yellow Peril, the devil from the Orient. If word reaches the populace about the enemy that we may be facing, Cheng fears he may fail as the chosen ambassador for our people."

"But how can you hope to contain it?" Dr. Pali asked. "These raiders do not appear as men who will disappear quietly into the night."

"I most certainly agree. But Cheng feels that Chinese security force can contain the issue. That is the reason for the call that he is on. But I fear that their aid will be too late."

Pali leaned closer, offering warm eyes and a sympathetic ear to take in her tale.

"There is a feared group of bandits known simply as the Hairless Ones. These men are much more than plunders, and raiders; they are a notorious sect of assassins and thieves who have served our nation's former warlords for generations.

"And these men are twisted. The Hairless Ones are feared because they recruit the perverse and the evil; murderers, boy-lovers, rapists. It is rumored that they even use some sort of chemical bath, a harsh depilatory, to strip all of the hair from their body, bonding them as one under their leader."

Pali pondered every word Mei just said. He then asked, "Last night, the bandits could have waited for the right opportunity to kidnap you. Why do it in such a bold manner?"

"That is their way," Mei responded. "They worship one thing: chaos. It is their god, and it is their weapon. For generations, it has been the mantra of the one who leads the Hairless Ones. No one knows who the man is, only referring to him by his symbolic name. They call him Nalgiri."

Pali knew too well the legend of Nalgiri. In Buddhist lore, Nalgiri was a fierce elephant, dispatched by a mortal enemy of the Buddha to spread chaos and destroy the Buddha. Drunk on spirits, Nalgiri was turned loose on Siddrath to destroy everything in its chaotic path; only the wise Buddha was able to use calm and compassion to stop the murderous elephant.

Dr. Pali looked deep into Mei's beautiful eyes. "My daughter, your honesty is most honorable. I will tell you this: I have friends, not in the police force nor among the authorities, but powerful people who may be able to assist in controlling this situation."

"I trust in what you say, Reverend," Mei said, raising her arm, to run a soft comforting hand along Pali's ruddy cheek. "I witnessed an amazing feat by your friend Jethro Dumont, and now you come to me, another source of both strength and comfort. I know that we are in good hands."

At that Mei turned to her security guard, and for a few moments, she was forced to lean up on her black heels to whisper in his ear. He looked at her for a moment and then nodded.

"My security chief Tan has given me permission to pass on one additional piece of information," she said.

"For a time now, Tan has feared that his cousin Qin-Li may be involved in the operation of an illegal opium den in your city's Chinatown. Tan also has heard rumors that Qin-Li is operating on behalf of a warlord clan."

Pali turned to Tan and then spoke to him directly in Mandarin. "My friend, please tell me where I may find your cousin in Chinatown. There is no time to waste in ending this dark threat. Help me to help your masters."

And help him he did.

Dr. Pali was gone.

In his place now walked the Green Lama.

His orthodox clergy garb was now covered by a hooded green monk's robe that had been secreted away in his briefcase, its dark, forest green silk seeming to capture any light that fell upon it.

The large hood cast deep shadows across his features, hiding the amiable visage of Dr. Pali, and revealing only the dark slash of a grim mouth above a crimson scarf wrapping his neck.

The Lama was moving along Mott Street in Manhattan's Chinatown. He was among the worst of New York City's opium joints. New Yorkers of all races and social bearing were known to patronize these places of stupefaction, none of them as opulent as their sinister sisters on the West Coast. These were working dens here in New York; simple, decadent hideaways where priority was placed on the high, not the surroundings.

Despite the occasional crackdown, the city's opium trade was never seriously threatened by law enforcement. Chinatown itself was hardly ever visited by police, and the opium dens were almost completely ignored. Caraway had complained of this several times to Dumont, remarking that occasionally, when the police department found itself short of funds, they would conduct some sort of raid on the dens, but for the most part, they were left unmolested. This was not an approach that Caraway agreed with, but as a street-smart member of the large metropolitan police force, he chose his battles wisely.

The Green Lama approached the address that Tan had supplied to him. It was a nondescript door under a tattered awning on Mott Street. Only a small, bent bell hung by the side of the door, a chain hanging from within, ready to make known that a guest waited at the door.

The Lama chose not to announce his arrival. Instead he simply entered the den, ready for whatever he might find. The door, much heavier than it appeared, opened easily, and he made his way within.

A small lobby area greeted him. Several old chairs were set back against the wall, and a grimy counter stood in front of a single door leading deeper into the den.

The Green Lama's highly sensitive hearing picked up a slight buzz from behind the door, indicating that he was standing on some sort of monitoring device.

It was only a few moments before the door opened, and a middle-aged Chinese man walked through. He was not the skinny, strung-out addict that the Lama had expected; rather this man was short and bespectacled, carrying a few extra pounds around his waistline.

"Yes?" he asked, in heavily accented English, a large smile on his face. "How can I help you, dear sir? Is there a need that I can meet?"

The Green Lama seemed almost to glide across the room, growing in both stature and strength as he moved closer to his host.

"I have been sent to meet the one known as Qin-Li. His cousin Tan has a message that only I convey. Can I see him?"

The smile on the face of his host grew even wider.

"Of course, of course. Qin-Li welcomes all guests to his place of business. Especially those sent by Tan the Powerful."

The host quickly turned to walk through the door behind him, waving the Green Lama around the counter to follow him.

They entered a long hall, doors aligned on either side. The smell of sin was strong here, a pungent mixture of aging teak woods and burning sweet syrups, with a slight hint of a decaying floral. The Lama knew that the scent behind the doors, where the opium pipes were burning, would be even headier.

His host turned to look up at him with an almost sinister smile. "What a pleasant surprise for Qin-Li. He will be most delighted."

With a laugh, he turned back on his intended path and then brought Dumont to a stop at a door near the first turn in the hallway.

Pulling a key from a ring hanging at his waist, the man opened the door and beckoned for the Lama to enter. It was a simple space, dark with a few candles burning and a long wooden shelf on the wall holding various forms of brass lamps and pipes. A stained curtain hung over one section of high-ceilinged wall, seemingly the room's sole decorative touch.

Only a single chair on the room's corner provided any form of seating, while tattered blankets laying on the floor were intended to play host to any partaking addicts.

"You wait, you wait," his host said. "I return soon with Qin-Li."

With that, he quickly backed out of the room, closing the door behind him. Though he attempted to do it faintly, the Lama heard him re-lock the door from the outside, tumblers falling into place.

The Green Lama did not have long to wait. Soon after his host departed, he sensed the steps of numerous feet in the hallway outside his room, his felt-soled feet feeling the vibrations carried through the teak floors.

The visitors paused for a moment or two. And then the Green Lama heard the cocking of firearms.

Bullets cut through the room, chewing up the wood, crisscrossing the small space in a symphony of death.

Round followed after round, seeking to extinguish the life of the room's lone inhabitant.

When the bullets stopped, the guns exhausted of their ammunition, the killers reloaded. The lock then clicked open, and three gunmen entered, the light from the hall spilling into the candlelit room.

Each was dressed in black; Mauser pistols extended forward and aimed low, hoping to make a kill shot if their target still existed. And like the raiders from the museum, each gunman was devoid of any hair on head or face.

Their eyes went large when they saw the destruction to the room, but no victim was to be found.

The Green Lama was gone!

The smiling host entered behind the gunmen. At first, he had a look of wide-eyed anticipation on his face. Upon seeing that the room contained no victim, only a single fallen chair lying on its side, his expression was replaced by one of fury.

"Where is he?" he yelled to the gunmen in Mandarin.

"We do not know, Qin-Li," one of them replied in his native tongue. "There was no time for him to escape prior to our strike! Even the door was still locked."

From outside in the hall, voices of the customers could be heard questioning what was happening, some fearing a police raid, others simply disoriented and responding to the chatter.

"He must have escaped into the labyrinth!" Qin-Li exclaimed. At that, he pulled back the tattered curtain hanging across the wall. Behind the curtain was a small wooden door cut into the wall. With one hand, he pulled down on a small cargo-style handle, and with the other hand, he pushed the door open.

"Go, go!" he demanded. "I'll handle the chaos up here."

One after another, the gunmen stepped through the dark opening as Qin-Li raced to pacify his confused clientele.

Having heard the guns being cocked, the Lama instantly suspected a trap.

With a trained grace, the Green Lama took one, then two, bounding steps across the room, and then using the chair to propel him, leaped up into the upper corner of the room.

Using a climber's technique that he had learned in Tibet, he caught both corners of the wall with his hands and feet. Tensing his body, he pushed his back up against the ceiling and held himself there.

Using a deep, internal yoga breath, he paused and waited. In this position, he could hold himself for an extended period of time. A long

"Where is he?"

breath in, a long breath out, fingers and toes extended, all working together to allow him to maintain his precarious perch.

Now a shadowy figure in the upper portion of the room, he watched the scene play out below. Tan's lead had been correct. Once the room was vacated, the Green Lama released his hands and feet, dropping swiftly to the floor in a dark crouch and quickly making his way to the passage entrance. Pulling down on the cargo handle as Qin-Li had done, the Lama pressed on the disguised door and felt it open to his touch.

It silently swung open, revealing a narrow passageway, small oil lanterns suspended along the wall. Although it would be easy to pull back and escape through the main halls of the opium den, the Green Lama knew that the answer was not to escape the problem, but rather to solve it.

With a single graceful step, he moved into the dark passageway.

The passageway offered insight into the way of the addict. As the Green Lama moved along the dimly lit crawlspace, he discovered several clandestine viewing holes set within the wall.

Covering each hole was a tiny brass swing panel, which when raised or lowered, allowed a single eye to view the inhabitants within.

Some of the addicts he witnessed were not much more than skin and bones. Others were a bit more robust, obviously more recreational users than the truly addicted.

Again and again, he witnessed men lazily watching nothing more than smoke curling up from their pipes. In other rooms, pipes had already been dropped and heads had fallen into deep opium trances.

Upon arriving at another door, the Green Lama found no viewing port. Rather than moving past it, he pulled on the door handle, which revealed a spartan room containing a desk, several filing boxes, an armoire, and a cork bulletin board covered with black-and-white photographs.

Curious, the Green Lama stepped into the room.

Only a few candles delivered any sort of light to this strange space. Moving silently to the desk and its bulletin board, the Green Lama stopped to survey the collection of photographs.

He was shocked by what he found. There were images of some of the most powerful men in New York City, men who lived on both sides of the law. Photos of notorious gangsters, powerful politicians, all were positioned on the bulletin board.

The Lama also noticed that while some remained untouched, others had been circled, and some crossed through. Even Lt. Caraway's photo had been hung, two large, red circles around his head, apparently made with some sort of grease pencil.

Next to the photos was a list of names. Several of the names at the top had been crossed through. These were the names of men involved in New York City's organized crime families; gambling, protection money, narcotics, all fell into the wheelhouses of these men.

But the name underneath was most intriguing. A simple American name, it proved to be of strong interest to the Green Lama.

The name was Jethro Dumont.

On the table were various newspaper clipping and magazines about New York City. The Lama also noticed something else. Here and there on the table, the Green Lama found lengthy black fibers. Twisting several in his fingers, the Lama found them to be of synthetic, man-made material.

His investigation proceeded no further; the doors to the armoire sprang open.

A dark shape hurtled out, dressed all in black. Before the Green Lama had a chance to defend himself, the invader slammed his head back against the teak wall, once and then again.

Prior to succumbing to the encroaching darkness, the Green Lama couldn't help but notice the massive head of his attacker....

Swaying. Lightly back and forth.

A cool, dank breeze rising up from below.

Another gentle sway.

Suddenly, the Green Lama was awake.

He was suspended upside down, pressure in his head coming from the blood rushing to his skull. His eyes looked downward only to be confronted by a black, rock-lined hole.

His hands and arms were free, but his feet were constrained. Straining to glance upward, he saw that his feet were tied together and apparently secured to a large hook on an ancient wooden winch.

The Green Lama's eyes strained to take in where he was. With the planked walls and the damp, earthen floor, he assumed that he was in the basement of the opium den. His inner sense told him he had been unconscious for mere minutes; too short of a time to have been removed from the premises.

And what of his captors? As his eyes took in the basement around him, the dim lighting of the room gave up nothing more than a trio of dark figures aligned along the wooden planks of a support wall.

And then, from out of the very blackness, a larger figure moved forth to stand in front of the captive Lama.

Almost freakish in its shape, it slowly moved closer to the bound vigilante.

The Green Lama's gaze appraised the bizarre creature that now stood in front of him.

This creature was an elephant.

Light played across its massive head, gray like that of a corpse, and mottled with a dense, leathery texture. A thick trunk hung lifelessly, rocking every so slightly every time the creature breathed deeply. Two dirty tusks of bone pointed downward from either side of its trunk, ancient and weathered, as if they had just been unearthed.

But these bizarre features on the hulking head did not disturb the inner calm of the Green Lama. But something else did provide a slight chill to his trained senses.

It was the creature's mad eyes.

Peering out through deep wells in the face, its eyes were alive with crazed passion. Blinking, wet, they almost sparkled in their clarity.

These were eyes that spoke of madness. And torture. And pain.

And they were now focused entirely on the Green Lama.

The creature's true size was hard to distinguish, as long, black robes covered its frame. Hands extended through the folds of the robes; long, thin fingers clasped together. Only the finger on the right hand made any sort of movement, slowly twitching in some sort of rhythm of anticipation.

"I am Nalgari," hissed the masked creature, his voice muffled by the head covering, yet containing the exotic sound of the Orient.

"This city is quick to tell mythic tales of its Green Lama," the creature continued in a dark whisper. "But I believe you to be more myth and mirrors than a worthy foe."

The Lama's only response was silence. Now was not the time to talk. Now was the time to listen, to ascertain his enemy's intention, and to find an opportunity to exploit their vulnerabilities.

"The Green Lama! The mystic scourge of the underworld! The holy protector of the innocent!"

The creature turned away for a moment as if in reflection.

"But what manner of man are you? Do you even know? Should I call you Dr. Pali? Or are you Jethro Dumont?"

For the first time, the Green Lama felt vulnerable. He was accustomed to the mad rantings of a lunatic. But this was different. Somehow this creature knew two of his identities.

Who was the beast in front in him?

"I've accepted your presence as a sign of what is to come. Like the still water that recedes before the tsunami, the death of the Green Lama will herald the great change that strikes without mercy to destroy all that's in its path."

Before the Lama could reply, Nalgari turned to the shadowy figures behind him and said, "Submit him to the ordeal."

With that order, the trio of men stepped out of the darkness. These were the hairless ones from upstairs in the opium den. They moved to the base of the winch from which the Green Lama hung suspended. Here they released the peg lock from a large crank mechanism.

The Lama's eyes followed the path of the crank mechanism to a rope running along the winch from which he was suspended. Looking down again, seeing a circular hole lined by stone walls, the Green Lama realized that he was hanging above an old well probably dug one hundred and fifty years ago when parts of Manhattan were still farmlands.

With a sudden lurch, he felt the rope release, and slowly, he was lowered into the well.

It took but a few moments for his head to descend past the lip of the well and into the darkness below.

Stacked and mortared stones were now his only view, and even that was fading fast, as he dropped deeper into the pit, any sight extinguished by the lack of light falling into the depths of the pits.

Secure that his entire body was now enveloped in darkness, the Green Lama claimed control of his core muscles, and in a singular motion, brought his upper body up to grasp the ropes securing his feet.

The knots were tight, but he was not daunted, for Jethro Dumont had been trained in the art of escapism by one of the Europe's most-esteemed escape artists, Sardo the Great. His fingers began to make quick work of the knotting structure, but the Green Lama was cautious with his progress.

He had no idea how far below him lay the well floor, and he had no interest in taking a mystery plunge into the void.

Suddenly his descent came to a violent stop, his body jerking hard. Looking above, the Green Lama could see a dimly lit circle indicating the opening of the well, which he now guessed was at least forty to fifty feet above him.

The smell had gotten much worse at this level of the well, a mixture of sickly sweetness and eye-watering bitterness. It was the smell of rot and decay.

He swung his body gently, moving his arms, trying to ascertain the size and nature of his surrounding. Stone walls seemed to surround him on all sides.

He then extended his arms straight down, and he was relieved to brush his fingers against solid ground. He much preferred having the earth below him while planning an escape.

But the relief was momentary. His fingers had continued to play over the ground, and he felt piles of odd, seemingly random pieces of wood. He picked up a few pieces in his hands, and he ran his fingers along their surface. Continuing his investigation, he felt mottled areas on the end of the object, forgiving and somewhat spongy to his touch.

Bringing the piece to his noise, the Green Lama gently breathed in and he was not pleased with the scent. He knew the smell. It was marrow.

The object in his hand was a bone.

Based on its size, it probably was that of a small animal. Dropping the bone back to the ground, he let his fingers once again play across the ground below him. As he suspected, what he had initially felt was a pile of bones, one atop the other, the discarded remains of many creatures who had been dispatched to this same pit.

The Green Lama then heard a sound break the silence of the pit. It was the sound of a shape slowly moving across the ground, disturbing the floor of bones, as it came toward him. To the Lama's hearing, its movements were both strong and cautious, as if attempting to ascertain its surroundings and the intruder in its midst.

And then the Green Lama heard it hiss.

The hairless ones began the process of raising the Green Lama.

They had waited patiently above the entrance to the well, hoping to hear cries for mercy from the pit. But none ever came.

They could only stand solemnly and watch the rope.

At first, the movement was ever so slight when the rope reached the base, just a simple sway that could have been caused by breeze or draft.

And then the rope seemed to come alive. Almost spastically, it quickly jerked and shuddered. It jerked again and again, and then it stopped.

No more movement came, and eventually the rope returned to its gently swaying.

The elephant head turned to his men, signaling them with outstretched hand to raise the body from below.

Slowly they did, bringing the rope up with each turn of the crank.

The body of the Green Lama cleared the lip of the well, and the hairless ones gasped.

For the sight before them was not only that of the Green Lama. His body was now entirely covered by the reptilian mass of a reticulated python.

Close to eight meters in length, the python coiled around the unmoving form of the Lama; its olive drab and fern green scale pattern melding perfectly with the man's green garb. The python appeared to have suffocated the human who had been dropped into its lair, constricting its coils to squeeze the very life out of the mystic warrior.

The python held its head high near the Lama's feet, as if preparing to ingest its victim. Turning its attention away from the Lama, the python's forked tongue darted out to test the air of the room, its head smoothly sliding back and forth.

And then, all at once, the python burst forth from the body of the Green Lama, flying across the room and directly into the assembled group of hairless ones.

Like lightning, the terrified beast struck out at the men around it. Hissing, while alternately inflating and flattening its body, it stuck out at the men with open jaw and dripping fangs.

At the same time, the Green Lama contracted his core muscles to bring his body up, his hands releasing the few remaining knots just barely holding him to the well's rope. Once free, he used his hands to swiftly pull his entire body up atop the winch.

Like a gargoyle, he surveyed the scene in front of him, his dark, hooded cloak hanging over the well below him.

For the first time, he saw the hairless ones moving in panic. Not a surprise though; even the bravest of men are not accustomed to having a nearly thirty foot python thrown into their midst.

A grim smile crossed the face of the Lama as he pulled the crimson scarf free from his neck. He then leapt into the fray.

When hanging in the well, the Green Lama had surmised from the sound of the slow, creeping movement that this was one large reptile. It sounded like the beast was using a rectilinear form of movement, the wide scales on its belly gripping the bed of bones while pushing forward with its other scales.

While in Southeast Asia, he had seen several large pythons move with this same method. And if it was a python moving on him, he knew exactly how it would intend to kill him.

A constricting snake kills its prey by suffocation. Moving in harmony with the victim's breath, the python squeezes every time its prey exhales, slowing getting tighter and tighter, until its intended meal can breathe no more.

At that thought, the snake struck. It must have reared back and shot its form directly at the Green Lama.

His body was thrown violently around the well, as the large snake quickly threw its coils around the Lama's body.

The Lama knew that his only hope for survival was to use a technique that came from years of yoga and meditation practice, one that instantly slowed his breathing and, in turn, his heart rate.

Immediately, he moved his thoughts away from the reptile constricting around him and conjured up vivid memories of diving into freezing waters. His mind instantly moved his body into an active diving reflex, allowing for his heart rate to slow down ten to twenty percent.

The Green Lama quickly exhaled and did a gentle uddiyana bandha maneuver, pulling the abdomen under the rib cage. This result in an increase to his levels of carbon dioxide, slowing his heart beat even further.

Calmly and with great care, the Lama than brought the tip of his tongue up to press against the back of his upper teeth and the roof of the mouth in a jiva bandha position. Once again, this yoga technique was used to increase the slowing of the heart.

Through its thick coils, a python can sense the heartbeat of its prey. As the heartbeat of the Lama slowed, the snake began to relax. This confused the reptile. It now found itself in a position that went against instinct; its warm-blooded prey instantaneously moving from quick breaths and rapid heartbeats to a state of non breathing with diminished cardiac activity. Should it continue to attack? Or was the struggle over? The simple-minded predator chose to wait for the answer to come from its prey.

And the Green Lama relaxed, hanging still in corpse pose, waiting for his chance to strike as well.

As the Green Lama prepared to take down his enemies, his feeling was one of elation. Following his intense survival meditation in the well, the sudden blood flow to his brain left the jade warrior with a sense of immense clarity and focused alertness.

It was exactly what he needed.

Two of the hairless ones were ina struggle with the great python; one wrapped in its constricting coils, while its large, fanged jaw head struck out at the other one.

The Green Lama had confused the poor, simple beast, and now the frightened predator sought to strike out at those it perceived as a threat.

As the Green Lama and the python were raised out of the well, the mystic allowed for his muscles to contract, bringing his arms closer and closer, allowing the slightest amount of slack to exist between his form and that of the snake.

When they came to a rest after clearing the lip of the well, the Green Lama brought his body to life. He opened his mouth, taking in fresh oxygen to his air-starved muscles. He then tensed and exploded, his arms suddenly pushing out against the now-relaxed coils of the snake around him, sending the beast flying from him and directly into his enemies.

The attack of the python left only one member of the hairless ones to deal with. The man, momentarily stunned by what happened, reached to his waist to draw a Mauser pistol from a belt holster.

The gun had barely cleared the leather when the Green Lama struck with his *kata*. Cleverly worn around his neck or waist, this five foot long ceremonial scarf was his offensive weapon of choice. Dense weights sewn into either end of the scarf allowed him to deploy it like a crimson whip, this time striking out at the gun of the enemy before him.

With a snap and then the sound of a cracking bone, the hairless one dropped the pistol to the earthen floor. Before he could begin to think about picking it up, the Lama was on him, his hands moving in a series of rapid ju-jitsu strikes to the face and chest, knocking him off balance, before turning into him, a hand wrapping around the man's back, only to slam him to the ground with a hip throw.

The Lama raised his head to find Nalgiri. The bizarre creature was at the far end of the sub-basement, running up a flight of old wooden steps in hopes of escape.

Reaching a door at the top of the stairs, the elephant man turned to look down at the Green Lama in pursuit, reaching the steps below him. Mad eyes embraced those of his enemy, and a hiss of hatred escaped from beneath the mask.

The Lama bounded up the steps, one and then two at a time.

But Nalgiri was faster. Appearing simply to want to escape, he suddenly spun on a single leg and drove an extended leg strike right into the chest of the Green Lama. The mystic warrior fell back, barely grabbing the rotting, wooden rail to catch himself from plummeting down the staircase.

This was all the time that Nalgiri needed. He quickly moved through the open door, slamming it behind him. The Green Lama heard the slam of a sturdy lock as he righted himself and restarted his ascent.

Upon reaching the doorway, the Green Lama did not waste time trying the handle. Instead, he turned his back to the door and then kicked like an angry mule, his foot hitting just under the doorknob.

Once, twice, and the doorjamb broke free.

The Green Lama once again entered the series of passages that ran behind the rooms of the opium den. He ran forward, and then turned a tight right, recognizing the initial passageway that he had passed through.

Racing down the hall, hoping to prevent Nalgiri from escaping, his pursuit was suddenly ended by an angry Qin-Li stepping out into the hallway, his gun drawn and firing.

Bullets chewed up the wall alongside the Green Lama's face, sending splinters of wood into his cheek. He did not pause, though, the *kata* in his hand shooting forward, its weighted end catching Qui-Li squarely in the nose with a loud pop.

Blood coursed from a now-broken nose, and the Green Lama continued to run toward him, closing the distance and hesitating only to leap into the air and slam into his chest with a fierce, running side kick. Qui-Li was propelled savagely against the door standing open, knocking it off its hinges, both falling still to the passageway floor.

The Green Lama swept into the room, his eyes and hands ready for another strike by the enemy.

But the room was empty. Moving out into the hall, he quickly looked left and right, hoping to find Nalgiri, but the beast appeared to be gone.

Standing behind the closed doors of a wooden phone booth, his hooded cloak returned to his briefcase, the Green Lama called Jean Farrell.

Moving swiftly out of Chinatown, he had entered an office building on Grand Street to avail himself of its bank of phone booths.

"Jean, this is the Green Lama," he said when she answered. "Were you able to find out anything about the woman who had been assaulted?"

Jean was enthusiastic to reply, “You bet I did! You were right; the police had her secured at New York Hospital. It was easy finding an extra candy-striper apron and then moving through the hospital until I found the poor thing. And boy, did she have a doozy of a store to tell!”

It turned out the woman’s name was Ava Carter, and she was a cocktail waitress over at the Stork Club. But it was the identity of Ava’s boyfriend—the man whose severed head was brought to police headquarters—that proved most interesting.

He was Al Marino, a hard man and a mob hard case. He was rising fast in the organization, known for quick, decisive moves while operating a narcotics ring out of Little Italy’s Mulberry Street that ran deep into the adjacent Chinatown area.

When Ava’s shift wrapped up on the night of the attack, she quickly donned her coat and joined Marino, who was waiting for her at the Stock Club Bar. Marino and Ava had just about completed their stroll to his apartment when they were suddenly attacked by a group of men who forced them into the stairwell of Marino’s building and then up to his studio apartment.

“The kid was really shook up, boss,” Jean told the Green Lama. “But it seemed like a relief to be talking. I felt a little bad sitting at her side and playing the role of concerned candy striper. But when I heard the rest of her story, I was glad that I was there for it.”

Ava knew little of why her boyfriend was being beaten back at his apartment. From the few words she could make out, it seemed to have something to do with drugs and turf in Chinatown. She knew that Al was mixed up in some bad stuff, and she feared that his criminal life had finally caught up to him.

The men had pulled Ava across Marino’s apartment to a small bath on the other side of the room. Her sense of smell was assaulted by a harsh, chemical odor coming from within. She was then raised over the tub and unceremoniously dropped into a bath of waiting chemicals.

“It burned her bad, boss,” Jean related. “It felt like her body was on fire, and not just her skin. Her eyes, inside her nose, mouth and throat.

“She fought to come came up from the liquid, gasping for fresh air, but it was hard to catch a breath over her own screams. But hands kept grabbing her by her hair and forcing her down.

“That was about all she could tell me,” Jean finished. “It seems like she went into shock and doesn’t remember anything beyond showing up at the police department, totally naked with her dead boyfriend’s head in a basket.”

This all made sense to the Green Lama from what he had encountered in his investigation. Starting with what he had learned from Mei, to his subsequent investigation and capture, the Green Lama told Jean of his personal encounters with the hairless ones.

He received a few hoots and whistles of surprise from Jean along the way, and he ended by telling her of the names that he had seen in the hidden room in the opium den.

"From what I've uncovered this all fits together," the Green Lama told her. "Nalgiri and his gang appear to have targeted anyone who could be an obstacle to achieving their dark objectives, and they are eliminating them in brutal, violent, public ways.

"I truly fear for the safety of a great many people right now, and I pray that we can act decisively enough to protect them."

Tsarong was fascinated by the Horn & Hardart Automat on 48th Street, its chrome-and-glass food-dispensers offered everything from sandwiches to apple pie.

Right now, he sat in a heavily lacquered table savoring a cup of the delicious H&H coffee. The restaurant made fresh coffee all day long, never allowing it to sit for more than an hour. And the delicious brew only cost him a nickel.

Yes, tea may be the drink of the enlightened, but a cup of fresh-brewed H&H coffee was his vice of choice.

After completing his coffee, Tsarong walked out on to and enjoyed the crisp night air. It was a beautiful night and he would try to savor every moment of it as he strolled back to Jethro Dumont's Park Avenue apartment.

Tsarong had all but completed his stroll when the assault happened. Looking up at the towering building that was his home, he suddenly sensed movement behind him.

Before he could fully turn around, a sharp pain exploded across his skull and everything went black for Jethro Dumont's valet and the trusted ally of the Green Lama.

The fist slammed once into Tsarong's cheek.

His head recoiled from the blow.

Fresh blood slowly trickled from the Tibetan's mouth. He was on his knees, hands secured behind his back, arms held at a painful angle.

He drew up his head and spat blood on the hard wood floor. The beating had been without mercy.

Regaining his focus, the same question was asked of him.

"Where is Jethro Dumont?" Nalgiri hissed. "I know that he is the one known as the Green Lama. Tell us where he hides."

Tsarong's answer was only muted silence.

His head was suddenly twisted to the side and pressed firmly against a rough, wooden table. Shards of wood splinters dug into his cheek, deep enough to allow for his blood to flow along the long grooves of the table's surface.

As a swollen eye strained to look forward, his focus fell upon a pair of strong, raw-boned hands grasping the handle of a weathered axe, its massive, chipped blade stained dark.

"His commitment is to be admired," Nalgiri remarked to another. "I suspect that he will tell us nothing, as his loyalty is too great.

"Be done with him."

At that, Tsarong watched the axe blade move away from his vision, rising upward, moving to a destination he assumed to be suspended above his strained neck.

Tsarong's reaction was immediate. A look of quiet serenity fell upon his dark features as a quiet Tibetan prayer escaped from bloodied lips.

And the axe fell.

"Om. Ma-ni pad-me Hum," he whispered.

The axe fell swiftly, but it never reached its target.

Tsarong's hands, which had been secured behind his back, were suddenly free, coming up to take hold of the handle of the axe upon its descent, and then swinging it away under its own momentum, carrying the executioner with it.

He was a large, heavily muscled man, wearing dark butcher's garb, a tattered black hood covering his head. He stumbled with the blade, but quickly regained his footing and turned toward the Tibetan, roaring in rage.

Suddenly he lunged forward, swinging the axe horizontally, in a move designed to eviscerate the innocent servant.

Suddenly he lunged forward, swinging the axe horizontally...

Tsarong leaped back, the axe blade narrowly missing the opportunity to disembowel him. While the vicious swing hung up the momentum of his intended executioner, Tsarong drove a heel into the side of the man's knee, brutally dislocating the knee by separating the femur and tibia.

A painful and traumatic injury, the executioner collapsed to the floor with a loud bellow, dropping the ancient axe in the process.

Tsarong immediately turned, ready the fight the man who ordered his death.

But Nalgiri was gone. He must have escaped deeper into the house while Tsarong was fighting to live.

Moving to the fallen executioner, still moaning and holding his destroyed leg, Tsarong reached down and yanked the tattered hood from his head.

He looked upon the visage of Tan, bodyguard to Mei and Cheng, and now traitor to his homeland.

This confirmed his suspicions. The kidnapping at the museum had been a set-up from the start. An effective way to move an involved player off of the playing board, and at the same time, building up a healthy bankroll with ransom demands.

Now he just had to find Nalgiri.

He was thankful that the elephant beast had not noticed him stealthily loosening the knots around his hands, using tricks taught to him by the great escape artist Sardo. He had been too consumed with torturing Tsarong to discover the location of Jethro Dumont.

But this could not happen, as he never had Tsarong in his clutches.

It had been simple for the Green Lama to switch places with his trusted friend.

Prior to contacting Jean Farrell to discuss her investigative findings, the Green Lama had called Tsarong to tell him he was in danger. From the notes and photos he found in the opium den, he knew that Jethro Dumont and anyone close to him were now priority targets of the hairless ones. He instructed the Tibetan to leave the Park Avenue apartment immediately and to take refuge in one of the Lama's safe houses throughout the city.

The Green Lama then headed to the apartment that he used as a front for his identity as Dr. Pali. Here, he returned to the make-up table to begin the careful transformation into that of his Tibetan valet.

To a close friend, the transformation would not pass inspection.

But the Green Lama was counting on the fact the Nalgiri and his men had never met Tsarong, and they would only know that a Tibetan servant worked closely with Jethro Dumont.

By dressing the part and using the right make-up application to conceal his true identity, he hoped his appearance would be convincing enough to pull off the intended subterfuge.

And in the process, bring him directly into the lion's den.

Quickly he moved to the front of the house. Opening the door that led to Lafayette Street, he whistled a queer tune. From out of the darkness, Jean Farrell ran quickly to the Green Lama. Around her waist, the Green Lama could see a holstered pistol.

When the Green Lama had spoken to Jean Farrell, he had ordered Jean to stake out Jethro Dumont's Park Place apartment, and keep an eye on the Tsarong impersonator as he went about his business.

At no time was she to intervene; her mission was simply to follow.

Jean rushed to the Green Lama's side. Seeing his battered face, Jean was taken aback.

"Oh my! Are you alright."

"Yes, I'm fine," the Lama said, smiling. "In fact, I believe that their fists probably look much worse than my face."

Jean chuckled and looked around at their surroundings. "Do you know where you are?"

"Yes. It is as I suspected," the Lama said. "I've been here before, but this will all end tonight. The beast is now trapped in its lair. We must break him."

Jean reached into a satchel secured over her shoulders and handed him a bundle of clothes as well as a small glass vial. "I brought what you requested," she said.

Taking the offering, he now held the hooded robe of the Green Lama, his red *kata*, and a vial of radioactive salts.

As soon as he donned the robe and brought the hood up and over his head, casting his face in the dark shadows of justice, Jean Farrell saw a different man.

The injuries from the beatings seemed to disappear; the abuse forgotten until another day.

Standing before her was a mythic figure, one that she would follow across the gates of hell if he asked her.

After securing Tan with some of the very same ropes that he had used to hold Tsarong, the Green Lama instructed Jean to keep an eye on the fallen bodyguard while he pursued Nalgiri.

He moved cautiously through the townhouse, checking each room, wary of a trap. The first level appeared to be clear, and as the Lama was moving toward the stairway to the second floor, he heard gunfire from upstairs.

First one shot, then another.

The Green Lama bounded up the stairwell, only pausing at the final step to ensure that he did not walk straight into further gunfire.

His nose suddenly detected the overwhelming, acrid odor of gasoline.

Planted against the wall to provide himself with the most cover, the hooded face of the Green Lama peered around to find the source of the gunfire.

He was stunned by what he found.

It was a large living space, and whereas the lower level was very traditional and western in appearance, this sumptuous area spoke of Eastern splendor. Scarlet paint graced the walls, and beautiful pieces of furniture made of lacquered wood were covered with pieces of ivory and Chinese pottery.

Yet throughout the room were large puddles of clear liquid. Some of the wall coverings also were covered in liquid, which dripped to the ground below.

The Green Lama knew that this was the source of the gasoline smell.

And toward the back of the room, lying on the floor in a pool of blood, was Cheng Yi-chuan, ambassador of the Republic of China to the United States of America.

Only he was dressed much differently than the times he had met Jethro Dumont and Dr. Pali.

He was now clothed in a black robe, which blended with the flow of blood spreading from beneath his body.

Behind his head lay the grotesque mask of Nalgiri, an elephant head left to stare blindly at the ceiling.

And above Cheng stood his trembling wife Mei wearing a casual floral dress with small Peter Pan collar and a Mauser pistol still aimed at the body of her dead husband.

The Green Lama moved to the side of the grieving widow, his hand reaching out to support her supple back.

She turned to him, her raven hair a perfect match to the long lines of black mascara that ran down her cheek.

She turned in to the Lama's chest, looking for some comfort in this terrible time, the scent of her jasmine perfume rising up to mix oddly with the scent of gasoline permeating the room. "I had to shoot him," she said through her sobs. "He is a horrible man, and he was going to burn the house down with me in it to facilitate his escape.

"I've wanted to kill him for so long, to escape his abuse, but I never had the strength. This gun has been hidden for months, waiting for me to find the strength to use it. When I learned what he was planning to do, I had to finally act."

The Lama pulled her closer, appearing to support this beautiful woman caught in a horrible ordeal.

But his actions said something different.

The hand on Mei's back suddenly snaked forward and closed around her neck. His other hand took hold of the wrist holding the gun, raising it toward the sky.

For he had seen Mei slowly raising her pistol, intending to shoot the Green Lama in his midsection.

The gun fired harmlessly into the air. The Lama swiftly found a pressure point located on the ulna nerve of the wrist. A pinch of the nerve against the bone, and Mei dropped the pistol.

But though the Lama had an arm around her neck, the struggle for the gun allowed Mei the opportunity to pull free. Standing free of his hold, the woman now faced the Green Lama, a look of hatred suddenly replacing what had been sorrow.

She took a few defensive steps back, kicking free of her round toe heels. With a few feet between her and the Green Lama, she reached up to pull the hair off of her head.

It was a wig, for Mei was one of the hairless ones.

Her bald head accented beautifully arched brows, now obviously drawn on, and thick false lashes.

Mei then clutched at her dress, tearing it from away her body in one swift move.

Now standing in front of the Green Lama was a lean warrior wearing only a mawashi loincloth. Now standing in front of the Green Lama was a man.

Intricate tattoos covered his torso in green and scarlet. Crashing waves, bladed weapons of death, ropes and other agents of bondage were all part of the intertwined design. And in the center was a black-garbed, elephant headed warrior, holding a sword in the air, the body of a whale speared on the tip of the blade.

A grim smile crossed the countenance of the Green Lama.

"Finally, I look upon the true visage of the one known as Nalgiri," he said.

Nalgiri simply sneered in response. "I thought you a simple fool, another man primed to comfort the poor woman presented to him. Yet you knew. How?"

"I was never sure of your exact role," the Green Lama replied. "Though once I fell into the trap at the opium den, I knew that someone within this household was to blame. Only the residents of this house knew where I was headed."

Nalgiri and the Green Lama began to circle one another, looking for exposed vulnerabilities.

"When I was investigating the hidden office in the opium den, I found several long black fibers lying among the notes. Examining these, it was clear to me that they were synthetic fibers used in wigs, and very similar to your own head of hair. You are not the only one who knows the artistry of disguise."

Nalgiri laughed, "And that was how your identity with Dr. Pali was made known to me! I suspected that all was not natural, and when I touched my hand to your face during your visit, it came away with a hint of dark foundation."

"Games on top of games on top of games," the Green Lama mused. "Though I must admit, I only imagined you in league with your husband. I did not consider you the beast that fed the machine."

Nalgiri sneered. "My husband. Don't sicken me with that term, nor provide him any more credit than deserved. He was a spineless puppet, nothing more. A weak academic who let me twist him to my plans, giving in to his own perverse desires."

The Green Lama was tired of the rants and moved on his enemy. Nalgiri brought his arms up in a defensive martial arts position, but the Lama struck swift and hard, moving up and under to deliver a fierce strike to the right flank.

Nalgiri recovered quickly. A fast drop kick savagely caught the Green Lama in the sternum. He staggered, scrambling to keep his feet under him. Crouching low, he allowed his free hand to take to the floor in order to regain his bearings.

Nalgiri moved in quickly though, ready to deliver another kick. The Lama continued to lean on the floor. Waiting, waiting. When the time was exactly right, he swiveled on his planted leg and delivered a devastating forked lighting kick, catching his enemy in the thigh.

The tattooed fighter's leg instantly went numb, allowing him to use it only for balance, not for support. The Green Lama used this opportunity to move in, grabbing Nalgiri by both throat and the arm, and savagely slamming him into the wall using a whirlwind throw.

Nalgiri lay still, stunned by the devastating throw.

"And who is the man who stands in my way? Jethro Dumont? Dr. Pali? Or someone else entirely?" Nalgiri asked.

The Green Lama had almost forgotten that he now wore the countenance of yet another man. "If we are to die together tonight, we should at least know each other's inner secrets."

At that Nalgiri's features softened, now again taking on the look of Mei, a heady mixture at once both demure and seductive.

"My material identity is one that you already know," the Green Lama softly said. "Our identity in the world is only a manifestation of our virtue or our vice."

At that, the Green Lama prepared to move in, ending the dance once and for all.

Suddenly, Nalgiri's hand came away from his mawashi loincloth, a lighter in hand, his thumb running the thumbwheel against the flint.

The flame ignited, and Nalgiri tossed the lighter toward a pool of gasoline.

The Green Lama reached to his shoulders, taking the *kata* hung around his neck and flicking it forward, hoping to hit the lighter in flight and divert it from its intended path.

But he was too late, and the weighted end of the crimson *kata* fell short.

Suddenly, the room burst into light and intense warmth as the gasoline ignited in flames. Harsh heat washed over the Green Lama.

But he knew he still had a dangerous enemy to contend with. Turning to Nalgiri, he saw the man scrambling toward the pistol where it lay on the floor, flames starting to close in.

He let loose the *kata* once again, sending it hurtling at the side of Nalgiri's bald skull.

His targeting was much more accurate this time, striking him hard directly at the temple.

The effect was instantaneous, Nalgiri's brain slammed violently against the skull lining, resulting in a total blackout.

In those few moments, more spreads of gasoline caught fire, quickly rising to ignite the fuel which had been splashed on the walls. The beautiful lacquer furniture also proved highly flammable, reacting instantly, and further fueling the fire.

The room was totally ablaze, a burning inferno which seemed to be everywhere.

The Green Lama knew he had to get across the room, to escape the flames, but a clear path was not evident to him. And though he was well trained in various mystic arts of the warrior mind, making himself fireproof was not one of them.

He suddenly remembered the vial of radioactive salts that Jean had brought him. Reaching into his green cloak, he removed the small tin vial and quickly swallowed its contents.

He would wait for a moment, letting the powers of the salts take hold in his body, for what he was going to do was sure to be a substantial.

Thick smoke was filling the air around him, turning the space into a darkening cavern. Tongues of flame continued to lick the walls, while the acrid smoke began to sear the eyes and lungs of the Lama.

He moved all of his concentration to the task at hand, his thoughts aimed at collecting his body's energy to move it lower and lower still.

And then he stopped. He turned to the unconscious form of Nalgiri lying behind him.

It would be so easy to leave the body here, to let it burn away with the multitude of sins that had existed here.

But that was not the way.

Vengeance. Destruction. That was not the path he chose. The man in the green cloak realized that the most valuable service is the one rendered to his fellow human being.

That is the way of the Lama.

He leaned down, taking up the unconscious form of Nalgiri into his arms.

The fire now had a life of its own, the roof now engulfed in flames.

Once again, the Green Lama made his mind go still. His focus moved through his body, first taking the active energy of his mind and collecting it into a throbbing bundle.

His concentration forced this bundle of pure energy lower and lower into his body, allowing it to absorb all of the body's vital energies that pulsed around it.

The heart, the lungs, each gave up its own energy so that his body was filled with the pulsating bundle. It then moved down his legs, attracted to the muscular strength of his legs, getting heavy with the mass of energy it absorbed, and then, coming to rest within his feet, before purging itself from his body in a concentrated burst of heat energy that flowed.

And the Green Lama rose.

His body began to levitate, one inch, six inches, a foot, raising above the floor, using the power of the radioactive salts to drive his body's heat energy out and under him.

Slowly he began to levitate across the flaming room. To anyone who saw the spectacle, it would be a miracle; a hooded man seeming to float across the room with ease.

To the Green Lama, it was an act of herculean strength. Every bit of fortitude in him, every bit of training, went into maintaining his concentration. One stray thought, one lapse in intensity, and both the Green Lama and Nalgiri would plunge into the flames below.

He felt the flames licking at his feet. Was he faltering, falling lower and lower, eventually lapsing into the flames? Or were the flames climbing higher, moving to a height that he could not rise above?

These random thoughts had to be banished, tossed away to the winds.

From deep within, a single prayer filled the mind of the Green Lama Om. Ma-ni pad-me Hum. Hail to the Jewel of the Lotus..

This was the mantra of Mahayana Buddhism. Its invoker to be protected from all dangers.

And this was all the Green Lama needed.

He came down hard on the floor just outside the stairwell. The flames had not spread this far, though he knew that the entire floor would soon be consumed, collapsing and dropping the flames into the first floor below.

He had to get out. Exhausted and drained, he threw Nalgiri into a fireman's carry over his shoulder and slowly made his way down the stairs, one foot in front of the other.

The first floor was already filling with smoke, debris beginning to fall from the ceiling.

The Green Lama tried to get his bearings, but the mental strain upstairs made it hard to concentrate. Thick, acrid smoke was everywhere.

Suddenly a hand reached out. It was Jean, her mouth covered with a damp towel, another damp towel over her head and shoulders. She wasted no time speaking; instead she took the Green Lama by his hand to the waiting front door.

The fresh night air of New York City was so sweet. Jethro Dumont did have warm memories of cool evenings in Tibet, just breathing in and out the fresh air of the Himalayas, savoring its pureness.

But no breath taken there was so satisfying as the evening city air that he now breathed deeply into his parched lungs.

He had been pleased to find that Jean had already dragged the body of Tan to safety on the small green lawn in front of the diplomat's townhouse.

Laying the unconscious form of Nalgiri alongside him, he tightly secured the man's hands and feet with his own *kata*.

Jean gave the Green Lama a questioning look after he laid the tattooed figure of Nalgiri in the grass.

"Meet your mastermind, Ms. Farrell," he said. "You might have met him earlier as the wife of Cheng Yi-chuan."

The Green Lama took simple pleasure in the utterly confused look that Jean gave him.

The sounds of incoming sirens signaled that both police and fire vehicles were on their way.

"Don't worry. When Lieutenant Caraway arrives, tell him that I will find a future opportunity to explain the whole case of the hairless ones to him, but he can rest assured that the immediate danger has passed."

The Green Lama did not want to wait for the authorities. Once Nalgiri was questioned, he was certain that claims would be made that the Green Lama was Jethro Dumont. Or perhaps he was Rev. Dr. Pali. Or even a Tibetan valet. As usual, confusion and slight of hand would be his best ally in protecting his identity.

All of these claims regarding the Lama's identity had been made at one time or another in the past; but for now, he intended to get home and secure a solid alibi for Mr. Jethro Dumont.

Jean continued to be perplexed by the appearance of Nalgari. She looked over the man; the young actress absorbed by the hairless body, the intricate tattoos, and what appeared to be a set of false eyelashes glued his closed eyes.

Turning with a bemused smile to the mystic warrior, she said, "I must say, this is one of the damnedest things that you've ever..."

But the Green Lama was gone.

The End

Blame it On Steranko

I was seven years old, and I discovered an amazing hero.

He was a hooded, caped figure in green, descending through a black sky, caught between the massive might of CC. Beck's Captain Marvel (a tiny Mister Mind atop his shoulder) and the fierce electrical bolts of Jack Binder's Pyroman.

The Green Lama may not have been the most dominant character illustrated by Jim Steranko on the cover of *The Steranko History of Comics, Volume 2*, but to me, this was one cool dude swooping through the air.

Inside Steranko's oversized pop culture reference guide, I read about the Green Lama's comic book adventures, and I was enamored by the book's black-and-white reproductions of Mac Raboy's art.

And it was in these pages that I first learned that Jethro Dumont originally appeared in the pulp pages of *Double Detective* magazine.

At the time, I was just getting into the Bantam reprints of Doc Savage, and I was fascinated by the idea of a character that started in the pulps and then found a new lease on life in the comics (a practice commonplace today!).

But where was a seven-year-old boy to find the prose adventures of the Green Lama in the early 1970s? I'd visit my local bookstores, searching the shelves, hoping to find his adventures in reprint editions, but my search was always in vain.

All was not lost though, as my hunt for the Green Lama led to me to discovering Pyramid Books' reprint of Walter Gibson's *The Living Shadow*, and I found my pulp-addled mind now obsessed with another costumed crime-fighter.

And of course, who else would have painted the cover to this reprint edition but the great Jim Steranko.

Fast forward nearly forty years, and I'm found myself in a new golden age for pulp fans!

Due to the hard work of pulp publishers John Gunnison and Matt Moring, I was finally able to consume all of the Green Lama's original adventures in issues of *High Adventure* as well as *The Green Lama: The Complete Pulp Adventures* collections from Altus Press.

Here I discovered Kendell Foster Crossen's novel-length adventures of the Green Lama from the pages of *Double Detective*. And what fun tales these were! Though not quite achieving the epic nature of the best of Doc Savage or the Shadow, these prose adventures tapped into something that Stan Lee made popular at Marvel Comics in the 1960s: they fully exploited the value of continuity.

In Crossen's Green Lama novels, characters and their relationships changed over time, the locale of one adventure could lead directly into the next, and previous tales were referenced within the current storyline. This was good stuff, way ahead of its time.

And although I continued to devour any pulp reprints that I could get my hands on, I was also finding great enjoyment in the booming New Pulp movement. The adventures of my favorite pulp characters had become 'infinite' in scope; lovingly cared for by a new generation of writers, artists and editors who respected the pulp heritage while bringing modern sensibility into these continuing adventures.

Having had the pleasure to become acquainted with Airship 27's Ron Fortier and Rob Davis at my annual pilgrimage to PulpFest, I eventually approached Ron about crafting a tale for his publishing house. I couldn't have been more thrilled when he told me of the need of a new adventure of the Green Lama!

I truly hope that the Airship 27 readers have fun with my take on the adventures of Jethro Dumont. For "The Case of the Hairless Ones," I wanted a title that would fit right in with Crossen's original titles for his Green Lama novels in *Double Detective.*

My goal was to incorporate the historical turmoil that China faced as it transitioned from centuries of Warlord control, and then blend these facts into one of my favorite pulp genres, that of the "weird menace" with its bizarre masked villains, impending tortures, and sinister acolytes.

This would be an intriguing setting in which to set loose the Green Lama, placing him in a situation where he would have to face down evil while remaining true to his own spiritual beliefs. I also wanted to honor the original pulp vision of the hero while demonstrating Dumont's inner motivations and actions (without halting the action too much!).

And if you don't like my take on the spiritual crime-fighter, just blame it on Steranko.

If it weren't for him clouding the mind of an impressionable seven-year-old, we may never have met on this road celebrating the pulp heroes of the past.

I'd love to hear from fans of the Green Lama, as well as any other readers and creators involved with all forms of pulp. Drop me a line at craigcreative@att.net or look for me on the pulp message boards!

Author Bio:

ROBERT CRAIG is the president and creative director of a Midwest advertising and digital marketing agency, as well as an associate design director for several affiliated marketing and media firms.

When not reading pulp fiction (classic, new, and anything in between!) or herding his three sons around to various academic and athletic events, Robert spends his spare time as an operating board member of the Bright Side of the Road Foundation, where he has helped to raise over $2 million for ALS research nationwide over the past several years.

The Old & the New

Several years ago we had the fun of publishing our first ever Green Lama anthology that featured three brand new stories. Peter Miller and Kevin Noel Olson delivered two great short adventures and Adam Garcia swung for the fences offering us a truly awesome novella. The book was published and to rousing critical success, thank you all very much.

In the meantime Adam had gotten the Green Lama bug in a bad way and offered to write a full length Green Lama novel for us. There was no way we were ever going to pass on that and thus was born our second GL title, THE GREEN LAMA UNBOUND. That book went on to win awards for both Adam and book illustrator Mike Fyles. That it helped cement Adam's rising star in the New Pulp world goes without saying.

But like all good creators, Adam wanted to do more. Lots more with this character. Lots more with this character than what he thought a small outfit like Airship 27 could offer, and so he began talking with a larger publisher about realizing his future Green Lama plans with them. They were receptive and that necessitated our parting ways not only with Adam, but his tales as well. Here at Airship 27 Productions, we allow our writers to maintain all rights to their work. So we had no qualms about Adam taking his novella and novel to another publisher; in fact we wished him then, and continue to do so now, all the luck in the world. As I pen these words, his first project for this other outfit has been released and we hope it does great for them.

Still, Adam's pulling his stories had a negative effect in that it also took both Peter and Kevin's great stories out of circulation. Something we felt was wrong and we set about finding a way to course-correct getting those stories back into print where they belong. In the end the solution was really simple: do another anthology. Only this time find two other writers to submit shorts and create a brand new Green Lama title offering up four stories, rather than three; the two reprints and two never before seen tales. I set out to recruit those new writers.

And I couldn't have been happier when both Nick Ahlhelm and Robert Craig signed on to be a part of this project. Of course, if the book was going to be a new edition, then we wanted to dress it up in a brand new art package as well. To that end we recruited the super talented Neil Foster to provide us with 12 fantastic new interior illustrations, all of which are stunning. Neil is one of our favorite artists here at Airship 27. To do the cover, I went to a young Pilipino artist named Isaac L. Nacilla whose work I'd seen on-line. He blew me away with his dynamic energy and once he turned in the cover, it inspired our new title: GREEN LAMA—MYSTIC WARRIOR, Vol 1.

So there you have it. How we were able to combine something old and something new and hopefully offer you a title filled with great stories and marvelous artwork in the grand pulp tradition you've come to expect from Airship 27 Productions. Of course if this volume does well, you can fully expect to see more of our Mystic Warrior in the future.

As ever thanks for your support, we couldn't do this without you.

HATS OFF TO THE SERIAL CLIFFHANGERS

The time is 1935. After a decade of fame as the Queen of the Serials, Hollywood actress Gloria Swann is dismayed to see her box-office numbers dwindling with each new production. Desperate to reclaim her popularity, she bankrolls her own film project; an over the top jungle adventure to be shot on location in the wilds of the Amazon rainforests of Brazil.

After the crew and cast arrive at their isolated destination, a series of accidents occur threatening the lives of several of the players. The main target of these unexplained mishaps is Swann's younger stunt double, Angela Morgan. She suspects there are evil forces lurking in the jungle that threaten their safety. Her only ally in this belief is veteran stunt coordinator Karl Braun. When Gloria Swann mysteriously disappears, Angela may be the only hope the Queen of Escapes has to survive.

Writer Curtis Fernlund's homage to the classic film serials of yesterday is a rousing, fast paced adventure that speeds from one danger-filled cliffhanger to the next. James Lyle provides marvelous interior illustrations and Andy Fish captures all the fun in his gorgeous cover painting, packaged and designed by Rob Davis.

Made in the USA
Charleston, SC
29 July 2014